GOING ALL OUT

By

DORIAN SYKES

RJ Publications, LLC

Newark, New Jersey

NOV 16   PA

The characters and events in this book are fictitious. Any resemblance to actual persons, living or dead is purely coincidental.

RJ Publications
www.rjpublications.com
Copyright © 2010 by RJ Publications
All Rights Reserved
ISBN 0981999840
978-0981999845

Printed in Canada

February 2011

1 2 3 4 5 6 7 8 9 10

Chapter 1

"You're nobody til' somebody kills you....I don't want to die."

The lyrics from the late great Notorious B.I.G. filled the SUV as the vehicle's three occupants rode in silence, each lost in his own thoughts. They drove deep into the suburbs of Michigan on Van Dyke Avenue. After ten minutes of antagonizing driving they finally reached their destination. Ollie, the driver pulled into an Olive Garden restaurant parking lot. He quickly scanned the lot for a spot, which was almost full due to it being lunch hour. They parked in the rear of the restaurant, each man simultaneously getting ready. Ollie pulled from the glove box a flat head screwdriver, surveyed the lot and exited the SUV. He removed the license plate in record time and replaced it with another.

Pharaoh and Tez the other two passengers were dressed for the occasion and ready for what follows. After Ollie climbed back into position in the driver seat, Pharaoh and Tez made their exit. Everything was going accordingly as they crept around the front of the Olive Garden and noticed the armor truck leaving the bank next door. They waited until the truck faded away into the lunch hour traffic and made a quick spring across the parking lot. Pulling down their ski-masks before entering, Pharaoh looked back at Tez who was holding a Tec-9, and said "You ready my nigga?" Without waiting for a response Pharaoh led the way.

Boom! The door of the bank slammed against the

wall violently, as Pharaoh ran full speed towards the two tellers working. He jumped the counter as if it were a hurdle in the Olympics. Almost falling he managed to grab hold of the white female teller's blouse to help keep his balance. "Bitch where the fuck is the money?" he demanded still clutching her by the collar. She began her stall game as she'd been trained to do, opening teller drawers handing over petty cash known as bait bills, which included die packs. Pharaoh took the money and looked at it in disgust, then slapped the teller with it square in the face, sending bills flying everywhere. "Bitch, you think this is a game?" He yelled, then continued, "take me to the vault before I make yo' funky ass a casualty." He motioned her towards the vault as if he'd been in there in the past.

Meanwhile Tez had everyone stretch out on the floor with their hands on their head, while he stood guard near the entrance waving the gun side to side like he was part of the S.W.A.T. team. There were only two customers, both of Oriental descent, a man and woman who appeared to be husband and wife. They laid in the lobby area, the man with his arm around the woman. Tez made the second teller come from behind the counter and get down. She was the only African-American in the bank besides the two men holding up the joint. There were eight additional loan officers in the conference room in the midst of a meeting when Tez tapped on the window with the barrel of the Tec-9, startling those inside. He also made them get face down. "Nobody tries to be a hero, and nobody dies" he said. Everyone complied fully with the man of the hour.

Once inside the vault Pharaoh stood back, as the teller typed in a key code accessing the lock. He began filling his nylon gym bag with stack after stack of money. "You didn't have to slap me" said the teller. Still filling the bag Pharaoh said "baby I had to make it look good." He finished filling the bag almost emptying the vault, then said

"I'mma call you later." He exited the vault and Tex noticed, "You ready my man?" he asked, looking at his watch. It had been three minutes, but seemed like an hour. "Let's make it."

They speed walked to the awaiting Ollie parked in the SUV, engine running. No one said anything, each man assumed his position realizing that the easy part was over. Now, they had to make it back to the city. Tez climbed in the hatch of the Chevy Trailblazer, while Pharaoh sat in the middle row, and Ollie driving. As they departed a young white boy who was on his lunch break sitting in his car with the door ajar, had witnessed the entire scene. Being the natural nosy superman citizen he was down to the core, he wrote down the plate number and description of the vehicle, along with what he had seen. The local police arrived on the scene, along with two FBI agents, to whom superman gladly handed over the information. The Warren Police Department was dispatched and notified to be on the look out for the hunter green Chevy Trailblazer tag # 000990.

The call had just come over the radio when Ollie passed a police cruiser tucked in the cut looking for speeders. The cop looked at the SUV and immediately hit his lights and sirens.

The three men inside all looked to the rear to witness what they had feared, but planned for. The chase was on! "Floor this bitch!" said Tez as Ollie dropped the Chevy into four-wheel drive. They were traveling on the back road that led back to the city. They knew if they could just make it across city lines they might have a snow ball chance in hell. Ollie gripped the steering wheel with both hands, constantly in the rear view mirror. Looking for an out he turned onto a busy street in hopes that he could weave in and out of traffic until losing the squad car. Pharaoh and Tez both cocked and checked their guns preparing for the inevitable.

Another police car joined the chase and they were still two miles from the city. Doing over eighty miles per hour Ollie drove expertly as if he were a Nascar driver. Tez ordered from the hatch that he turn left, "Nah nigga keep going" ordered Pharaoh. Tez saying one thing, Pharaoh saying another, and Ollie kept looking in the rearview mirror, he didn't know what his next move would be. When it happened a loud bang erupted through the SUV, sounding like thunder. Ollie ran a red light and collided into a crossing eighteen wheeler head on. The impact sent the SUV spinning like a bottle several times, coming to a violent halt after side swiping two other vehicles.

Tez and Pharaoh both exited the vehicle as if nothing happened, guns in hand, with the gym bag in the other. "Get down! Freeze!" yelled the four officers as they attempted to inch forward. *Fa. . Fa.. Fa…* Tez let off the first series of rounds as Pharaoh joined *lakaa.. lakaa..* The cops fired minimum rounds back as they ran for cover. Their Glott 27's weren't nearly as efficient as the twin Tec-9 Luger's equipped with 30 round clips and cooling systems, Tez and Pharaoh were handling.

Pharaoh held the cops at bay, while Tez ran into traffic spotting an old white woman sitting at the light unphased by the current events. Tez blindsided her, smashing the driver's window in with the butt of his gun. All in one motion he reached inside, unlocked the door, opened it, and snatched the old hag out sending her scratching against the cold winter salt pavement. "Let's ride my nigga!" he yelled, as Pharaoh made his way to the car still busting. *Lakaa.. Lakaa..Lakaa..*

The police were still hiding behind their squad cars when they witnessed Tez and Pharaoh pulling off into traffic. They couldn't shoot because it meant taking the chance of hitting someone innocent, and they couldn't give chase because Pharaoh had shot their tires flat and sent a few shells to their engine blocks. As Pharaoh constantly kept looking back for any other cops, he finally realized for the first time that Ollie wasn't present. "My man, turn around!" he said.

"For what?" asked Tez.

"Cause we forgot Ollie, we can't leave the nigga."

"You know how it go. We got away he didn't."

The statement may have been harsh, but it was true. That was the code of the street. Tez continued on breaking the brief silence, "how much we get?"

"I don't know yet, we've got to count it."

They drove back into the city and ditched the recently borrowed car getting low on foot. They were on 7 Mile and Mound Road back on familiar grounds, but still uneasy. "So what now, my nigga?" asked Tez. He and Ollie always asked Pharaoh for the next move, he was without a doubt the brain behind any and everything they did. "Catch that cab right there," he suggested. Tez flagged the Checker cab to a stop. "Take us to the downtown bus station" said Pharaoh as the cab driver promptly asked for a deposit. Pharaoh reached inside the bag and handed the driver a crispy hundred dollar bill. The cab driver pulled from the curb, mixing in with traffic.

"Where we going my nigga?" asked Tez sounding like a curious first-grader going on a field trip. "Shit somewhere, we damn sure can't stay here."

They arrived at the Greyhound bus station in downtown Detroit. People were everywhere, coming and going. Once inside they looked at the buses leaving within the next hour on the schedule at the front desk.

"May I help you?" a clerk asked. Pharaoh still reading the board, he turned to Tez and asked, "Have you ever been to Arizona?"

"Nope."

"Well that's where we're going."

"Two tickets to Phoenix, Arizona please." Pharaoh paid the woman and she handed him two tickets.

"Have a nice trip" said the clerk as Tez and Pharaoh left the counter.

Tez, like a big baby, raced to the back of the bus, which was full to capacity. He wanted to sit near the window. It made no difference To Pharaoh, he was just happy to be aboard and departing. They took their seats, Pharaoh trying to become familiar with his surroundings, he eyed everything and everyone. Every face had a story to tell.

Chapter 2

Days before....

It was mid-December of 2001 and the weather in Detroit was a typical below zero degrees. The streets were frozen, six inches of snow covered the entire city from a recent blizzard, and the people outside were at a minimum. For the two men inside the red bungalow, it was just another day in the spot. They sat in the living room in their favorite love seats dressed in several layers of clothing, hooded sweaters, hats, and winter boots. Both bundled up under thick comforters in an attempt to stay warm, they rubbed their hands together in front of a kerosene heater watching their ritual classic movie "New Jack City" quoting lines from the script as if they wrote it.

The house was owned by the city, it was taken due to back taxes. Old lady Edna was its last legal occupant, she and her late husband used to live there. One day she came in from her daily walk and found her husband lying on the kitchen floor beaten to death, for reasons which still remain a mystery. The loss of her husband traumatized Old Edna, so she moved out of the house neglecting it altogether. She would often stop by and pitch a bitch claiming to still own the house, demanding money from the young hoodlums as she often referred to them, who were using the house as a crack headquarters. The house was on the verge of being condemned. There were several holes in the aging roof; plastic covered the windows, and there were only two small bedrooms more like cells. The kitchen was at the back of the house with a small bathroom sat the corner. There was no basement, nor an upstairs. Everything was centered in the living room where the two men sat as a familiar knock sounded on the front door. Both men looked at each other with a look on their faces that said "you get it." Neither wanting to budge from their comfortable little nooks the older of the two, Pharaoh, said "my man get yo' musty ass up and get the door, it's your turn." The man he was giving sarcastic orders to was Tez, he reluctantly got up "who it?" he yelled. "Boo-Baby." Boo-Baby was a local crack head and a regular at the one stop shop crack spot.

Tez took the two boards off the steel door and quickly let her in. She wore her favorite blue jean stonewash coat, and matching pants. Her black cotton skull cap looked more like grey, it was covered with lint balls and soiled spots. "What you trying to get?" asked Tez, holding out a hand full of dime rocks, and a 40 cal. in the other.
"Let me get six for fifty," said Boo-Baby. She stood with her ass up in the air leaning over, fingering each rock. "Damn bitch, they ain't gon' change," yelled Tez, as Boo-Baby quickly selected her six rocks and handed Tez a soakimg wet fifty dollar bill.

As Boo-Baby made her departure Ole' Tony Rome entered. Despite the weather, the spot hadn't missed a beat. The crackheads were coming rain, sleet, or snow. "Tony mothafuckin' Rome...," Pharaoh said with a bit of rhythm. "Do that dance baby." Ole' Tony Rome broke into his patented two steps, with a spin and a clap. Tez and Pharaoh both watched and laughed, but still with high respect for the former playa!
"What you need Rome?" asked Tez.
"See that's the thing, right." Ole' Rome always had a story. "I only got eight dollars baby, work with me."
"Hook em' up Tez," ordered Pharaoh.
"Alright baby, now ya'll be smooth," said Ole' Tony Rome.

As Tez put the boards back on the door the phone began ringing. It was a burn out, Pharaoh had it turned on using some stolen I.D. and social security number. Tez answered on the fourth ring. "Who this?"

"Can I speak to Juan?" it was the voice of a Caucasian woman. Tez tossed the phone to Pharaoh a.k.a. Juan. He told all his broads his name was Juan.

"Hello."

"Hey baby how's it going?"

"Everything's, everything you know just here at the studio thinking about you." Pharaoh recognized the voice and snapped into playa' mode. It was Tamara, his new recruit to what he referred to as his starting five.

"When can I see you," she asked.

"Well, I was actually wrapping things up; I'll see you in let's say a half hour." Tez looked at Pharaoh with a look of "you're not going anywhere."

"Sounds like a plan," said Tamara.

"I'll see you in a minute."

Tez immediately said what he was thinking, "My man, you ain't 'bout to leave me up in here all day while you go lay up?"

"You know me better than that. This is strictly business. Remember the white hoes we met at Fairlane Mall a couple weeks ago?" Tez tried to jog his memory, but he smoked entirely too much weed to possibly remember.

"The bitch was bout five feet, stacked real neat, with an ass like a '57 Chevy. She was the one with them Apple Bottoms on."

"Bingo," Tez recalled, "Oh yeah" he said with a smile looking into space as if he was still at the mall.

"Well listen, the bitch is a teller at a bank out in Honky land and she game on letting us hit it."

"Square business?"

"Yeah, I been drilling the bitch and it's definitely in the works. She said it's at least two hundred thousand in that piece, and all we got to do is go pick it up."

"What about security?" asked Tez.

"Ain't no security guards in Honky land, they so far in the suburbs that they feel safe out there. Trust me my nigga I been plotting hard, I been out to the bank and everything the lick is sweet. You know I wouldn't have us on no dummy mission my man."

"I know my nigga."

"So is you with it?" asked Pharaoh.

"Two hun'd g's, I wouldn't miss it for the world."

They both broke out into a high pitched laugh. Pharaoh grabbed his keys to his 85' Chevy Caprice, which he called Midnight because she was triple black, and ran like a stallion. "Good, now we need to holla at Ollie. Me and you gon' go in and he'll drive."

Tez agreed with everything Pharaoh said, he was sold once he heard the amount of money at stake. As he let Pharaoh out and locked up he was already planning what he would do with his share. Pharaoh scrolled through his phone and stopped at Kellie, another one of his starting five. The phone rang once and she answered as if she'd been waiting by the phone all day,

"Hello."

"What up doe?" asked Pharaoh, .a.k.a. Juan,

"Where you at?"

"On my way to see you, be ready." Pharaoh hung up before she could respond. Kellie was his old head, that's what he called her. She was 32, no kids, single, worked at Ford Motor Company, and had her shit together for the most part. Kellie was golden brown, hazel eyes, full dick lips, jet black hair which came down her back, all ass and no titties. She stood about 5'5", 140 pounds. Pharaoh was 19, but acted like an old man. He was indeed a lady's man 6'3 , 195 pounds, light brown skinned, deep 360 brush waves, perfect white teeth, and very smart. He was the pretty boy of the clique; Tez was 18 stood 6'1", black to death 200 pounds, muscular build, and a temper out of this world. Ollie was also 18, light skinned 165 pounds, about 5'10", he was a shy guy, but was pretty lose when with his boys.

Pharaoh arrive at Kellie's apartment on 9 Mile and Greenfield next to the Northland Shopping Mall. She was waiting at the entrance and came out when Pharaoh pulled up. She was dressed to impress. She wore the latest Al Wissam_leather with fur around the hood and a pair of high heel gator boots to match the coat. She was dressed as if they were going to an event and Red Lobster afterwards. Pharaoh had a fetish for manicured hands and toes so he complimented Kellie on her freshly French manicured nails. "Where we going?" She asked after giving him a wet passionate kiss.

"Up here to the rental car place. I need you to get me a rental." Pharaoh could tell that her mood had changed by the shift in her weight as she readjusted herself in her seat.

"That's all you ever want me to do, rent you a car, where is it this time Chicago?" she said with a bit of sarcasm.

"Actually, Minnesota. I gotta go on some business, but I promise we'll spend some time together soon as I get back."

With that Kellie lightened up because Pharaoh was a man of his word. They arrived at Enterprise Car Rental at Northland Mall conveniently two blocks away. Kellie knew the drill, go in get an SUV any kind, pay her money, get insurance and the hole nine, while Juan sat in the car for her to return. She pulled next to his Caprice in a hunter green Chevy Trailblazer. He hopped out and got in with her taking the driver's seat. "You know I'm going to miss you right," he said lining up for his next punch line and he continued, "why don't you bless a nigga before I hit the road." Kellie knew damn well what he meant and she went for what she knew. She unbuckled his pants and pulled his limp dick through the hole of his boxers. She began stroking him until he came alive. Looking him in the eye

with a seductive slutty look on her face, she teased the head
of his dick flicking her tongue back and forth then
swallowed it entirely. He leaned back and enjoyed the
warm moisture, which felt almost like heaven. Kellie
gobbled him up like a seasoned vet for what seemed like an
eternity. She took his dick out her mouth and began jacking
it. "You almost there baby?" she asked in her softest voice
looking him in the eye. She knew how to make him bust,
she was a pro. "Ahh-shit!" squirmed Pharaoh a.k.a. Juan as
he began ejaculating. Kellie put his dick back in her mouth
and swallowed every drop, sucking him softly. A parking
lot security guard tapped on the window with a flash light,
startling Pharaoh which caused Kellie to scrape the head of
his dick. "Fuck," Pharaoh mumbled.

"Excuse me, but you're going to have to exit the premises
sir," said the guard.

"Alright man we were just finishing up" Pharaoh said with a
slight grin of satisfaction.

"How long you gon' be gone baby?" asked Kellie.

"Just two days, I'ma see you when I get back okay."

"Alright," Kellie exited the vehicle leaving in Pharaoh's car.

        No time to waste, Pharaoh made his way to
Tamara's crib. She stayed on 15 Mile and Gratiot in a
recently built subdivision in a double wide trailer. She was
from Iowa, 25, and moved to Michigan to study medicine at
Wayne State University. She worked part time at the bank
as a teller to help fund her education. Tamara was gullible
and Pharaoh a.k.a. Juan could and would exploit her.

        He arrived and parked the SUV in one of her parking
spots. By the time he reached the front door she was
opening it. They embraced as if they were husband and
wife, him coming in from a long days work. He kissed her
romantically while palming both ass cheeks and squeezing.
She pulled back all smiles, "I ordered Chinese food your
favorite peppered steak, shrimp fried rice, sweet and sour

chicken. It's in the oven."

"Thank you, baby."

"I'm going to take a quick shower and slip into something a little more comfortable," Tamara said as she disappeared into the shadows of the trailer.

Pharaoh washed his hands and retrieved his food from the oven. He sat in the living room and tuned in to a Pistons basketball game. He heard the shower water begin to run, so he flipped his cell phone and called the other three starting five playas on his team. "Let me check my rat traps," he said to himself as he scrolled through the long list of names stopping on Danielle. He spoke briefly with her arranging a future booty call, and did the same with Kim then Cinnamon. He then called Kellie back and let her know that his boy would be picking up his car.

Ring... Ring... the phone in the spot rang twelve times. "Where the fuck these niggas at?" Pharaoh said frowning at the thought of noone being at the spot then relaxed once a familiar voice picked up.

"Say something" it was Ollie's simple ass. "What up doe, my man?"

"Hey, dig, pay close attention, matter of fact get a pen and piece of paper....you ready?"

"Go ahead."

He gave him the instructions to call Kellie and go get his car just in case shit went sour on the lick. "Got cha' you my nigga," said Ollie waiting for further instructions. Pharaoh heard Tamara coming from the back and ended the conversation quickly, "Look I'mma be through there early in the morning, be there," he said and closed his phone, stuffing it into his pants pocket.

Tamara emerged looking like a cool million and smelling even better. She wore a lavender lace matching bra and panty set. "Did you enjoy your food baby? " she asked, looking at the food spread on her coffee table.

"Yeah it was A-1, what's for dessert?"

"I was hoping you, me and some chocolate syrup" she said spinning around so Pharaoh A.K.A. could get a full visual of the total package.

Without hesitation he undressed still wearing his socks, he stood in the living room ass naked, dick on missile. She escorted him into the kitchen where she sat him down and got the chocolate syrup from the cabinet. She kneeled down knowing first thing's first; she grabbed his dick like it had never been handled before and started bobbing. Not too fast, not too slow, but an even sincere pace almost as if she was making love to it. She uncapped the syrup and poured it all over his chest, watching it drip down to his balls. She started at his balls and licked her way back up to his chest.

Now, it was Tamara's turn, Pharaoh sat her on the kitchen counter and repeated the same performance on her. He then climbed onto the counter and assumed the 69 position. Tamara was dripping wet after having multiple orgasms. They slid down onto the floor where Pharaoh put Tamara in the superman position, knees to shoulders. They fucked all night, making their way to the bedroom and passed out.

It was 7:00 a.m. and Pharaoh was awakened by the sound of Tamara singing in the shower. He quickly got dressed and found a towel. He retraced his steps through the trailer the night before, dusting any possible fingerprints of his. Tamara found him sitting in the living room fully dressed. She too was dressed and ready for another day's work at the bank. "Are your ready?" she asked.

"Ready when you are," answered Pharaoh.

"Listen make sure that you're at the bank no later than 12:00 p.m. and remember you've got four minutes tops," she informed.

"We'll be there." He kissed her good-bye as if it was their

last kiss. They parted ways, she on her way to work, and Pharaoh on his way to the spot.

He arrived in the city and rode down Kelly Road, turning onto 7 Mile. After five minutes of constant lights and traffic police at every corner, Pharaoh was in the hood. He did his usual rounds bending each corner of his twelve block hood, and then made his way to the spot. Tez and Ollie both were inside sleeping, tired from the all night traffic. Pharaoh did his coded knock and Ollie's eyes popped open instantly. He unboarded the door then snatched it opened.

"What up doe?"

"Ain't shit my man," Pharaoh said giving his boy Ollie dap, then slapping Tez's leg awakening him.

"Wake up boy," Pharaoh was all business. "Look, I got the SUV outside, Ollie I need for you to try and find a truck similar to that one and take the license plate off it. If not, we'll use a temporary tag. Tez you go get the Tec's and I'mma go to the dollar store and get some masks and gloves. Let's go, everybody meet back here by 10:30 a.m., it's 8:00 a.m. now so let's get to work."

"One more thing Tez did you run the lick down to Ollie?"

"Yeah man," said Tez.

"We all on the same page?" Pharaoh asked looking from Tez to Ollie. The both nodded in agreement and with that they all made their exit.

Chapter 3

Back at the bank, two FBI agents were conducting interviews with each employee, and Tamara was up to bat. She was a nervous wreck and her eyes told it all. "Ms. Morley," said one of the agents as he stood in the open door way looking down ready from his clipboard. Tamara stood and said, "That's me." "Right this way ma'am," the agent said, ushering her into a conference room, and closing the door. "My name is agent Jim Fleming, and this is my partner agent Bill Opperman. Please have a seat. We're conducting an investigation on the robbery that occurred this afternoon. We need to ask you some questions, and if you would please try and remember as much detail as you can. Before we get started can I offer you something to drink?" She shook her head, no.

Tamara was sweating bullets. Sweat beads were literally visible on her forehead and nose. Agent Jim Fleming was sitting and handling all the questions. He was clearly in charge of the meeting, while Bill stood next to Tamara reading her body language, almost studying her. Her story sounded too rehearsed as if she was in a rush to end the meeting. She gave simple answers, but agent Bill sensed that Tamara was holding back. He interrupted and asked his partner Jim if he could speak with him in the hallway. They politely excused themselves.

"She's involved," said agent Opperman no sooner than the door closed behind them talking in a very low tone. He had nothing to go on besides his instincts and experience. "She's acting too shifty Jim."

"Well good cop, bad cop."

With that they re-entered the conference room and immediately went to work on Tamara. Jim who appeared first as a calm, fair guy changed his mood as if he received a fax or something disclosing her guilt. He walked to where he was originally sitting, and picked up the notes, he'd been jotting down. He read its contents briefly then slammed it on the table frightening Tamara. This was agent Opperman's cue. For the first time in the meeting he said something. "Ms. Morley you need to help yourself." The ambiguous statement blindsided Tamara as she was at a loss for words. "What do you mean?" her eyes bucked like she'd just hit a rock of some premo. They would go back and forth drilling her until she cracked. Bill would make a vague statement, leaving it out there to hang in the air while she tried to figure out exactly how much they knew. Agent Fleming was feeding off his partner's energy, drawing theories. He was in one ear, and Opperman in the other, both standing with their sleeves rolled up looking down their noses at Tamara.

"We know all about your involvement in the robbery Ms. Morley. Your boyfriend has already told us everything. There was a high speed chase in which they crashed. He's doing exceptionally well, but he's already thinking of himself. We recovered the money taken in today's robbery, leaving him and his buddies caught red handed," said Agent Fleming.

Opperman took over, "listen we know he forced you into this Ms. Morley, and we can help you only if you're willing to help yourself. We believe that he's responsible for a string of other bank robberies. What he does is meet women who work at banks, and seduces them until they'll do anything he wants," said Fleming. "Do you honestly believe that he met you by coincidence? No, he followed you somewhere outside of work and casually met you. He does this to all the women. We just so happened to catch them on the scene this time," said Opperman. "Don't you see you've been manipulated?" Tamara's nervousness turned to anger instantly. They were playing on her intelligence and emotions. Never once did they say who he was, no name, or description. It was all bullshit, but she figured she had a way out, and she felt used .

"It was Juan and his boys," she said as Fleming darted to the table and scribbled the name Juan quickly.

"Where does Juan live?" asked Agent Fleming.

"I'm not certain," answered Tamara realizing for the first time she didn't know where Pharaoh a.k.a. Juan lived.

"What's his last name?"

"I have not the slightest clue." The more questions they asked, the more Tamara came to realize that she know nothing about Mr. Juan.

"Do you at least have a number he could be reached?"

"It's (313) 893-****."

Agent Fleming wrote the number down. "Where did you meet Juan? Did someone introduce you to him, if so who?"

"No. I met Juan at Fairlane Mall."

"Was he with anyone?"

"Yes, he was with two of his friends." Agent Opperman retrieved a booking photo of Ollie from a manila envelope and handed it to Tamara.

"Do you recognize this man?"

"Yes. He was one of the two men with Juan when I met him."

Ollie was in the hospital with two broken legs, a dislocated shoulder, minor bumps and bruises. The Warren Police Department had two officers on stand by waiting for clearance that Ollie was innocent. He told them that he'd been carjacked and forced to drive the two gun men. Agent Opperman immediately notified the two officers not to release Ollie, and to bring him to the station when released by the doctors. A check was run on the SUV and it was discovered that it was a rental from Enterprise, which was rented by a Ms. Kellie Todd. She knew nothing about the robbery, and the agents didn't explain to her off hand that the truck was involved in the robbery. They initially told her that the driver had been in a serious accident. "Oh my God!" Is Juan Okay?" she asked them expecting the worst case senerio.

"Oh, he's fine. He managed to jump out and run, shoot four officers, carjack an elderly woman, and escape, all after robbing a bank. Have any idea where we might find Ol' Juan?" asked Agent Fleming with every ounce of sarcasm he could muster.

Kellie realized then that it was too late to deny knowing Juan, besides she did say his magical name, to top it off the SUV was in her name. "I have not a clue. He told me he was going to Minnesota, that's why he needed the rental. Juan said he'd be back in two days." They showed her the same picture of Ollie they had shown to Tamara. She I.D.'d him as the guy who picked up Juan's car. "What kind of car does he have?" asked Fleming, ready with his notepad. "A black Caprice."

"You wouldn't happen to know the tag number?"

"I'm afraid not."   She gave them his number, which was all she had just like Tamara.

With that they departed and ran the phone number through their database. The number came back to Eugene Smith address 19248 Mound Road, in Detroit, MI. They immediately got a warrant signed and raided the house a.k.a 'the spot.' Nothing, no one, not a trace. Pharaoh had cleaned the place of any evidence that could reveal any of their identities. The only thing agent Fleming could hope for was somehow they'd catch em' at the spot, or maybe Ol' Ollie would give em' what they wanted and needed. They arraigned Tamara on aiding and abetting in a bank robbery and 924 (c) the use of a firearm in a robbery. They

promised to drop the gun charge if she continued to so-
called help herself, and let her go on bond in hopes that Mr.
Juan would attempt to contact her.

Chapter 4

Pharaoh and Tez arrived at the downtown Phoenix Grey hound bus station. It was damn near 80 degrees and it was December. Both of them looked out of place by what they wore; Timberlands, Carhart working coats, thick jeans, and hoodie sweaters. They not only looked out of place, but they felt out of place as well. They didn't know a soul in Arizona, but they were still alive, and had a duffle bag full of money. They exited the bus and headed for a cab parked along side the curb. Pharaoh exhaled, looking up at the partly cloudy blue sky and sun shining down. It felt like summer. "Where we goin' my nigga?" asked Tez.
"Shit we gon' get a room somewhere first, you know then hit the city," Pharaoh answered as they climbed into the taxi.

The cab driver quickly turned on the meter. "Where to my friend," asked the driver in a heavy Spanish accent. He was Mexican. He stood no more than 4'10" and weighed about 90 pounds soaking wet. "Take us to the best hotel you know of," answered Pharaoh. The driver cranked the engine and slowly departed, trying to milk the meter. He tried making small talk.
"So….where are you guy's from?"
Tez quickly answered, "Where the cabs don't stop." He and Pharaoh bust out laughing. "Where?"
"Milwaukee, "answered Pharaoh hoping to avoid any further talk.
"Well, my name is Hernandez." Neither Tez nor Pharaoh bothered to introduce themselves. They ignored Hernandez and began talking in code.

"Here we are, my friend." They pulled into a parking entrance of the Double Tree Hotel. "That will be $32.80." he said.

"A'ight my man, you be smooth," said Pharaoh handing Hernandez a fifty dollar bill. Before getting out he asked, "say would you mind driving us around later?"

"Hernandez is always on the clock my friend," he said speaking in third person. He gave Pharaoh his cell number to reach him.

Pharaoh and Tez entered the hotel lobby and checked into a presidential suite. "This is the life my man, I can get used to this," said Tez as he fell back on the enormous bed in the master bedroom. "If we flip this money right we can hange our lives," said Pharaoh, pouring the money onto the bed. They both stood in amazement at all the money. It was more than either one had ever seen at once. Pharaoh counted it fast totaling $196,000 and some change.

"Man we get sixty-five G's each," said Pharaoh.

"Dog we get more than that."

"Man, just 'cause Ollie didn't make it, whatever the outcome may be whether he's locked up or dead, this sixty-five belongs to him." There was a slight pause. Tez broke the silence.

"You right man."

"Look I'mma take a quick shower, you should do the same boy you smell like hot baby shit," said Pharaoh in a joking manner, attempting to lighten the mood. Tez laughed as the both went and jumped clean.

It was still fairly early in the day, and Pharaoh wanted to get out and see the city, meet some chicks, go shopping, and get something to eat. He hated being bored. He walked over to the phone and began dialing the number that Hernandez had given him.

"Hernandez," he picked up on the first ring and still talking in the third person. "Hey my man, this is Juan, the guy you dropped off a the Double Tree earlier...I need for you to drive my boy and me around, can you do it?"

"Hernandez will be there my friend." Tez emerged from the bathroom with an unlit cigar in his mouth, with two hands full of hundred dollar bills, pretending as if he was counting it.

"You got change for a hun'd" he asked Pharaoh.

"Let me see," Pharaoh replied reaching into his pants pocket pulling out a donkey knot. He flipped it open and began to shuffle through it. "All I got is hun'd," he said, as they both joined in laughter.

"So now what my man?" asked Tez. "Shit I just called that cab driver, Hernandez and told him to come scoop us. We need to jump clean and hit the mall."

"That's a bet, but what we gon' do, just stay here in Arizona?" Tez was ready to go back to Detroit so he could stunt out on niggas in the hood.

"Man we gone parlay at least until we find out what's what, you feel me."

"Yeah,"They met Hernandez at the curb as they exited the hotel. It was like he never left because he arrived so quickly.

"Where to, my friend?"

"Man take us to a mall and turn on the radio Amigo," ordered Pharaoh. Hernandez clicked it on and some Mexican garbage filled the cab.

"Nah, nah my man, turn that shit on some rap," said Tez "You know baby, cop and flip, cop and flip. Shit, I'm a copp alright. I'm a copp me a 'Lac soon we hit the D," said Tez.

"Dog you gon' be broke in two days," laughed Pharaoh.

"Damn man what the fuck is this shit?" asked Tez, as he browsed through the off brand department store at the local mall, and the off brand clothing.

"Man I don't know, but I'mma cop me some crispy white Air Ones and a rack of white T's. Nigga can't go wrong with that my man," said Pharaoh.

"Yeah, but what about pants? I'm not rocking no Old Navy, my man."

"Shit, let's copp some Dickies and keep it moving."

The dress code in AZ was far different from what Tez and Pharaoh were used to. They walked through the mall cracking on folks' clothes and shoes, referring to them as 'odd balls.' "Look at them chicks in there my man," Tez said stopping dead in his tracks gawking at the two beautiful Latino women inside a department store. Pharaoh made his entrance and addressed the one he found most attractive. It was really a toss up, either way a brother couldn't go wrong. "And who you might be," he asked as he leaned up against a rack of clothing the two women were eyeing.

The woman examined him starting from shoes to face, and smiled pleased with what she saw. "My name is Rachael." She was absolutely flawless she stood about 5'6, weighed probably 140 pounds, nice tits, long black silky hair, and an onion booty that could make a brother cry.

"I'm Juan. Listen, I'm new in town and I was hoping you'd be kind enough to show me around." "Are you asking me out?" she asked, obviously flirting?

"Yes. I was thinking maybe a movie, dinner, night spot, anywhere as long as you are present. I mean queen you shining like the pyramid of Egypt."

"I'd love to," she said blushing from ear to ear.

Tez was on baby girl like a pit bull. She was all smiles as he ran down his spill, sealing the deal by paying for her outfit. Her name was Lisa. She was equally built as Rachael, and ready. They exchanged numbers; Pharaoh gave them the number to their hotel suite.

Hernandez was waiting outside with the meter moving a mile per second. He drove them around downtown, and through a few other areas, almost like a tour with him pointing and speaking 'bout any and everything, anything to keep the meter running. They stopped at a cell phone shop and bought pre-paid phones and a rack of phone cards.

"Amigo, where can my friend and I get some fake I.D's?" asked Pharaoh mocking Hernandez's accent.

."I don't know what you speak of my friend." Hernandez looked in the rear-view mirror nervously. Yeah, right his ass couldn't be legal. He knows damn well where to get some at, and Pharaoh knew exactly how to get it out of him.

"I bet you know 'bout this, huh Amigo?" He asked as he flashed a donkey roll of hundreds, spreading them apart. He watched the greed come alive as Hernandez's eyes widened, then continued. "Listen my friend," this time dropping the accent. "You don't have to worry about myself and my friend here. We're just trying to spend some money with you, that's all."

This was a language he understood very well. Without a word he took a right turn and headed into a more rural area. They arrived at some rinky dink dilapidated gas station/towing service. You would have thought it was the Feds from all the computers, printers, and high tech digital cameras. They got their official bootleg Arizona license made in alias names. The shit was legit though. It looked as good as any other fake they had seen. Pharaoh's was of course in the name of Juan Johnson. Tez's was Rick James. That nigga was out his hook up. If he could've, he would have put 'bitch' on the end.

The sun was going down and it had definitely been a long day. Pharaoh couldn't stop thinking about Rachael since he met her. He turned on his new phone and searched his pockets for her number. After locating it he phoned her.

"Hello" she answered on the third ring in a sincere soft voice.

"Hey this is Juan."

"Oh hey…I was just starting to think you changed your mind on me. So are we still on for tonight?"

"Of course, what did you have in mind," asked Pharaoh?

"They just opened a new bar and grill called 'The Zone.' I hear it's nice, good food, music, and a decent crowd."

"It sounds good to me. Do you want us to meet ya'll there?" asked Pharaoh, it was sorta like a double date. Sure how soon can you guys get there?"

"We're in a cab right now. I can have him drop us off."

"See you in a few," she said as they ended the conversation.

"I'm fenna get some pussy. I'm fenna get some pussy," said Pharaoh in a rhythm. "Who was that, the hoes my man?" asked Tez.

"Yeah, man. Hernandez, you know where a spot called 'The Zone' is at?"

"Hernandez will take you there my friend."

"My man, why you always talking in the third person?" asked Tez in a funky ass tone of voice.

Hernandez shot him a look of confusion, and headed for 'The Zone.' They arrived at the bar. It was pretty packed, hoes everywhere. Pharaoh scanned the place for Rachael and Lisa. He didn't see them so he took a seat at the bar, Tez taking an open stool next to him. "Can I take your order Papi?" asked a waitress holding a pen in one hand and a pad in the other.

Pharaoh looked up starring into her seductive green eyes. "Uh! I'll have a bottle of Don P, and whatever my friend is having," he said. Tez ordered two double shots of Remy Martin 1738. "Girl right!" said Tez admiring the waitress ass as she walked down the bar. "Yeah man, I might have to get on her my man," said Pharaoh also enjoying the view. "Here you are Papi" she said returning with their drinks. She popped the cork professionally with almost a mute sound. She had two champagne glasses; she poured Pharaoh a glass then poured herself one. What's the occasion, she asked with a smile holding her glass out for a toast.

"Life, everyday's a celebration," replied Pharaoh as they clinged glasses.

"I'll drink to that," she said after swallowing half her glass. "What's your name Papi?"

"Say that again," said Pharaoh.

"What, "Papi?"

"I love the way it rolls off your tongue," She said it even more enticing than before. Pharaoh smiled and introduced himself. "I'm Juan and this is my parter T-Love."

"I'm Sasha, pleased to meet you." Sasha was Mexican 'bout 5'7 and weighed 140 pounds give or take, green bedroom eyes, long jet black hair, perfect smile, and a body put together by no other than God Himself. They flirted in between her other customers, both obviously feeling the other.

Tez noticed Rachael and Lisa entered and tapped Pharaoh on the arm pointing with his glass in their direction. Tez got up and met them in the middle of the floor, giving Pharaoh enough time to excuse himself. "Sasha I no doubt would love to see you again, possibly outside of your work," he said. She leaned over the bar revealing two nice sized prizes, then reached inside her bra and pulled out a piece of paper with her information already on it. "Use it Papi," she teased.

Pharaoh found Tez and the hoes sitting in a booth towards the rear of the bar. He slid in next to Rachael. "Damn my man, what you do take a shit?" Tez asked trying to play it off.

"Hah, hah, hee" said Pharaoh. "What ya'll drinking?" he asked trying to make sure they got ready for the aftermath. They both ordered several shots of Tequila, downing them like champs and ordering a second, then a third round.

"I'm nice," said Tez referring to his buzz.

"Me too" Pharaoh said looking at his watch. "So… what ya'll got planned for us next?" asked Pharaoh.

"What did you have in mind?" asked Rachael as she reached her hand under the table and rubbed Pharaoh's leg up to his piece. "That sounds like a good idea," he said they ordered food and made small talk. They listened to the music provided by several local artists, from jazz to Latin Tex-Mex.

They all piled into Lisa's Honda Accord and went back to the hotel. Tez went right and Pharaoh went left taking Rachael into the master bedroom. Tez was in the bathroom running some water in the hot tub. It was all business in the bedroom. Pharaoh laid Rachael down on the bed and slid her shirt over her head. She wasn't wearing a bra; Pharaoh rubbed her stomach, and played with her belly button ring. He began kissing her softly as she laid back and closed her eyes. He inched his way up, not missing a spot until he reached her firm D cup titties. Her nipples were a pretty light brown. He cupped the right one with one hand putting it in his mouth. Sucking it like an infant, he used his free hand to maneuver his way down in her pussy. She was wearing skin tight low-rider jeans. He expertly unbuttoned them to discover she wasn't wearing any underwear either. Rachael had no hair on her pussy, just like Pharaoh loved it. He slid his index finger into his ear then rubbed the skirts of her click. This is an old test to see whether or not she's burning. She didn't jerk or make any unusual movements, so she was clear. She was wet as shit. Pharaoh couldn't handle any further foreplay. He stood up and undressed, while Rachael did the same. Pharaoh had a rule against condoms, he didn't wear them. He couldn't bust a nut wearing a condom .

As he positioned himself on top of Rachael he told her to put it in. She reached down and guided him inside.

"Ah…" they both said as Pharaoh entered. He slow stroked her until she relaxed, then began deep stroking, concentrating on her left wall. He delivered consistent, even strokes until she reached her climax. His would soon follow…he sped up as he could feel it cumming. Rachael had her nails embedded in Pharaoh's back. "Ah..Ah.." he said in satisfaction as he bust a luggie in her. He continued to stroke until his dick went limp.

Tez and Lisa were in the hot tub filled with bubbles. He laid back smoking a cigar watching Scar Face, pretending to be Tony Montana. While Lisa rode him like a champ, he stood up in the tub with Lisa still riding him, legs wrapped around his waist. Besides the plasma TV in the wall, the bathroom was surrounded with mirrors. He looked in one direction and she looked in the other, both watching each other get fucked. Tez's hands were slippery as he palmed both of Lisa's ass cheeks, pushing up and down on his dick. They fucked like mad Russians all night.

Pharaoh was still asleep when he heard the loud voice he knew oh so well. "Wake up my man!" said Tez, as he threw a pillow at Pharaoh. It was 11:00 a.m. and Rachael and Lisa were already in traffic.

"Where the hoes at?" asked Pharaoh still half sleep.

"Oh they got low, but they want to hook back up fo' sho.'"

"Where have you been?" asked Pharaoh noticing that Tez was fully dressed. Tez pulled a sandwich bag full of weed from his pants pocket, "they took me to get some greens." He took out two buds, enough to roll a decent sized blunt and attempted to put it back in his pocket. . "How much that hit you for?"

"A light forty dollars.

"Straight?

"Yep. and it's some good shit," said Tez while he tossed the bag to Pharaoh.

Pharaoh examined its contents. It was an ounce or

better and it sure was some goods. It was lime green, all buds and no seeds. It was so fluffy it reminded Pharaoh of popcorn. An ounce back in Detroit was going for $100.00 depending on who you know. Pharaoh started doing the math, wondering what a pound was going for. He figured you'd have to get a deal if he were to buy a pound. And an even better deal if you bought in large quantity. He settled on a figure of $500.00 per pound, give or take a little. He realized how he was going to flip his money.

Chapter 5

Two months had passed and Pharaoh was starting to get a feel for Arizona. He purchased an '87 Chevy Monte Carlo Luxury Sport and rented an apartment. Tez caught a flight back to Detroit. It was killing him being away from his baby mama Annie. He and Pharaoh called home and found out that Ollie was in jail, charged with bank robbery among other things. No one mentioned anything about the feds looking for them but they still wouldn't disclose their whereabouts. Pharaoh contacted Ollie's mom and arranged to pay for Ollie's attorney. He was not leaving Arizona without a weed connect.

Pharaoh met the barmaid Sasha he had met at the bar & grill "The Zone" at the local high school. They had been meeting there for the past month at 8:00 a.m. Sasha was a health nut. She jogged three miles every morning and it was serving it's purpose. Pharaoh a.k.a. Juan reluctantly agreed to jog with her. It wasn't that bad. He'd trail her enjoying the view of her perfectly shaped ass, bouncing with every movement. He was in fair shape considering he didn't smoke, and only drank occasionally. They ran their final lap, then began to cool down with a walk.

"Are you working today?" asked Pharaoh.

"Yeah, but I'm only working until 12:00 p.m."

"Let's do lunch."

"Sure."

They departed. Pharaoh went home to take a shower. The weather was beautiful, so he got his car washed then rode around. He called Rachael and lined up some pussy for later. It was almost time to meet Sasha for lunch so he headed towards 'The Zone.' He sat at the bar waiting for Sasha to punch out. Four well-groomed Mexican men entered and approached the bar, all wearing black business suits. They remained standing as one of the men asked one of the barmaids to phone Toro. "And whom might I tell him is here?" she asked "Valdez."

The barmaid disappeared into the back office, while Pharaoh watched the episode. The guy who referred to himself as Valdez was wearing a masterpiece platinum Rolex, with baguette diamonds in the bezel of the watch. The barmaid reappeared and said, "he'll see you, right this way gentlemen." She ushered them around the bar and pointed in the same direction in which she had returned. She leaned on the bar and said, "God damn Mexican mafia." There was no one else at the bar, so Pharaoh assumed she was talking to him or perhaps herself, either way he wanted to know more.

"What's the Mexican mafia?"

"The biggest Cartel in the state of Arizona. They probably supply half of the damn country." "With what?" asked Pharaoh.

"Gotta go!" said the barmaid as she noticed Sasha approaching.

"Are you ready Papi?"

"Yeah." He was still thinking about the cartel, and what it was they were supplying.

They went to *Chili's* for lunch. Sasha ordered a chef salad and some grilled shrimp appetizers. Pharaoh ordered a platter, with chicken burritos, steak burritos, and some special cheese dip.

"Papi my family is having a reunion Saturday, I would like for you to come,"

"Is there gon' be food?" Pharaoh said joking.

"Yes."

"Then I'm there!" .

"Good! I'll buy us some outfits," said Sasha.

It was Saturday, the day of Sasha's family reunion. She bought matching outfits so to speak, royal blue Ralph Lauren Polo shirts and white khaki shorts also by Polo. It was a nice day, it was heading into spring and the temperature was rising. Pharaoh was to pick Sasha up from her apartment, so he could take her to the grocery store and do some last minute shopping for the affair.

Pharaoh bought some hair clippers and cut his own hair like a professional. He had seen some of the local's haircuts, and they were deemed to be "Timmy's" a.k.a. a bold haircut. He showered and jumped clean putting on his new Polo outfit and some crispy white on white Air One's. Inspecting himself in the mirror and removing his doo- rag, he was pleased with his attire. He splashed a bit of his favorite cologne on called 'Lucky You,' when the phone rang. It was Sasha, her sister Ambria's husband's car wouldn't turn over and they needed a lift to the reunion. Pharaoh made his exit and headed for the $2.00 car wash. Since he would be having back seat passengers, he vacuumed the car out and sprayed some air freshener. He then picked Sasha up and headed for the grocery store. She had to buy some hot dog buns and cutlery.

Sasha directed Pharaoh to her sister Ambria's house. He pulled into the horseshoe driveway in complete astonishment. He admired the colonial style mansion, the 500 SL parked out front. He wondered how this car could possibly not start, and further how come they only had one car living in a home of that caliber. "I'll be right back," said Sasha. She got out and rang the doorbell. Pharaoh could see a Mexican woman open the door and hug Sasha. They stepped in and closed the door.

Five minutes or so later the front door of the house reopened. Sasha came out first carrying some plastic Tupperware. She was followed by her sister Ambria, two small children, and last Ambria's husband. Pharaoh got out and opened the trunk for Sasha and she introduced everyone. "Juan, this is my sister Ambria, and this is her husband Valdez and my two nephews." "Nice to meet you," said Pharaoh extending his hand to Valdez. Pharaoh recognized him from the other day at "The Zone" as one of the Mexican mafia boys. Valdez on the contrary showed no signs of remembering Pharaoh. They all piled into Pharaoh a.k.a. Juan's Chevy Monte Carlo and headed for the family reunion, which was at Sasha's parents house. They drove making small talk, Pharaoh wondering again what it was this guy and his cartel buddies supplied. After a forty-five minute drive, they were in Tucson, Arizona, in one of the most expensive areas. Pharaoh pulled into an estate even more mystified than when he pulled into Ambria's driveway. "This is your parent's home?" asked Pharaoh. "Yeah" answered Sasha as she opened the door and helped her sister and nephews out the back seat. Pharaoh hadn't budged, he was still in amazement. "My friend would you mind letting me out?" asked Valdez, breaking Pharaoh's trans. "Oh my bad" he said. Pharaoh popped the trunk to retrieve the Tupper ware, then headed for the front door with the rest of them. Luxury cars were everywhere, anything from BMW's, to 600's, to Bentley's. Sasha had never mentioned anything to Pharaoh about her family being wealthy.

They were greeted at the door in Spanish by Sasha's mom. She was aging but she could still get it Pharaoh thought to himself, looking at her ass as she escorted them inside. They were led to the backyard/garden where the festivities were taking place.

Sasha introduced Pharaoh A.K.A. Juan to all her cousins, mostly female. They would all snicker in Spanish after meeting him, with a look in their eyes that said, "So your Juan, I've heard about you." Before Sasha could introduce Pharaoh to her father, Pharaoh spotted Valdez kneeling and kissing the forehead of an older Mexican man who was sitting a plush deck chair near the pool. He wore an identical Rolex watch like the one Valdez was wearing.

The entire festivity was centered around this old man. Sasha approached him with Juan on her side. "Hi, daddy!" she said as if she were still a little girl. The old man's face lit up like a Christmas tree, as he said something in Spanish then stood up and kissed his daughter. He had shown disdain for everyone else who had approached him, but it was obvious Sasha was still his little girl. After their embrace, Sasha introduced Pharaoh. "Daddy this is my boyfriend Juan" and Juan this is my dad", she said. Pharaoh extended his hand, "Nice to meet you sir." "Please call me Toro," said the old man. Pharaoh had heard this name before he thought, but couldn't quite place where. Sasha mixed and mingled while Pharaoh sipped some Crown Royal and watched the old man from the bar.

They were fresh out of ice, and Pharaoh volunteered to make the trip. Valdez said he would ride with him, after Ambria suggested it. On the way to the store it hit Pharaoh where he had heard the name Toro. He started replaying the scene from 'The Zone'. Toro was who Valdez and company where there to see. It was all starting to make sense. Toro was the mob boss, that's why Valdez had kissed the old man, and it explained why everyone was puckering up to kiss his ass. This all brought Pharaoh back to his earlier question. What was it that they were supplying?

"So Juan what do you do for a living?"

"I specialize in pharmaceuticals," answered Pharaoh.

"Really?" asked Valdez. He gave the impression that he knew what Juan was referring to.

"And what is it that you do, if you don't mind me asking."

"Well I'm a gardener and distributor," answered Valdez.

"Really? Tell me more." There was a slight pause in the

volley of a convo they were having. "Let's just say we're not too far apart." Pharaoh chewed on that ambiguous statement and came to the conclusion that they, the Mexican mafia, were supplying weed.

"So how'd you get into what you call it, gardening?" asked Pharaoh as if he had just figured out what Valdez's occupation was.

"Well once I asked my wife Ambria to marry me, Toro pulled me in. It's sorta like a family business. He wanted to make sure I could provide for his little girl, and any grandchildren we might have," answered Valdez.

"How thoughtful? Do you have a card? You know just in case I may need some gardening done." Valdez didn't have a business card so he wrote his number on a McDonald's napkin Pharaoh found in the glove box. Pharaoh examined the number then tucked it away neatly into his jeans pocket. He patted it for safety, guarding it with his life.

They arrived back at the reunion. Everyone was still kissing Toro's ass. Pharaoh, however, was anxious to leave. He endured several more hours of irritating entertainment, courtesy of some off brand Mexican band. They performed live song, after song, after song. Finally, Sasha was ready to leave. They said their goodbye's and departed. During the drive back Pharaoh said little. Sasha went on and on, asking questions.

"So Papi, did you enjoy yourself?"

"Uh-huh." Pharaoh was in another world. They arrived at Sasha's apartment building. Pharaoh pulled up to the entrance and parked leaving the car running.

"Aren't you going to come up, Papi?" Sasha asked with a confused look on her face,

"Nah baby, I'm tired. Plus, I've got to get up early." Sasha wanted him to stay, but it was part of her custom not to argue with her man.

"Okay Papi, but please call me to let me know you made it

home safe."

"Promise."

Sasha exited the car after kissing Pharaoh. He watched to make sure she made it inside before pulling away from the curb. He turned up his sounded and came alive as he raced home enthusiastically. He weaved in and out of traffic, singing along with the stereo. "If it ain't no platinum in ya' Cartier, switch ya' frame. Ain't no manicures on board, switch ya' plane." The lyrics from Pharaoh's favorite rapper Jay-Z. Pharaoh was indeed feeling himself. He pulled into his apartment complex, parked his car and speed walked to his apartment. Once inside, he went straight for his stash spots. He hid half the money in cereal boxes, the other half he put in the vacuum. He sat on the edge of his bed and counted out $40,000. He then reached in his pocket and recovered the napkin with Valdez's number on it. Pharaoh leaned over his bed to grab the cordless phone. He dialed the number on the napkin and waited patiently as the phone rang.....

"Hello." Pharaoh stood to his feet full of anticipation.

"Yeah, can I speak with Valdez?" he asked.

"Speaking."

"This is Juan, Sasha's boyfriend."

"Oh what's up, my friend. What can I do for you?"

"I was hoping that we could meet somewhere."

"Tomorrow my friend, meet me at Denny's on Liberty. Be there at 8:00 a.m. we can talk over a good mornings breakfast," said Valdez.

"See you then."

Pharaoh turned on his stereo full blast. He stood in front of his dresser mirror counting money, and popping his collar. He remembered to call Sasha so he turned the music down and phoned her. He didn't talk long, he just wanted to let her know he'd made it home. Pharaoh stayed up all night planning what he'd do if everything panned out tomorrow with Ol' Valdez.

Pharaoh watched the clock on his bedroom wall tick. He lay stretched out across his bed starring at the walls unable to sleep. It was 7:00 a.m. the sun was up and Pharaoh could hear the spring morning birds chirping. He rolled off the bed and headed for the shower. He had pulled an all nighter and was still full of energy. After showering he selected one of the many outfits Sasha had bought him. He quickly dressed and was out the door.

It was 7:45 a.m. when he arrived at Denny's. The restaurant was almost full with the regulars, sipping coffee and reading the paper. Pharaoh spotted Valdez tucked off in a booth towards the back. "Damn" Pharaoh thought to himself. It was his intention to beat Valdez there. He approached the booth Valdez had food everywhere, everything from Western Omelet, to French toast. "Juan," he said with a smile. He pointed with a hand, "Please have a seat." A waitress appeared and Pharaoh ordered steak and eggs, and an orange juice.

"So, what did you want to see me about?" Valdez asked in between bites.

"I'ma cut to the chase because you seem like a very busy man," said Pharaoh. He removed a large manila envelope from his coat and pushed it across the table towards Valdez. "It's $40,000 in there." Valdez quickly cuffed the envelope, but said nothing. "Look, what can you do for me with that?"

"Let's take a ride" answered Valdez. Pharaoh picked up the tab, leaving a tip and phone number for the pretty young waitress. They drove in Valdez's 500 SL. It was cocaine white with peanut butter interior. Pharaoh sunk down into the butter soft leather passenger seat. They drove nowhere in particular. Valdez broke the ice by asking.

"Where are you from?" Valdez asked, trying to break the ice.

"Detroit."

"And what brings you to Phoenix?"

"Opportunities."

"I see," said Valdez. He was still a bit hesitant, but he still hadn't returned the money either. "Look man, I'm not a cop, I'm not working with the cops. Hell I don't even like the cops. You don't have to worry about me," said Pharaoh. This was music to Valdez's ears. He knew if Juan was a cop that it would be deemed entrapment if they proceeded in any transactions. Pharaoh continued. "So what can you do for me for the forty G's.?"

"One hundred pounds," answered Valdez. Pharaoh almost jumped out his seat. That was a hundred dollars less than his initial calculation.

"I assume you'll be dealing in Detroit?"

"Right."

"How long will it take you to get rid of the marijuana?"

"A hun'd elbows in 'bout a week," he answered.

"How about transportation?" Pharaoh had thought about it, but couldn't come up with anything solid. The long pause told Valdez that Juan didn't have the means. "Don't worry about it, but it's going to cost you."

"How much?" asked Pharaoh.

"A hundred dollars per pound goes to the driver."

"When can we get started?" asked Pharaoh.

"Today!"

Valdez dropped Pharaoh back off at his car. They were to meet later at a warehouse so Pharaoh could meet his driver. Pharaoh's cell phone rang. "Hello."

"Where are you Papi?" asked Sasha.

Pharaoh had missed their daily jog. "Ah man, I had to take care of some business this morning. I should have called you, I apologize, baby," he said.

"Will I see you today?"

"Of course baby, but it'll have to be tonight, I'm still on

something right now."

"I get off at 10:00 p.m. so call me and let me know something."

"A'ight," I should be finished by then.

Pharaoh hung up realizing it was almost time to meet Valdez at some warehouse. Valdez had given him the address and directions. Pharaoh drove for twenty minutes down a familiar road. He pulled into a gas station/towing service. It was the same spot Hernandez took him and Tez to get their phony ID's. He learned that it was also a distribution company. He noticed Valdez's Benz parked near the entrance. Pharaoh pulled in behind it. He got out and walked inside the very busy warehouse. Mexicans were everywhere talking in their native tongue, scurrying across the floor like little mice at work. They were so busy, noone noticed Pharaoh's presence. He walked over to Valdez where he stood talking to a middle aged clean cut white man. "Oh hey! Juan, I'd like for you to meet Eric. He's your driver," said Valdez. They greeted and waited for Valdez to finish talking, he was orchestrating everything. "Follow me," he said.

They went out back where all the eighteen- wheelers were located. They were brand spanking new, equipped with bunk beds, TVs, DVD players, the whole nine. Valdez showed Pharaoh the secret compartments. He said that the trucks could hold 3,000 pounds easily. Pharaoh day dreamed about the day he'd be pushing 3,000 elbows at a time. Next, he took Pharaoh back inside and showed him what he had purchased. The two entered a dim storage room. Valdez opened one of the several boxes on a wooden table. Pharaoh examined the contents and discovered it was the same weed Tez had shown him months prior. He closed the box and nodded in agreement. "Eric is leaving for Detroit this afternoon. He should arrive there in two days with your package. You need to catch a flight there so you can meet him," said Valdez. "A'ight," said Pharaoh.

Everything seemed to be going smoothly. Pharaoh was satisfied with Valdez's plans. He left the warehouse after exchanging numbers with his driver Eric. He went straight to 'The Zone,' Sasha was still on the clock, but Pharaoh insisted she leave early so they could spend some time together. He drove back to his apartment trying to think of a way to break the news about him leaving. They sat and watched "Baby Boy" Sasha's favorite movie. The sex scenes made her horny. She began rubbing her foot up Pharaoh's leg until she felt a bulge. They were lying on the couch in the living room. Sasha was laid one way and Pharaoh the other. She sat up and began kissing him, whispering sweet nothings in Spanish. She lifted his shirt and removed it over his head.

Now, she was sitting on his lap with her legs wrapped around his waist in a riding position. She began kissing Pharaoh's bare chest, and rubbing him passionately. She unbuckled his belt and then unbuttoned his pants. By know Pharaoh had started pre-cuming. Sasha pulled his boxer's down to his ankles. She began playing with Pharaoh's dick with her index finger, using his pre-cum as lubrication. Pharaoh took her hair and wrapped it around her ear so he could watch as Sasha tongued teased his dick. "Ah," said Pharaoh. Sasha was deep-throating him, while making seductive moans. "Umm," she sucked. Pharaoh slid his hand down her pants from the back. He began playing with her click trying to get her ready. He felt himself almost there, so he pulled her head up. Pharaoh wanted some pussy. Sasha stood up and undressed as Pharaoh remained sitting on the couch with his dick sticking straight up gleaming with saliva and cum. Sasha smelled like strawberry Bath and Body Works. She climbed on top of Pharaoh's awaiting dick and began riding him. She moaned and groaned in Spanish, as Pharaoh took over. He gripped her by the ass, slid her up and down on his dick, while looking up at her go crazy.

"Oh Juan, Oh, Oh!" she screamed. Pharaoh couldn't last another stroke. "Uh.. Ah!" he grunted sending violent spurts of cum off inside Sasha, while still stroking. His dick finally went limp. Sasha wanting more, started sucking him again, trying to get him back up. He managed to say, "baby I got something to tell you." She was still at work. Pharaoh pulled her up and continued. "Baby I'm leaving for Detroit in the morning."

"What? Why?" she asked.

"Business."

"When will you be back?" There was a pause. Pharaoh really hadn't planned on coming back, at least not to live.

"Are you coming back?" asked Sasha.

"Of course," answered Pharaoh.

"Well then, I'll see you when you get back."

Pharaoh kissed her. He thought she was so understanding.

Chapter 6

Back in Detroit, Tez was living his dope boy fantasy. Only problem he wasn't selling drugs. He was steady spending money, but wasn't making any. He bought a platinum colored Cadillac Seville, mink bomber, and several pair of Cartier glasses. Tez had his fronts up, but was practically broke. He was driving in his caddie on Jefferson Street. He had just come from Belle Isle. The weather was starting to break, and the sluts were coming out.

He drove west heading towards downtown. He was a bit hungry so he decided to go get a burger from 'Fuddruckers.' He pulled into the parking lot, 'Fudds' was located in a strip mall. He parked and got out going to the carryout entrance. The restaurant had a dining area with a second entrance, but Tez wasn't trying to stay. He ordered his burger and potato wedges, with a frozen treat.

As he waited for his order, he so happened to look in the dining area, and saw his baby momma, Annie. She was at a table hugged up with Rolo, h was a nigga from the West side who was getting major money. He was also Annie's first baby daddy. Tez became furious and left before getting his food. He went home and called Annie's cell phone.

"Hello," she answered after two rings.

"Baby listen I need for you to come home it's an emergency. Dana is having an asthma attack."

"I'm on my way." Tez knew if he said it was a an emergency that she would coming flying home.   .

"What's wrong?" Dana was Rolo's son. He sounded sincerely concerned.

- 45 -

"Nothing major, I'll see you tomorrow," said Annie, then kissed Rolo goodbye. She knew not to mention Dana because Rolo would have wanted to come, that's exactly what Tez was banking on.

There was nothing wrong with Dana. In fact Dana nor Tez's daughter Princess were there. Tez closed all the blinds to the house, and turned up the stereo on full blast. "*Me against the world. I got nothing to lose, it's just me against the world,*" were the lyrics from the late great 2-Pac. Tez paced back and forth in the living room, steady peaking out the blinds to see if Annie had arrived. The font door opened, as Annie barged in looking like a concerned mother. "Where is he?" she asked scanning the front room. "Dana," she called as she walked towards the back of the house. Tez made sure the door was locked, and peeped out the window to make sure no one was sitting in her car. Annie returned to the front room, and asked more like demanded. "Where is Dana, Tez?" Tez pulled from his waist a 40 cal. Smith & Wesson, and pointed it in Annie's face.

"Bitch, where you been at?"

"What?"

"You heard me, bitch!"

"Who the fuck you calling a bitch? Yo' momma's a bitch!" shouted Annie in total disregard for the gun in her face.

Tez cocked back and slapped her t o the ground with the butt of the gun. Annie laid on the floor screaming, holding her face. Blood was everywhere. He had struck her on her forehead. He split her shit to the white-meat. "You pussy ass nigga! Look what you've done to me!" hollered Annie. Tez went into a rage. "Shut up bitch!" he said, then grabbed her by the legs and dragged her through the kitchen, and down the basement stairs. Hitting her head on each step, Annie kicked and screamed, but to no avail. He pulled her into the wash area onto a comforter with a thick sheet of plastic he had put there earlier. "Whatcha' gon' do, kill me?" asked Annie in a hurry up and get it over with tone of voice. Her lack of fear infuriated Tez.

"First things first, bitch!" he yelled pulling out a pair of scissors. He bent down and reached for Annie's head when she kicked him in the shin. "Ah, you stupid bitch," said Tez. He pimp-slapped her before she could scramble to her feet sending her back to her position on the comforter.

Tez grabbed Annie's hair, wrapped it around his right hand in a knot and used his left hand to cut off a great portion of it. He stood up and threw it down on her and said, "Look at cha'." He pulled the 40 cal. back out his waist band and pointed down to Annie's torso. He let off four rounds, lodging bullets in her stomach and heart. He then stood closer and sent two rounds to her head. Tez looked at Annie's dead body, gun in hand, adrenaline pumping. "Funky bitch!" he yelled at Annie's dead corpse.

"Ring! Ring!" Tez's cellphone went off.

"Hello" he answered.

"What up doe?"

"Where you at my nigga?" asked Tez returning to his senses.

"Shit, I'm on my way to see you. Where you at?"

"I'm at the crib come through. I need you to help me do something anyway."

"A'ight in a minute," said Pharaoh. He had just landed at the Metro airport, and rented a car. He sped in his Suburban rental bumping the radio. It felt good to be back in the city. The sun was out, and so were the hoes. Pharaoh made it back to the city, and he exhaled at the sight of all the oh so familiar abandon buildings, crackheads, panhandling, tricked out cars parked at various car washes all on 7 Mile Road.

Tez lived on Syracuse, two streets over from the crack spot on Mound Road. Pharaoh bent the corner of 7

Mile and Syracuse, nothing had changed. All his childhood friends Twon, Rell, Bone, Remy, Pope, Damon, Floyd, and a couple other off brands were huddled at the "Sunoco" service station on the corner shooting dice. They didn't notice him because they were too involved with the craps game. Pharaoh continued on down three blocks to see all the neighborhood kids playing b-ball on one side of the street in a park, and some dope fiends kicking it on the monkey bars at the park across the street. Tez stayed in the middle of the block. Pharaoh pulled out his cell phone.

"Come open the door my man," he said. By the time he parked and made it up the stairs, Tez had opened the door.

"What up doe?" said Pharaoh.

"Ain't shit," said Tez as he looked past Pharaoh up and down the street. "Come in, come in," he said.

"I see you done copped the Lac', my manz."

"Yeah, man," said Tez.

"What's wrong my nigga?" asked Pharaoh. He could tell by the look on Tez's face that something was bothering him.

"Man, follow me," said Tez. He led Pharaoh through the kitchen and down into the basement. They entered the laundry room and Pharaoh saw Annie's bloody lifeless body lying there.

"My man what you done did man ah... nah... man," said Pharaoh.

"I caught the bitch up at 'Fudd's' all hugged up with that lame Rolo.

"Look at 'cha'" said Tez talking to Annie. Pharaoh stood there and watched Tez, and thought to himself 'This nigga done flipped.'

"So what you want me to do?" asked Pharaoh.

"I need you to help me throw this bitch in my trunk so I can bury her funky ass somewhere."

"Man you lucky you my nigga. Dog, come on."

They wrapped Annie's body up tightly in the

comforter and plastic. Tez took some grey duct tape and
wrapped it around her head to toe. Pharaoh pulled Tez'c car
to the back door and together they put the body in the trunk.
Tez cleaned the spattered blood from the walls and floor,
and changed clothes. He went in the garage and found a
shovel.

"You ready my nigga?" asked Tez.

"Yeah, but I'mma drive my car. I'll follow you."

Tez drove to a vacant lot across from a scrap metal
shop where crackheads took stolen aluminum siding. Tez
parked and grabbed the shovel. He found a decent spot that
he thought to be a burial site, and dug a shallow hole. He
returned to his car and drove next to the grave. Pharaoh
followed. They quickly removed the body from Tez's trunk
and threw it in the grave. Tez shoveled the dirt back over
Annie's body and said "see you in hell bitch!"

Chapter 7

Tez's incident spoiled Pharaoh's surprise and good news. To take his mind off what he just experienced, Pharaoh decided to hit "007". He and Tez drove down 7 Mile and turned on Outer Drive pulling into a parking lot. Pharaoh valet parked the rental and entered the club. It had been a good minute since he played his favorite spot.

A lot of new faces were in the place. But that wasn't why he was there. The place was wall-to-wall asses and titties of all shapes, and colors. "Home at last," Pharaoh said, settling in the V.I.P. section of the club. A short waitress approached him, wearing titties and a garter belt.

"Can I take your order?" she asked.

"Yeah. Um, let me get a bottle of Dom, your number and whatever my boy here is having," said Pharaoh looking on in approval of the waitress's assets. She smiled and asked Tez. "And what will you be having."

"Let me get a bottle of Remy 1738."

The waitress walked off to fill their orders. Pharaoh watched her every step. "I'm hitting that, man," he said, then looked at Tez who was still a bit shaken up. It had dawned on him what he had really done.

"Relax my nigga. We can't change it, but I do have something that will make you feel better."

"What in the world could possibly make me feel better?" Tez asked, looking at Pharaoh in disbelief.

"Freeze the game," said Pharaoh because the fine red bone waitress had returned with their drinks.

"Anything else?" she asked sitting the drinks down.

"Just your name and number," said Pharaoh.

"My name is Chyna, as far as my number if you're a good boy we'll work on that," she said and turned walking away, throwing that ass in every which way.

"Like I was saying what could possibly make me feel better my manz?" ask Tez.

"Nigga we 'bout to blow like Ali Ba Ba. I got a weed plug, my manz. I bought a hun'd bows and it'll be here by tomorrow."

"For real?" asked Tez.

"Yeah, man. You know you got a spot on the team my dude."

"Good 'cause I'm bout' broke." They both laughed.

Two young ladies dressed in nothing approached Pharaoh and Tez, and asked if they would like lap dances. "Sure why not," said Pharaoh. The broads pop, locked and dropped it to the "Yin Yang Twins" among other club bangers. Pharaoh and Tez sat back like kings, enjoying the perks of being what they considered to be made niggas. A few hours had passed and Pharaoh was feeling nice. Chyna the waitress came to check up on them, especially Pharaoh, since he was draped with another hooker.

"Are ya'll okay? she asked.

"Yeah, we good ma," said Pharaoh.

"Matter of fact we 'bout to get up out of here. Can you please get our bill?" asked Pharaoh.

Chyna turned and went towards the register. Pharaoh removed three hundred-dollar bills from his wad, giving the two dancers one each. He wrote his cell number and a.k.a. Juan on the third one.

Chyna returned with the bill and Pharaoh paid it. He left the hun'd with his information on it on the table. "Let's be up my manz," he said to the drunken Tez. Chyna looked at Pharaoh's back as he exited the club in disbelief that he didn't pursue her phone number. As she cleaned their table, she saw the hun'd and picked it up relieved to see Pharaoh a.k.a. Juan's math. They rode around politicking the come up, and who would play what role. Pharaoh did the majority of the talking. Tez nodded in agreement, glad to be back on. "A pound going for a thousand am I right?" asked Pharaoh.

"Yep, but sometimes twelve hun'd."

"Well we gon' let em' go for an even thousand. It's all about a quick flip, ya' feel me?"

"That's what's up, but exactly what do you want me to do?

"Every mob needs muscle and you're it. Your job will be security, and to instill fear in these cowards. We 'bout to take the city on the weed end of things. If niggas ain't getting it from us, than they ain't getting it!" said Pharaoh putting a battery pack in Tez's back.

"Okay I feel you now my nigga," said Tez.

"I'm 'bout to buy some choppers with hun'd round drums, some bulletproof vests, and whatever else you need to war. Niggas gon' try and buck, but once they see niggas dropping, and coming up missing in action, they gon' fall in line. Niggas nowadays ain't built like that. It's called 'realistic fear.'"

Pharaoh was charging Tez up. He drove West on 7 Mile Road until he reached Moenart Street. He pulled over and parked in front of "B.B.'s Diner." Pharaoh and Tez got out and crossed the street, they were going to "Al's Barber Shop." Pharaoh rang the bell, a few seconds later they were buzzed in. No one was cutting hair, it was after working hours. Everyday after closing, and sometimes during the day it'll be a craps game jumping in the back room.

"Can't get right," said Mo' referring to Pharaoh. Mo' was about 5'9, light brown skin, medium build. He was in his early 30's. Pharaoh used to clean up hair in the barbershop when he was a youngin'. He would sit around and soak up game from all the major players such as Mo', Rich Bo, Redman, Old man Bob, and of course Al.

Maurice, Mo' for short took to Pharaoh. He gave Pharaoh the handle 'Can't get right" because he stayed in trouble.

"What's up Mo?" asked Pharaoh.

"Losing right now, but the night's still young."

Mo' escorted them into the back room. There were at least twenty plus bodies in a small room, all of whom had some clout on the streets. It had to be at least a million or better back there, them niggas weren't betting nothing less than a thousand. Over the years Pharaoh had witnessed hundred thousand dollar lock outs. Each man had to have a hun'd G's or better to get in. Niggas have lost everything from houses to cars in Al's.

Pharaoh hadn't come to gamble. He was looking for Dee his barber/business associate. Dee had just done a ten year bid, but was out and on a mission. Pharaoh spotted him crammed in a corner trying to crawl up a nigga's leg, betting only certain points. Pharaoh signaled Dee from the entrance, and it was right on time. Dee was winning and looking for an excuse to leave without seeming petty. Dee was in his early 40's, gap teeth, wore a bold fade, about 5'10 and weighed about 180 pounds.

"What's up baby?" asked Dee.

"You gotta be up my man," said Pharaoh.

"A little something, something light weight ya' dig?"

"That's what's up, but dig this, I got them pounds of popcorn, no seeds all buds for a stack."

"Square business?"

"Yep. I know you be fucking with the weed so you know get at me before you copp again."

"For a G-ball, when can I copp?"

"Get at me tomorrow when you get off."

"That's a bet."

Dee walked Pharaoh and Tez to the door and let them out. Pharaoh drove to Highland Park a once beautiful place to live, but it had been taken over by the crack era, better known as the 80's. Pharaoh turned the corner of Rhode Island and spotted the man he was looking for. Mike was his name; he was one of Pharaoh's associates who was much older than him, probably thirty-five. Mike was walking down the driveway of a crack house towards his Impala. Pharaoh hit the horn and Mike scanned the truck as if it was the police. Mike was 6'5", 200 pounds solid, high yellow nigga, about 25 years old. Tez let the passenger window down as they pulled in front of Mike.

"What up doe boy?" said Pharaoh leaning over Tez. Mike recognized the voice and relaxed. "Oh what up my nigga? I ain't know who ya'll was." Pharaoh pulled over and got out leaving Tez in the truck. He and Mike gave each other dap, and kicked the bo-bo's for a few minutes.

"But yeah man I came through to let you know I got them elbows for an even thousand. All buds, no seeds may man," said Pharaoh.

"I'm trying to get ten of them like immediately. My guy charging me twelve hun'd sometimes thirteen."

"Well look I'mma get up with you tomorrow early."

"Bet that," said Mike giving Pharaoh dap before hopping in his car.

'Two down, four to go,' Pharaoh thought to himself. He climbed back in the Suburban and got in traffic. He rode around to every spot he knew of and any nigga who was fucking with the weed. Pharaoh drove back East on Grand River and Gratiot. He turned down Helen Street going south. He pulled into the driveway of a two family flat red brick duplex. The man inside on the first floor peeped out the curtains, holding a 357 in his right hand.

"Who that?" he said talking to no one in particular. Pharaoh exited the SUV and cut across the grass.

"Oh that's my nigga," said the man inside rushing for the door. As Pharaoh walked up the stairs he could hear chains and boards coming off the door. The door swung open. The man used his key to unlock the storm door, and then another security gate.

"You must be sitting on a mint, with all these damn locks and boards you got my manz," laughed Pharaoh.

"What it is my nigga?"

'Ain't shit just come to holla and rap a little with you. You know you're still my nigga." The man was Tone, Pharaoh's high school friend. They were from two different hoods, but they clicked while going to Osborn High School.

"Come on in baby," said Tone putting all the locks and boards back up. Tone was 20 years old 5'11", weighed about 195 pounds and was silly.

"That won't be necessary, I can't stay, I just came through to let you know it's going down my baby. I got them elbows of them goods for a G-stack," said Pharaoh.

"Word?"

"Yeah, man look it's time to expand. You got this spot banging, but you can do better. It's all about the pyramid my nigga."

"What you mean?" asked Tone.

"Nigga I got it where you can have a house on every block…yeah man."

"I'll have to kill a nigga on each block to get it too."

"Let me worry about that. All you gotta do is point, and it's done. I'm on some other shit! So is you with it or what my nigga? I'm a front you all the work you need, so don't worry about that."

"It's whatever. So, when all this supposed to be taking place?" asked Tone.

"Tomorrow. I'mma drop something nice on you."

"A'ight get with me," said Tone as he watched Pharaoh safely to his truck.

Pharaoh headed for the North end. He pulled out his cell and called his uncle "Killer B.," he was getting a little money on the weed. He lived on the West side though.

"Hello" answered Killer B.

"Nigga quit trying to sound hard. You ain't no killer fo' real," said Pharaoh. In all actuality, he wasn't. His name was Brian. He gave himself that name. He had never killed anyone, the nigga was soft as pussy. He was shit black, 6'1" weighed 230 pounds of bad body and 45 years old.

"What up nephew?" he said dropping the act.

"I'mma be through there to see you in a few."

"Come on, I'mma be here."

Pharaoh pulled into the parking lot of the "Outkast," which was one of the known ruthless motorcycle clubs on the North end of Detroit. He and Tez got out and quickly headed for the door. They were frisked by two "WWF" looking niggas manning the entrance/exit. Once inside Pharaoh and Tez headed for the bar where they parked on two stools.

"What ya'll having?" asked a barmaid who looked more like a man.

"I'm good, but you can give my boy whatever he's drinking, and could you please tell Chris that his boy Pharaoh's out here?"

Tez ordered his usual Remy Martin 1738, double shot. The barmaid disappeared into the back. Pharaoh and Tez sat at the bar and watched as the members of the club acted a donkey. There was a stage/dance floor in the center of the club, that is where it was going down. The women, who mostly resembled me, were lying on their backs, while the real men drank shots of cheap whiskey, and hard liquor from the women's stomach. "Woo!!!" they screamed repeatedly. Everyone was dressed in worn out skin tight leather outfits, the coats read "Outkast" with their symbol of a skull and bone. "These mothafuckas on the sipidi boom," said Pharaoh.

"Chris will see you now, said Butch the barmaid retuning

and handing Tez his drink.

"I'll be right back," said Pharaoh.

Pharaoh walked around the bar and was escorted upstairs to an office by a no neck bouncer. The bouncer pushed the door open and stepped back, allowing Pharaoh to enter. The bouncer closed the door remaining outside. The guy Pharaoh was there to see was Chris. He was playing a game of pool by himself. He took a long swallow of his "MGD" beer when he noticed the door open. Chris was in his mid 50's, but looked an easy 35. He was 6'3", 180 pounds, fairly skinny, brown skinned and wore his hair brushed to the back.

"Pharaoh! And what do I owe the pleasure?" he asked.

"Ah.. man cut it out."

Chris was Pharaoh's father's best friend--well used to be. Pharaoh's dad who was known as "Weasel" was shot and killed during a bar brawl in '87. Pharaoh was only four when his father passed. Chris looked out for Pharaoh and his siblings here and there, but Pharaoh was nobody's charity case.

"I need some guns Chris, some vests, the works." There was a slight pause.

"For..." Chris was about to ask for what, but caught himself. "You done grew up boy, look at you," he said with a smile.

"Yeah, but look Chris you know me man, I got cash," he said pulling out several thousands, trying to cut to the chase and bullshit.

"Well I guess if I don't sell 'em to you, somebody else will," said Chris in attempt to justify his greed. He walked over to a wall and pushed a button. The wall turned 360 degrees. When it stopped there was enough ammunition to figth Vietnam. Pharaoh selected two Mack 90's, a replica of the AK-47, equipped with hun'd round drums, two bulletproof vests, and two thousand shells.

"One more thing," said Pharaoh. "I got the weed now, not no dime bag shit. I got a connect and I know you dib and dabble here and there."

"What a pound going for?" asked Chris.

"For you…"

They both laughed at the often used phrase niggas used when trying to sell something.

"I'll let you get em' for a thousand even, but only 'cause I fucks with you," said Pharaoh.

"What is it?"

"I call it popcorn, all buds, no seeds."

"I want fifty of 'em. When can I get on?"

"I'm,a get up with you tomorrow," said Pharaoh.

Pharaoh wrapped his newly purchased guns and shells in an old dingy sheet Chris had in his office. He was escorted by No-neck back down to the bar, where he spotted Tez on the dance floor ticking and gettin.' Pharaoh laughed, then signaled him that it was time to leave. They climbed back in the Suburban, putting the gun's and vests in the hatch. It was three o'clock in the morning, but Pharaoh had two more stops to make.

Pharaoh's uncle Killer B. didn't stay too far from the "Outkast." He took the Southfield Freeway and came up on exit 9 the infamous Joy Road home of the "Joy Boys" and a host of other money gettin' niggas. Pharaoh drove west until he reached Grandville. On the corner sat a 24- hour eatery famously known as Coney Island. He turned left and pulled in front of Killer B.'s crib which was the third house off the corner. Pharaoh and Tez got out and rang the doorbell. Moments later, Killer B. opened the door wearing nothing but his boxers. He stepped back rubbing his stomach as Tez and Pharaoh entered the house.

"My man put some clothes on. You around here like you that nigga," snapped Pharaoh, as he and Tez took a seat on a couch.

"Boy, I bet I could pull one of yo' lil' hoes."

"Not looking like Virgil Tibbs from *In the Heat of the Night.*"

"Ah, you got jokes huh?" laughed Killer B.

"Nah check it though. I got them pounds of that popcorn for a stack."

"Nigga I ain't got no money."

"Quit pump faking for once in ya' life nigga, I'mma let you get 'em at a playa' price."

"And what's that?"

"A thousand a piece," laughed Pharaoh.

"Man, I might fucks with you boy."

"Look I'mma drop ten of em' off tomorrow, have me ten thousand ready boy!" said Pharaoh heading for the door.

Pharaoh shot to southwest Detroit. He had covered every section of the city except this one. He pulled into the parking lot of the "Perfect Beat" a little off brand bar niggas only from Southwest went to. It was almost four o'clock in the morning, but the bar was still jumping. They were supposed to stop serving drinks after two o'clock, but yeah right! The owner Mel would lock the doors so the police couldn't just walk in. He had cameras at every corner of the club inside and out.

Pharaoh walked to the door and pushed the buzzer. Tez had fallen asleep. Mel looked at one of the many monitors mounted on the bar. He pushed the entry button after recognizing Pharaoh. Pharaoh was searched by the doorman, and then let into the bar. Hoe's were everywhere. Hood rat's who used to be top notch filled the small dance floor with drinks in their hands. They were doing the hustle. Pharaoh walked up to the bar where Mel was standing.

"What it do, my peeps?" asked Mel. He was a very heavy set black Mexican almost 350 pounds.

"Just come to check you out man. Can we go somewhere and kick it?" asked Pharaoh.

Mel came from behind the bar and walked towards the back of the bar. There was a back patio so to speak at the rear of the bar, surrounded by a ten foot brick wall. Mel closed the door behind them. It was only them two of out back.

"So what's up?" asked Mel.

"Hey look, I know you got Southwest pretty much sowed on the weed, but I got a proposition for ya'."

"I'm listening."

"I got some goods and I'm letting em' go for a G-stack."

"Man I'm already getting 'em for the low low's, and it some goods," said Mel. Pharaoh thought for a moment on how much Mel could be paying for his weed, and how much he could afford to drop the price.

"What if I let you get 'em for nine hun'd a pound," he said.

"My baby I can let you get 'em for nine hun'd."

Pharaoh saw that his efforts were to no avail and decided not to press the issue. He changed the subject and kicked the game around for a few. He looked at his watch and it was going on five o'clock. Pharaoh politely said his goodbye giving Mel some dap. He jumped back in the SUV. Tez was still asleep, slobbing like a baby. He started the car and headed for the Lodge Freeway driving back east.

Chapter 8

  Pharaoh and Tez made it back to the east side. Tez was still asleep. Pharaoh started to relax as he bent the corner of 7 Mile and Syracuse. He drove down three blocks until he reached Tez's house. The scene from earlier with Tez's baby momma, Annie, replayed itself in Pharaoh's mind as he pulled into the driveway. He turned the truck off, and nudged Tez.
"Wake up my man."
Uh" Tez said awakening, but still in a state of delirium. He realized that they were at his house. He opened the door after gaining his senses. They entered the house carrying the guns and bulletproof vests.
"Where yo' kids at my manz?" asked Pharaoh.
"They at my mom's house."
"You know you got to go file a missing persons report on Annie."
"Yeah, I'ma do that later on when the sun come up," said Tez as he opened the refrigerator.
"Cook something," said Pharaoh.
"Nigga what I look like , Chef Boyardee?"
"Nah. You look more like Aunt Jemima," laughed Pharaoh.
  Tez took out some wing-dings and fries from the freezer. They pigged out until the sun came up. Tez jumped in the shower while Pharaoh watched the morning news. His cellphone rang. Pharaoh picked it up and recognized the number of the caller.
"Hello!" he answered sitting down.
"Juan, it's me Eric. I'm like twenty minutes outside Detroit in Ann Arbor. Where do you want to meet?"

"Uh..Uh.. meet me on East Outer Drive and Mound Road at this warehouse called 'Randazzo's'". Pharaoh gave Eric further instructions and told him to park in the rear of the place.

"See you in a minute," said Eric.

Randazzo's was an old abandoned fruit market and warehouse. There was still traffic there, so it wouldn't be out of the norm to meet there. Pharaoh grabbed his keys off the coffee table and hollered through the house at Tez.

"I'm up my man!"

Tez didn't respond, and Pharaoh wasn't sure whether or not Tez heard him. He didn't bother to repeat himself. He was too geeked that his package had arrived. He let himself out, and locked the door behind him. He hopped in the SUV and backed out the driveway. 'Randazzo's' was only two blocks from Tez's house. Pharaoh arrived at the warehouse. He drove around back and parked. He waited for what seemed like a lifetime, but it had only been fifteen minutes. He heard the roaring engine of an eighteen- wheeler.

A cranberry truck bent the corner and headed towards Pharaoh's SUV. Pharaoh jumped out waving the driver, Eric, to a stop. Eric put the truck in park, leaving it running an climbed down.

"How's it going?" he asked.

"Glad to see you!" said Pharaoh smiling from ear to ear.

"Let's get to work," said Eric walking to the rear of the truck. He opened the cab and started undoing the secret compartments.

Pharaoh pulled the SUV up to the rear of the truck, backed in and opened the hatch. Eric began tossing him plastic bags. Pharaoh filled the hatch until he couldn't fit anymore. He then filled the third and second row seats.

"All done," said Eric as he climbed out the cab and locked it's doors.

"And this is how much?" asked Pharaoh.

"One hundred pounds."

Pharaoh handed Eric an envelope filled with hundred dollar bills.

"And how much is this?" asked Eric.

"Ten thousand. It's all there, but look man I'mma get out of here. Thanks and be safe," said Pharaoh as he jumped in his rental and pulled off.

It had been several months since Pharaoh had last seen his mother a.k.a. "Mom Duke's". He drove east on Outer Drive until he reached Lappin Street. He took the side street passing several busy streets, Hoover, then State Fair. He turned down Alcoy until he reached his mom's crib. Pharaoh's mom lived in a decent neighborhood for it to be in Detroit. A few whites remained, but they had "for sale" signs stacked in their front lawns. They were running deeper into the suburbs.

Pharaoh pulled his truck all the way to the back of the house. His mom's car wasn't there. She was still at work. Pharaoh hopped out and walked to the side door. He fumbled with his keys, he located the right one. He unlocked the door and stepped in. His older brother Donald was at the kitchen sink washing dishes. Neither one spoke to each other. They stayed feuding about basically nothing. Donald had Pharaoh by three years. He was a momma's boy, in school, and on the ball. He and Pharaoh were entirely two different beings, they favored except Pharaoh was much taller. Pharaoh walked past his brother and walked through the kitchen into the hallway. He went into his mom's room, and opened the patio door. He then went outside and opened the hatch of the truck. He began unloading the bags and taking them inside through the patio. After he finished he took the bags into his room located next to his mom's room. There were two bedrooms on the main floor, and the master bedroom upstairs where Donald slept.

Pharaoh closed his door and locked it. He leaned against the door for a second. "A'ight let's get to work,"he said, talking to himself. He flopped down in a black beanbag and started opening the bags. The pounds were already in individual Ziploc bags. Pharaoh pulled out his cellphone and called Dee from Al's Barber Shop."

"Hello" answered Dee.

"What up doe?"

"Oh what boy, you still coming through?"

"Yeah, but what you want me to bring you from the store?"

"Uh, shit bring me two bags of chips."

"A'ight in a minute." Pharaoh scrolled down to Mike from Highland Park's number. He hit the call button. The phone rang twice when a female picked up.

"Hello."

"Can I speak to Mike."

"Hold on, Mike!" the woman hollered.

"Damn bitch" Pharaoh said in a low tone of voice. The woman wasn't courteous enough to take the receiver away from her mouth before hollering.

Mike grabbed the phone. "Who this?" he asked.

"Pharaoh."

"What it is?"

"Ain't shit. I'm coming your way what you want me to bring you from the store, same shit?"

"Yeah."

"Ten right?"

"Yep."

"I'll be through in a minute."

Pharaoh called the "Outkast." It was still early in the day, and most of the Bikers including Chris were still in bed. Pharaoh clicked off and dialed his uncle's number, Killer B. The phone rang ten times. Pharaoh hung up and pushed redial. Killer B. answered on the third ring.

"Hello," he said in a dry raggedy voice. He was still in bed.

"My manz, get yo' old ass up. I'm situated."

"What you want me to bring you?"

"Man I got thirteen stacks," said Killer B.

"A'ight I'll be through there."

Pharaoh did the math. He had sells for 75 pounds, 50 went to Chris, 13 to Killer B., 10 to Mike, and 2 to Dee. "I got twenty-five left," said Pharaoh talking to himself and thinking on his next move. "A'ight, I'ma give these twenty-five to Tone." He reloaded the truck and headed out. It was now eleven o'clock in the morning. The sun was out and traffic was starting to pick up. Pharaoh took 7 Mile this time being careful of the speed limit. He pulled up in front of 'Al's Barber Shop.' He flipped open his phone and called in to Dee. "I'll be out in a minute," said Dee. Seconds later Dee emerged out the front door. He climbed in the SUV after looking east then west. "What up my manz?' asked Pharaoh. He had Dee's package on his lap. He handed it to Dee. Dee quickly inspected it, and was in congruence. He, in return, handed Pharaoh a brown paper bag. Pharaoh looked inside to discover all five dollar bills. They both nodded and Dee looked in the passenger mirror before making his exit.

Pharaoh pulled back into traffic. He drove on, heading west. He took the Davison Expressway and came up in Highland Park. He turned on Rhode Island Street and pulled in behind Mike's Impala. He dialed Mike's number on his cell phone. It rang twice; Mike recognized the caller and didn't bother answering. He looked out the front window of the house, and noticed Pharaoh sitting in the truck. Mike exited the house and approached the SUV. Pharaoh saw him and unlocked the doors. Mike pulled out a grocery bag from under his hoodie sweater. Pharaoh could see all green through the plastic bag, he reached in the back seat and grabbed Mike's package. "That's them goods right there," he said handing it to Mike.Mike could smell the

strong aroma coming from the weed. He opened it and attempted to stick his nose down in it. "Woo!" he said coming up for air. He handed Pharaoh the grocery bag and reached for the door handle. "Be safe my nigga," he said.
"A'ight you, too, be smooth," said Pharaoh.

Pharaoh drove further west taking back routes. He reached for his cell phone and scrolled down to Killer B.'s name. He pushed the call button. The phone rang six times. "Damn this nigga done went back to sleep," said Pharaoh.
"Hello," answered Killer B. on the seventh ring.
"Hey, come open the door, I'm bout to bend ya' block in a minute."
"A'ight."

Pharaoh turned down Grandville and Joy Road. He pulled into Killer B.'s driveway. Killer B. was still in bed asleep. Pharaoh got out and rang the doorbell. He grew impatient, and walked around back to Killer B.'s bedroom window. He banged on it almost breaking the glass with a closed fist. Killer B.'s eyes widened from the noise, he peeked out the bedroom window and saw Pharaoh on his cellphone. Killer B.'s phone was ringing.
"Hello," he answered.
"My man, come open the fuckin' door." Pharaoh walked back to the front of the house. He retrieved Killer B.'s package and walked up the stairs. Killer B. was standing in the door still in his boxers. Pharaoh barged in still upset. "Man, you'd get a nigga knocked. If a nigga was running from the police, he'd be assed out if he was to run to your house," Pharaoh said, setting the weed on the coffee table.
"Where my money at?" he asked.
"I'mma give it to you when I flip it," said Killer B. as he walked over to the coffee table and attempted to pick up the package. Pharaoh stopped him in his tracks.
"Nah, you gone pay me right now. You think you got all the sense."

Killer B. went in the back of the house for a few minutes. He returned carrying a Nike shoe box. He handed it to Pharaoh. Pharaoh took a seat at the coffee table where he dumped the money inside the shoe box. He began counting.

"It's all there except five hun'd."

"You stay on bullshit. You should of said that before you gave it to me, you was gon' let me leave with it."

"I got you nephew."

Pharaoh calmed down and pulled out his cellphone. It was going on two o'clock and he was hoping Chris had made it to the "Outkast." The barmaid/man answered.

"Hello" she said in a deep voice.

"Chris?" said Pharaoh joking.

"Nah, this is Tammy."

Pharaoh laughed to himself. 'Don't you mean Tommy?'

"Oh my bad. Is Chris in?" he asked.

"Hold on."

She transferred Pharaoh to Chris's office.

"Hello."

"What's up man, this Pharaoh, we still on?"

"Yeah slide on through," said Chris.

"In a minute." Pharaoh stood up gathering the money back into the Nike shoe box.

"It all better be here may manz, and I'll be back to get that other five hun'd tomorrow." He said.

"You out?" asked Killer B.

"Yeah, let me out. Be smooth," said Pharaoh as he walked out the front door and down the stairs. He jumped back in the SUV and pulled out. He took the Southfield Freeway heading north coming up on 8 Mile Road. He stopped at a cell phone shop on the corner of Livernois. He bought four phone cards and a new Nextel phone.

After leaving the cellphone shop he drove south on Livernois until he reached the North end. Pharaoh pulled in front of the "Outkast" and parked. There were only two motorcycles at the club, and the parking lot was empty.

Pharaoh exited the SUV carrying Chris's package wrapped in the same sheet he used for the guns the night before. He hurried to the front door pushing the buzzer. A few seconds later Tammy a.k.a. Butch opened a slot on the steel door and recognized Pharaoh. She undid the bolts and locks, then let Pharaoh in. She locked up behind him, and disappeared behind the bar. Seconds later she returned and ushered Pharaoh up to Chris's office. "Thanks Tammy," said Chris as she closed the door.

"Here you go," said Pharaoh handing the weed to Chris.

"Oh man you could have kept the sheet baby," laughed Chris. He sat the sheet on the pool table, and walked over to his desk. "You want a drink?" he asked.

"Nah, I'm cool." Chris removed five stacks of hund's from the bottom drawer and tossed them to Pharaoh. Pharaoh fanned through each stack wrapped in thick blue rubber bands.

"It's ten G's in each stack," said Chris.

"A'ight man let me get up out of here. I'mma get up with you later," said Pharaoh as he stuffed the money in his pants pockets.

"This shit is already accounted for. When can I re-up?"

"Hey man, give me a couple days," answered Pharaoh.

Butch let Pharaoh out. He was grinning from ear to ear as he drove back east. He only had twenty-five pounds left, and he was on his way to drop them off to Tone. He drove east on Gratiot Avenue until reaching Helen Street. He drove south on the crack-infested block down three streets. He pulled in the driveway and hit the horn. Tone peeped out the window, then bolted for the front door. He undid the locks in record time. Pharaoh pulled Tone's package from under the passenger seat, and exited the truck. Tone was waiting on the porch.

"What up my baby?" he asked as Pharaoh cut across the front lawn.

"Ain't shit, got a lil' something for you."

They entered the house. Tone only put a few locks on the doors. He was anxious. Pharaoh walked into the dining room and sat the weed on the glass table.

"Look, this is twenty five pounds. I want twenty-five thousand back."

"A'ight that's a bet," said Tone.

"How long you think it'll take you to dump this lil' shit?"

"Nigga I'm doing like three pounds a day, so I say 'bout two weeks give or take," answered Tone.

"Who else selling weed around here?" Pharoah asked thinking two weeks was too long. .

"This hoe ass nigga name Jimmy, and his manz Curt."

"Show me where their spot is at."

They locked up and got in the Suburban. Tone directed Pharaoh two blocks over and pointed out Jimmy and Curt's weed spot. "See this bitch shaking," said Tone referring to all the traffic going and coming from the house. Pharaoh drove Tone back to his house/weed spot.

"Look man, don't even worry about them niggas," he said as he parked in front of the spot.

"Good looking out my nigga," said Tone.

"Don't worry about it, but check it I'm 'bout to get in traffic, just get with me when you're done."

"A'ight."

"One" Pharoah and Tone said at the same time.

Pharaoh drove off content with his accomplishment for the day. He had $74,500 and $25,500 still in the street. 'Not a bad flip,' Pharaoh thought to himself.

Chapter 9

"May I help you sir?" asked the desk sergeant. Tez had bubble guts as he stood at the front desk of the 11th precinct on Nevada Road. The place was crawling with cops, and Tez hated cops. Sergeant Chapman sat in a reclining leather chair. She had a funky build, all chest no butt. She was in the middle of eating her hourly donuts when Tez entered. She looked down over her thick '88 Cazel reading glasses.

"Sir may I help you?" she said repeating herself. Tez snapped back to reality and focused on Sergeant Chapman for the first time.

"Uh, yes I would like to file a missing persons report on my baby mother, Annie..." Before he could finish his sentence she handed him a form.

"Fill this out front and back," she said.

Tez took the form and walked over to the waiting area. He took a seat next to an elderly woman. He scanned the form before filling it out. He stopped on the section that read: *Where was the last place you seen the missing person? And with whom?* Tez quickly put at home on such and such date. He said that Annie told him that she was meeting her ex-boyfriend/baby father at "Fuddrucker's" to discuss child support issues. He volunteered and wrote that Annie and Rolo had a history of domestic violence. Tez smiled as he walked to the counter and handed Sgt. Chapman the form. She looked on both sides of the form, then placed it in a tray with a bunch of other forms.

"That's it?" asked Tez.

"That's it," answered Sgt. Chapman eating her fourth donut.

Tez exited the police station. While he was walking to his car, his phone rang. He
looked at the caller I.D. then pushed the talk button.

"What up doe?" he asked.

"Where you at boy?" asked Pharaoh.

"Shit just leaving the 11th."

"Word, everything straight?"

"I guess. What's up though?"

"Meet me at yo' crib."

"In a minute."

Pharaoh and Tez pulled up at Tez's house minutes apart. Tez had just locked the door when he heard the horn of the SUV in his driveway. He walked over to the front bay window and looked out. Pharaoh hopped out and made his way up the stairs. Before he could knock Tez had opened the door. "Yeah man" said Pharaoh pulling out all the money he'd rounded up during the course of the day.

"That's how you do?" asked Tez.

"Finished! All that is gone."

"All hun'd pounds.

"Yeah man, I'm ready to re-up. This time I'mma snatch two hun'd elbows," said Pharaoh. Tez became silent. He walked over to the couch and flopped down. Pharaoh was like Tez's big brother, he knew when something was bothering him.

"What's wrong my nigga?" he asked.

"Shit what I'm suppose to do?" asked Tez.

"I told you. You on security and your job is to put fear in these niggas, which brings me to why I wanted to meet. Look I need you to go see Mel's fat, funky, half breed ass."

"What you want me to do?" asked Tez.

"Put his ass out of commission!" Pharaoh counted out five thousand and handed it to Tez. "That's five G's. I got to use the rest to get back on and get right. I'm damn near broke. Every time we flip you gon' get hit with bread. The more we cop, the more you get," said Pharaoh.

"Good looking." said Tez stuffing the money in his pocket.

Pharaoh pulled his cellphone out, and flopped down on the love seat across Tez. He phoned Valdez to let him know he was ready to re-up.

"Your ready already?" asked Valdez.

"Yeah. I'mma catch a flight tomorrow."

"See you then," said Valdez, then hung up the phone.

"Look I'mma catch a few hours of sleep, wake me up at five," said Pharaoh.

Tez went in his bedroom and got one of the two Mack-90's Pharaoh bought from Chris. He sat on the edge of his bed, and loaded 100 rounds into a special made drum attached to the assault rifle. He grabbed his 40 cal., the same one he used to kill Annie and laid it on the bed next to the Mack-90. He went to his closet and retrieved a black hoodie, and some black Timberlands. He took off the Polo shirt he was wearing and tossed it on the floor. He tucked his white T-shirt he wore into his pants. He grabbed one of the bulletproof vests and strapped it to himself. Tez grabbed the 40 cal. and put it in the waist of his jeans. He picked up the hoodie and slid it over his head. He looked in his dresser drawer and scrambled through socks and boxers. He located the black leather gloves he was searching for and looked in his dresser mirror to check his appearance. Pleased with what he saw, Tez turned and grabbed the Mack-90 off the bed. He wrapped it up in the bed comforter after wiping his prints off. He walked into the front room to find Pharaoh asleep. He didn't bother to wake him. Tez exited the house locking up behind him.

It was after eight o'clock when Tez reached the 'Perfect Beat.' He parked in the rear of the parking lot next to an S-10 Chevy pick up. There was only one other car. It belonged to Mel, a 420 SL Benz. Tez wrapped the Mack-90 around his waist with the belt of the rifle. He pulled his hoodie down over it and exited his car. Tez casually walked across the parking lot and to the front door. He pushed the buzzer. Mel sat up in his office chair and looked at the video monitor, he recognized Tez. "Let him in!" he hollered.

Tez heard this and clutched the handle of the rifle under his hoodie. The bouncer, Mel hollered and unlocked the door. Before he could fully open it Tez sprang into action.

Wakaa..Wakaa..Wakaa. Tez let out several rounds through the door. The bouncer was hit three times in the chest, sending him flying back and hitting the floor hard. Tez forced his way in, sending shots in every direction of the bar. Mel jumped up and grabbed a .38 revolver out of his desk. Tez inched his way towards Mel's office, clearing each section of the bar. As Tez walked around the bar, Mel who was kneeled, down saw Tez's shadow. *Boom! Boom"* Mel sent two shots in Tez's direction, one hitting Tez in the stomach. The impact sent Tez stumbling back, but he remained on his feet. Tez let off what seemed like fifty rounds through the wall of Mel's office.

Mel was forced to lay flat on his stomach. He pointed his gun at the entrance of the door. He had only three shots left. Tez figured Mel had to be hit, if not dead. He continued to let the Mack-90 rip. Mel couldn't hear Tez's foot steps as he entered the office. But he did get off his last three rounds. "Boom! Boom!" Boom!" Mel planted three shells in Tez's chest at close range. Tez was plunged backwards and slammed against the wall. His adrenaline was pumping, and that's what kept him from falling. Tez saw Mel trying to get up. He was pulling the trigger repeatedly but to no avail. *Click, Click, Click.* Mel was out. Tez looked Mel in the eyes before squeezing the trigger. He could see the death in Mel's face. He knew it was over and why.

Wakaa. Wakaa.. Wakaa.. Tez filled Mel's big frame with multiple rounds. Mel buckled down to his knees and fell over on his face. Tez walked up closer and extended the barrel to Mel's head. *Wakaa.. Wakaa..* He sent two shells into Mel's dome, exploding it, sending blood everywhere.

Tez, satisfied with his kill, made a casual exit. He peeped out the front door. The parking lot was the same as when he went in. He quickly made it to his car tucking the rifle. He hopped in his car and mashed off.

Pharaoh was still asleep on Tez's loveseat when his cellphone rang. He fumbled around for his phone, finally locating it sitting right in front of him on the coffee table. He pushed the talk button. "Say something, " he answered.

"Can I speak with Juan?" asked a sexy female voice.

"Who is this?"

"Chyna." Pharaoh sat up at attention for the name. He had remembered Chyna from "007" as the sexy waitress.

"What you doing?" asked Pharaoh.

"Shit bored as hell."

"You working tonight?" asked Pharaoh.

"I'm always at work, but I won't be at the club if that's what you mean."

"So where you at right now?"

"At home."

"Yeah, what you got on?" asked Pharaoh as he stuck his hand in his boxers.

Chyna turned on her bedroom voice. "Just a T-shirt," she teased.

"For real, well look I'm a cut to the chase. I'm trying to see you," said Pharaoh.

"Do you know where the "Alterwood Apartments are?"

"Do I? What's your apartment number?"

"Seven."

"I'll be there in let's say twenty minutes."

"I'll be waiting," teased Chyna.

"I'm fenna get some pussy. I'm fenna get some pussy," said Pharaoh as he jumped to his feet. He rushed in the bathroom and took a quick bird bath. He went in Tez's bedroom and found some new socks and boxers. He removed a brand new white T from an opened four pack, slapped some "Izzi" on and was out the door. Pharaoh arrived at Chyna's apartment complex. He stood in the lobby and rang doorbell number seven.

"Who is it?" Chyna's voice asked across the intercom.

"It's me Juan."

Chyna buzzed Pharaoh in. He walked up a flight of stairs and turned right. Chyna was standing in the door of her apartment wearing exactly what she said she was wearing, a white tight T-shirt. It revealed her shapely hips and her perky nipples.

"Hey," she said with a smile.

"What's up? You lookin' good."

"You too" said Chyna as she stepped aside to let Pharaoh in.

Pharaoh stopped in the hallway and turned around as Chyna locked the door. Her white T was revealing her camel toe as well. "Oh" Pharaoh said to himself at the sight of Chyna's fat monkey. She stood about 5'4, 135 pounds, short wavy hair, brown eyes, she was right. "Come on in. Have a seat," said Chyna escorting Pharaoh into the living room. Her apartment was top flight. Girl had wall-to-wall deep plush tan carpet, leather couches, marble granite tables, she was doing the damage.

"You like?" she asked spinning around in a circle waving her hands.

"Yeah this real playa' like."

"Can I get you something to drink?"

"Nah, I'm good," said Pharaoh as he took his coat off and had a seat on the couch.

Chyna took a seat next to him, almost in his lap.

"So where ya' man at, cause I ain't into no domestic

violence," said Pharaoh.

"I'm single."

"Any particular reason? Crazy, deranged, skitso?" joked Pharaoh.

"Oh you got jokes," laughed Chyna.

"Nah, I'm just fucking with you, but uh, what's the business? We here on business or some social shit?"

"If it was business, I wouldn't have invited you to where I lay my head," said Chyna.

Pharaoh lifted Chyna's white T over her head leaving her butt naked. He stared in amazement at Chyna's beautiful bronze colored frame. He began sucking her titties, while Chyna held her head back and clutched his head. Pharaoh unbuckled his pants and slid them down to his ankles. Chyna helped him pull his boxers down. Pharaoh was standing at attention. Chyna gently grabbed his dick and leaned over. She put his entire dick in her mouth and held him with one of her manicured hands and sucked up and down passionately. Chyna was a professional head doctor. Pharaoh had to sit up and stop her because he wasn't ready to bust just yet. He directed her into the cowgirl position. He helped Chyna as she slid down on his dick. She began grinding on him using her hands as a brace on Pharaoh's knees. Pharaoh sat back and watched in awe as Chyna's ass jiggled every which a way.

Chyna was soaking wet, after her umpteenth orgasm. She leaned back on Pharaoh's chest, with her left hand wrapped around his neck. "Fuck me fuck me" she moaned in Pharaoh's ear. Pharaoh gripped her by the waist and bounced her up and down violently on his dick. He could feel the bottom of Chyna's pussy. "Ah.. Oh!," screamed Chyna. "Ah.. Ah, " said Pharaoh as he bust a fat nut inside Chyna. He continued to raise her up and down until he ejaculated every drop of semen. "Damn girl you got them goods," said Pharaoh as he sat back on the couch exhausted.

Chyna smiled and laid her head against Pharaoh's chest. She curled up and fell asleep. Pharaoh's cellphone rang, he picked up on the fourth ring.

"What up doe?" he said.

"It's done," said Tez.

"Where you at right now?"

"On my way over my mom's house to pick my kids up."

"A'ight well look I gotta hop a flight back down the way. I'mma get up with you when I get back."

"A'ight, my nigga."

"Yep."

"One" Tez and Pharaoh said then hung up.

"Wake up sleepy head," said Pharaoh as he nudged Chyna.

"I wasn't sleep, just a little nap."

"Look I gotta get ready to go."

"You can spend the night. Come on let's go in the bedroom," said Chyna getting up leading Pharaoh into her bedroom.

Round two!

Chapter 10

Pharaoh's plane landed at the "Freeport" air terminal in Phoenix, Arizona at two o'clock in the afternoon. Before leaving Detroit he rode around to several party stores and post offices and purchased money orders in the amount of $1,000.00 each. Pharaoh exited the terminal carrying a brief case, which contained the money orders in secret compartments. He approached an awaiting Lincoln Towne car. Valdez hired a driver to take Pharaoh to the warehouse. Pharaoh clutched the brief case for dear life as he tried to relax in the back seat of the car. There was a car phone mounted on the back console. Pharaoh hadn't noticed it until it began ringing. He looked at the driver through the rear view mirror. "Aren't you going to answer it?" asked the driver. He was a young white man, couldn't have been older than 21. Pharaoh reached down and picked the phone up.
"Hello."
"Are you enjoying the ride?"
"Yeah, man thanks, Val."
"Well that's how we drive,first class. I'll see you in a few."
"Okay," said Pharaoh as he hung the phone up.

Pharaoh relaxed at the thought of being tied in with the mob. The driver took the now familiar rural route. They drove for about twenty minutes until the service station slash all- purpose warehouse appeared. The driver pulled into the gravel parking lot. He stopped at the front door, and hopped out to open Pharaoh's door.
"What do I owe you?" asked Pharaoh standing outside the car.

"It's already been covered."

"Well here's a lil' something extra," said Pharaoh handing the young man a fifty dollar bill.

"Thanks Man!" he said excitedly.

Pharaoh tapped on the front door before pushing it open, there was no one in sight. Pharaoh walked to the rear of the warehouse, it was like another world, wall-to-wall amigos. Pharaoh walked over to the storage room Valdez had taken him in previously.

"Juan!" what are you doing here?" asked Hernandez the cab driver.

"Ah..what's up amigo. I'm here to see Valdez. Have you seen him?"

"Yeah he's in here," answered Hernandez as he walked towards the storage room. He knocked once and then turned the knob. Valdez turned from what he was doing.

"Juan glad you made it. Thanks Hernandez," said Valdez.

"Here you go," said Pharaoh handing Valdez the numerous money orders. "It's seventy thousand," he said.

"Money orders?" asked Valdez. There was a moment of silence. Pharaoh wasn't sure whether or not he had messed up. "I like it, more convenient," said Valdez walking over towards several boxes. Pharaoh followed. Valdez opened one of the large boxes and removed a Ziploc bag of marijuana.

"Same as last time," he said.

"So what can you do for me?" asked Pharaoh.

"Seeing as though you got rid of that first hundred in what a day, two at the most, I'm going to let you get two hundred." That's what Pharaoh was hoping for. He smiled in agreement.

"How soon will you be ready to receive it?" asked Valdez.

"I plan on leaving for Detroit in the morning."

"That's why I like you Juan, you're all business. I'll have Eric set out for Detroit as soon as he gets back. He'll be a little pissed, but twenty grand should ease any grief.

"Can you give me a lift to my apartment?" asked Pharaoh.

"Sure."

  Pharaoh's Monte Carlo was still parked in its spot. He smiled as he walked past it and up to his apartment. He thought to himself, had he left his car parked out in the open in Detroit, it would have without a shadow of a doubt, been stolen. Pharaoh immediately took a shower and changed into some fresh clothes. For the first time in a few days he thought about Sasha. He felt bad for not calling her. He flipped out his cell phone and dialed her number. No answer. He tried again and the same outcome. "Umm," Pharaoh said. Maybe she left her phone somewhere, he tried to reason with himself. He flopped down on his cotton couch, and reached for the remote on the coffee table. He flicked on the TV, trying to catch Sports Center, seconds later his cellphone rang. He picked it up and smiled, it was Sasha.

"Hello," he answered trying to sound calm, cool, and collected.

"Juan?"

"What's up mommie?"

"How come you haven't called me?" asked Sasha with a bit of an attitude mixed with concern.

"I know baby. I lost track of time. Can I see you?"

"I guess so," said Sasha still trying to sound upset.

"Where are you?"

"At home."

"Be there in a minute."

"Hurry Papi."

  "I'm fenna get some pussy. I'm fenna get some pussy," said Pharaoh as he turned the TV off, and snatched his keys off the coffee table. He locked up his apartment and hopped in his luxury car. He drove about four miles north until he reached Sasha's apartment complex. He pulled in and parked next to Sasha's Lexus 430. He rang her apartment buzzer, Sasha buzzed him up. Pharaoh walked up two flights of stairs and was greeted by Sasha in the hallway. She looked even better than the first time Pharaoh layed eyes on her. She was looking very edible, wearing an elegant sundress and heels. Her hair was pulled into a bun.

"You look--wow!," said Pharaoh as he attempted to embrace Sasha. She pulled back.

"I'm still mad at you."

"You know you can't stay mad at me," said Pharaoh as he pinned Sasha on the wall and kissed her.

"Ah..." sighed Sasha in satisfaction as Pharaoh kissed her neck. She managed to push him back. Her eyes were now filled with passion. She looked up and down the hall. "Come inside," she said grabbing Pharaoh's hand.

She locked the door behind them. Pharaoh was on her like a lion on its prey. He pressed her up against the door and tongue kissed her, while holding her face. Sasha took a pin out of her hair, then shook it, letting it fall down her back. Pharaoh unbuttoned her sundress, and helped her slip out of it. She wasn't wearing a bra, her titties stood firm. Pharaoh teased her nipples with his tongue. He stepped back so he could take a look at Sasha's voluptuous frame. He grabbed her hand and spun her around in a full circle. He slapped her on the ass.

"Oh Papi."

"You've been a very naughty girl, haven't you?" asked Pharaoh.

"Yes."

"Well you know what happens to naughty girls don't you?"

"What happens Papi?" asked Sasha playing along.

Pharaoh ripped Sasha's panties off. He got down on both knees and kissed her stomach.

He gripped Sasha's ass with both hands as he tongued kissed her pussy.

"Ohh..." sighed Sasha as she looked down at Pharaoh. She gripped his head, directing him to her satisfaction. Pharaoh focused primarily on Sasha's clit. He flicked his tongue violently across her pearl. All in one motion Pharaoh laid flat on his back, pulling Sasha down on his face. She had her way and went crazy. She grinded on Pharaoh's mouth for over ten minutes, screaming at the top of her lungs, while she had orgasms after orgasms. She came to a point where she stopped and pressed down with all her weight. She bust a nut so big, Pharaoh thought that she was pissing on him. He got up face looking like a glazed donut. He wanted some pussy bad, but he wanted to make it all about her. Seeing that Sasha was now in good spirits, Pharaoh thought this might be a good time to tell her.

"Mommie I've got something to tell you." Sasha had led him into the living room, and turned the TV on.

"What is it Papi?" asked Sasha taking a seat.

"I'm not sure if I'll be living here in Arizona anymore."

"So where does that leave us?" asked Sasha.

"That's just it. I'm not sure about that either."

"So you're breaking up with me?"

"No not at all. The choice rests solely with you. I want us to be together, but you've got a life here in Phoenix and I have a life in Detroit. There's a conflict of interest. I don't expect you to leave your life behind," said Pharaoh. There was a moment of silence, then Pharaoh continued, "Listen, I came to Phoenix on vacation to get away from some things, but I've rectified things back home. I tell you what, let's take things one day at a time, and see what happens. I've never been in a long distance relationship."

"Me neither," said Sasha.

"I'm willing to try if you are."

"Me too," smiled Sasha.

"That's my girl," smiled Pharaoh.

"So when are you leaving?" asked Sasha.

"In the morning."

"Already, can I ask when you'll be back?"

"Soon mommy, soon," Pharaoh answered trying to assure Sasha he would return.

Chapter 11

Pharaoh slept the entire flight to Detroit. He landed at the Metro Airport just after noon. He rented another SUV, except this one was a Cadillac truck. He was still a bit tired, he hadn't had a full night's sleep since Valdez put him down. Pharaoh drove on I-94 north back into the city. He was damn near broke after dropping seventy stacks on Valdez, so he headed over Tone's. He took Gratiot Avenue down to Helen Street. The sight of the many sluts in skirts and tight outfits gave Pharaoh the boost he needed. He sat up high in the SUV and cranked the radio up. "Oh Boy!" were the lyrics of a local hit by the "Chedda Boyz." Pharaoh popped his collar, rocking side to side. He was indeed feeling himself. He pulled up in Tone's driveway and hopped out, leaving the truck running. Tone peeped out the front window, with the 357 in his hand. He hadn't left the spot in God knows how long. Tone unbolted the front door. He met Pharaoh as he climbed the stairs.   Tone swung the door open wide.

"That's how you doing it?" asked Tone pointing at the Caddie truck.

"That's just a rental. I'mma drop that Range Rover on niggas. Just give me a minute."

"Come in, said Tone.

"So what it do?" asked Pharaoh stopping in the hallway.

"Hold on, I'll be right back", said Tone. He ran in the back room and within seconds he returned carrying a duffle bag. He handed the bag over to Pharaoh. "That's $20,000.00, I still got $5,000.00 left."

"So that leaves us a five stack, "said Pharaoh.

"Right, I should be done with this by tomorrow."

"A'ight, look I'mma swing through and touch you up with something in a couple days," Pharaoh said as he headed for the door.

"A'ight, be smooth my nigga," said Tone locking up behind Pharaoh.

Pharaoh drove to his mom's house. Her car wasn't in the driveway, so he figured she was still at work. His brother Donald's car wasn't there either. 'Good,' Pharaoh said to himself. He pulled the rental up to the bumper of his Caprice. He looked at his car and vowed never to drive an old school ever again. He hopped out the SUV carrying the duffle bag Tone had given him, and made his way into the house. As he expected no one was home. Pharaoh raided the fridge hoping to find some leftovers. He was in luck, he removed a tray of macaroni and cheese, and some fried catfish. Pharaoh warmed his food up in the microwave. He sat in the living room and enjoyed his meal while watching the Detroit news. After finishing his meal, he dumped the money from the duffle bag on the table and began counting the small bills. As he counted the money, he flipped out his cellphone and called Tez.

"What up doc?" answered Tez.

"Ain't shit. What's the word?"

"Ah, man just came from the police station. They wanted to ask me some questions. "Everything cool?"

"Yeah, but if they come at me again I'mma get a lawyer."

"You ain't heard nothing about Ollie?" asked Pharaoh.

"His mom's said he's got a court date coming up."

"How is it looking?

"Ain't no telling, nigga just gotta wait and see."

"Yeah, I'mma try and go see the nigga."

"Shit not me, I got warrants," said Tez.

"But uh, where you at?"

"On my way to the crib.

"I'm a see you in a minute."

"Yep."

Pharaoh met Tez at his house. He pulled in the driveway and hit the horn. Tez peeped out, then made his exit. He climbed into the SUV.

"You switching up like clothes nephew," he said referring to the SUV.

"Ah, man when you getting money, you gotta look like money." Pharaoh backed out of the driveway and headed east. He drove down to Tone's hood. He showed Tez the weed spot Jimmy and Curt was selling out of. "This is where them two niggas be at," said Pharaoh. He pointed to the house. A young female was coming down the stairs.

"Pull over," said Tez.

"For what?"

"So I can get ole' girl's number."

"Nigga, we on business. These two niggas is in the way," said Pharaoh.

"Don't worry about it Godfather, I'mma handle it," said Tez being sarcastic.

"Yeah, well these niggas must go. Like I said, the more we sell, the more you get paid," said Pharaoh. "There they go right there," said Pharaoh pointing at Jimmy and Curt standing on the porch. Pharaoh casually drove past the house, and turned off on Gratiot, then drove east, back towards Tez'd house.

"You hungry my nigga?" asked Pharaoh.

"A little bit."

"Let's go get some steaks at "007", said Pharaoh.

He turned on Outer Drive, looking for an excuse to go see Chyna. They pulled in the parking lot, it was damn near empty because it was during the day. They valet parked and made their entrance. Pharaoh scanned the entire club as he and Tez stood at the front door. Chyna spotted him and headed in their direction. She ushered them to a booth. Tez asked for one hundred singles. He was tipping two red bones on stage. Pharaoh took a seat in the booth and ordered two steaks, one for him and one for Tez.

"You can't call nobody?" asked Chyna, after taking Pharaoh's order.

"I mean you're a very busy woman."

"What does that mean?"

"It means I'm on your time," said Pharaoh.

"Umm.."

"You looking good as usual."

"Thank you, so when will I see you again? asked Chyna.

"Shit we can hook up tonight, of course after you get off work, but like I said, I'm on your time."

"Let me go get ya'll food," said Chyna. She turned and walked away, throwing her ass from left to right.

Pharaoh looked up to see Tez arguing with Rolo. "Bitch ass nigga, why you lie and tell the police me and Annie had domestic violence issue," yelled Rolo. Tez didn't bother to respond. He slapped the dog shit out of Rolo. He didn't fall, but stumbled back a few feet. He was every bit of 6'8" and weighed 230 pounds solid. He lunged at Tez catching him with a right, then a left. Pharaoh jumped to his feet and ran to help Tez. By the time he reached the two, they were locked up scuffling. Pharaoh grabbed a half full Corona beer bottle and cracked Rolo in the head. The bottle shattered, but seemed to have no affect on Rolo. "Boom! Boom!" Two gun shots rang out. Pharaoh thought it was a bouncer shooting, until Rolo fell backwards landing on his back. He clutched his stomach with both hands covered in blood. Tez walked up next to him, and dumped the rest of the clip into Rolo's head and body. Pharaoh looked around the club, and no one was in sight. The bouncer had retreated, along with the few dancers.

"Ah man let's get the fuck up out of here," Pharaoh said, grabbing Tez by the arm. They ran out the club and located the valet driver. Pharaoh grabbed the keys, and rushed for the SUV. They skirted off taking several side streets back to Tez's house.

"My man you ain't have to kill the nigga. At least not in there," said Pharaoh driving expertly while looking in the rear view constantly.

"Man fuck that nigga. He called me a bitch," said Tez.

"What am I going to do with you?" asked Pharaoh. He pulled the SUV all the way in the back yard behind Tez's house. They entered the house through the side door.

"Where yo' kids at?" asked Pharaoh.

"Where else, at my mom's crib."

"Have you told them that their mom is missing?"

"Nah, I figure they'll figure it out, they're smart enough."

"You out yo' shit fo' real ain't you?" asked Pharaoh. He looked at Tez as if he'd lost his mind. "Fucking with you my manz, a nigga still hungry," he said raiding Tez's fridge. "Ain't too much of nothing left in there. You know Annie used to do all the shopping," said Tez.

Pharaoh opened the freezer and removed some chicken wing-dings, and a gab of French fries. He tossed them to Tez. "Cook these," he said and walked in the living room. He flopped down on the couch after turning on the t.v.

"Breaking Story" flashed acrossed the television. A news anchor woman was standing outside the "Perfect Beat." Pharaoh sat up and hollered for Tez. Tez looked at the t.v. and turned the volume up: "Two black men, in their mid-twenties were found slaughtered this morning in the night club. The owner Melvin Cherry was found in his office on the floor, with multiple gunshot wounds to the head and body. His bodyguard whose name isn't being released right now, was gunned down at the door. Police believe it's drug related," said the anchor. Tez turned the volume down, and waited for his praise.

"My Manz, you went through there like that?" asked Pharaoh.

"Yeah, man," boasted Tez. "They say they believe it was drug related, so we don't have to worry about no thorough investigation."

The sound of Pharaoh's cellphone disrupted their conversation. Pharaoh grabbed his phone and looked at the caller's name. "Chyna" it read. He was skeptical about answering, but picked up anyway, "Yeah," he answered.

"It's me Chyna."

"Where you at?" asked Pharaoh.

"At home, they sent everyone home."

"I'll be through there in a minute."

"I'm out to get in traffic my manz," said Pharaoh as he stood up.

"You ain't gon' eat? You done had me fry all this shit."

"I'mma take some with me," said Pharaoh. He wrapped his food up and headed out. Pharoah stopped at the door and looked at his friend. "You a'ight my nigga?" he asked.

"Yeah, I'm good."

"Sure."

"Yeah, I'm straight."

"A'ight, call me if you need anything," said Pharaoh as he walked towards the SUV.

Truth is Tez wasn't okay. He was in fact losing it. Every time he killed someone, he felt like he gained more power. Tez locked up and headed for his closet. He removed his black hoodie, bulletproof vest, Mack-90 assult rifle, and his 40 cal. He placed everything neatly across the bed like he was getting ready for work, in his mind he was. He walked over to the dresser and pulled out a fresh white - T, and his black leather gloves. He suited up then checked himself in the dresser mirror before leaving. It was a quarter to seven and the sun had just set. Tez drove in his own car. He had no regard for the law whatsoever. He turned down Hamlin Street off Gratiot and headed south. He pulled across the street from Jimmy and Curt's weed house. Tez left his car running, and got out.

He crossed the street casually and walked up the stairs of the spot. He put his hoodie on and clutched the Mack-90 underneath. He knocked on the door three times repeatedly. He could hear someone walking towards the door. A young boy swung the door open without asking who it was, or looking out first. Tez grabbed the young boy, who couldn't have been more than 15 years old. The boy tried to run as he realized it was a robbery, at least that's what he thought it was. Tez put his hand over the boy's mouth and walked him towards the living room. "Who that at the door?" asked the voice of an older man.

Tez walked into the living room, and pushed the young boy into the center of the room. The boy fell forward, landing on the wooden coffee table. Two men who were seated on the couch playing NBA Live on Play Station attempted to get up, one reached for a handgun on a night stand. *Lakaa...Lakaa..* Tez caught him twice in the rib cage. He turned and shot several rounds at the second man, who was now trying to exit the room. *Lakaa..Lakaa..Lakaa..* Tez shot the man all in the back and ass, sending him face first to the soiled carpet.

"Please don't kill me," pleaded the young boy.

"You know I got to kill you, but it won't hurt, I promise." *Lakaa..Lakaa..Lakaa..*

He shot the young boy in the throat, then in the chest. He walked over to both men, and emptied several rounds into both of their already dead bodies. After killing the men, Tez turned to leave and noticed a freshly rolled blunt in the ash tray. He picked it up and lit it. He took one long pull and coughed as he exhaled. "This some good shit," he laughed talking to the dead men. *Knock, knock, knock.* Someone was at the door. Tez, still wearing his hoodie, walked to the door. A young man said to Tez, "Let me get two dimes." Tez walked back into the living room and picked up two bags off the coffee table. He walked back to the front door and handed the man the weed.

"Here you go," he said.

"Can I get two for fifteen?" asked the man.

"Two for fifteen? Nah..my manz, no shorts, no loss." Tez laughed to himself as he tucked the twenty dollar bill. He sat there in the spot playing Play Station, selling weed until he ran out. "I'm a catch ya'll later," he said to the dead men as he made his exit.

Chapter 12

Pharaoh stood in the visiting area on the sixth floor of the Wayne County Jail waiting for Ollie. He had an eerie feeling, it reminded him of when he entered a hospital. Pharaoh had never been to jail before. He thought jail was for dummies. He waited for over an hour before ringing the buzzer. A guard appeared who had let Pharaoh into the visiting area.

"Who did you say you were here to see sir?" she asked.

"Ollie fuckin' Hayes," said Pharaoh. He said each syllable with as much sarcasm he could muster.

The guard gave Pharaoh a look of "you lucky I'm at work, otherwise I'd cuss yo' ass out." She turned on her heels and disappeared. "Boot mouth bitch," Pharaoh said. The other visitors turned in his direction staring. Moments later the guard escorted Ollie to a visiting cell. Pharaoh smiled at the sight of his friend. He quickly dropped the expression as he watched Ollie get the handcuffs removed through the bars of the cell. "Thirty minutes!" screamed the guard.

"What up my baby?" asked Pharaoh. There was a wall separating the two. They talked through an eight inch glass with small holes.

"Ain't shit my manz," said Ollie.

"Step back boy, let me look at you. Damn you putting on weight, you working out?" asked Pharaoh.

"Yeah, picking up my spoon," laughed Ollie.

"But, seriously, my nigga, how you holding up?" asked Pharaoh.

"I mean, it is what it is. I'm cool, considering."

"What the lawyer talking about?"

"It's 50/50. The only thing they got me on is them two hoes."

"What two hoes?" asked Pharaoh.

"The bitch at the bank for one, and the bitch Kellie. She told the Feds I came and got our car from her the day before the lick."

"Don't worry about it. That's all they got though?"

"Pretty much, without them I walk," said Ollie.

"Hayes, time!" yelled the guard.

"Man it ain't been no damn thirty minutes," Pharaoh said.

"Don't trip, she stay on bullshit."

"Bitch need some dick!" Pharaoh said loud enough for the guard to hear.

"I'mma get on back here before she have a sucka' stroke."

"Tell Tez I said what up doe."

"A'ight my nigga, be smooth."

"One" Ollie and Pharaoh said as they put their fists on the small glass.

Pharaoh drove east on 7 Mile Road. He checked his voicemail because he had to leave his phone in the truck to enter the county jail. He had messages from Dee, Tone, Mike, and Chris. Each one was out of weed and needed to re-up as soon as possible. He called each one back, starting with Dee. He let them know he would be back on tomorrow.

"Hello."

"What up doe, where you at my manz?" asked Pharaoh.

"Shit at the crib," answered Tez.

"What, you sleep?"

"Yeah, come through."

"In a minute," said Pharaoh.

Pharaoh pulled into the parking lot of "Fat Burgers" on 7 Mile Road. He saw some PYT's inside through the picture window, and bust a u-turn. He parked the truck and went inside. The young ladies turned in Pharaoh's direction as he approached the counter. They stared at him as if he was a burger. "Damn you fine," said one of the three women.

"Thank you baby," replied Pharaoh. He continued on for the counter, then paused looking up at the menu. A guy Pharaoh's age, whom he went to middle school with appeared from the back of the restaurant.

"What's up Pharaoh? Long time no see."

"What it is Alvin?"

"Same ole', same ole' you know. Them hoes on yo' dick," whispered Alvin, pointing towards the three women.

"I'm not fucking with them. They jail bait." Alvin laughed. Pharaoh saw the news playing on a small television mounted next to the cash register. "Hey, turn that up," said Pharaoh.

He caught the tail end of the story. They showed the weed spot which belonged to Jimmy and Curt. In the background Pharaoh could see police bringing three dead bodies out of the house on stretchers. He smiled to himself, and thought, 'Tez putting in major work.'

"What you ordering? asked Alvin.

"Let me get two fat burgers and some of ya'll famous fries."

Pharaoh got his food and headed for the door. "Bye cutie," the young women said.

Pharaoh only smiled at the young women as he pushed the door opened. He walked towards the SUV and saw the jump outs sitting in the alley. The jump outs were narcotics officers, who wore plain clothes. They stayed on garbage, beating niggas, planting drugs and guns on people, and sometimes shooting folks. They felt justified in their doings, because they figured, you're a drug dealer anyway.

Before Pharaoh could hope to God that they wouldn't fuck with him, they swooped out the alley. They pulled right in front of Pharaoh as he walked to the SUV.

All four cops a.k.a. dick suckas jumped out at the same time. Pharaoh stopped dead in his tracks. His first instinct was to run, but he hadn't done anything, at least nothing they should know about. "License, registration," said one of the white dick suckas. Pharaoh's hands were full with food, so he attempted to place it on the hood of the SUV. One of the dick suckas drew his gun, and pointed it in Pharaoh's face.

"Calm down man, I'm getting my license out."

"Shut your fucking face boy. You don't move or say nothing you got that?' asked the head dick sucka in charge.

The one cop didn't bother to drop his gun. He held Pharaoh at bay, while two other officers searched his pockets. One of the cops found Pharaoh's driver's license. He handed it over to the head cracker in charge, whom examined it carefully. "Run it," he said handing it to another cop. The cop walked back to the unmarked car and got in.

"The registration--" Pharaoh tried to say. The cop who found his license slapped the spit out of Pharaoh's mouth. "Didn't I tell you to shut your fucking face boy."

Pharaoh gained his composure and looked the cracker square in the face. He spat a luggie right between the cop's eyes. "Bitch! Fuck you!" he screamed. The two officers who were searching Pharaoh pulled out their flashlights and struck Pharaoh in the head. He didn't fall, but it dazed him a bit. He knew if he fell it was pretty much over. Pharaoh swung wildly with all his might and caught one of the officers in the jaw. He flatlined the second one with an upper cut. The officer who was holding the gun couldn't get off a clear shot without jeopardizing one of his partners being hit. He stood there with the gun shaking in his hand. The head dick sucka joined the scrap. He hit Pharaoh in the back with his flashlight. Pharaoh fell forward, but landed on his knees. The cop who went to run Pharaoh's license also joined in. He raised his boot as high as he could, and stomped down on Pharaoh's back. By that time a uniformed black officer who was working traffic pulled into the parking lot, jumped out and assisted Pharaoh. "That's enough!" he screamed as he pushed the dick sucka's back.

Pharaoh managed to jump to his feet. He staggered for a moment burling insults. "I'ma kill all you cracker ass crackers!" he yelled. One of the officers attempted to strike him again, but the black cop intervened.

"You're lucky punk."

"Fuck that he's still going to jail," said dick sucka number one.

"What's the charge?" asked the black cop.

"Fighting with an arresting officer."

"And why was he being arrested?" There was a long pause.

"You're not our fucking sergeant!" screamed dick sucka number one.

"Yeah," but he's black just like me, so whose report do you think he'll believe?" The cops were fuming. They reluctantly had to leave Pharaoh alone, at least at the moment.

"We'll see your ass again," said one of the cops as they piled into their unmarked car, then sped off. Pharaoh flipped them off, as they exited the parking lot. He could barely stand up straight.

"You alright man," asked the officer.

"Yeah, I'm good. Thanks man," Pharaoh said as he grabbed the food off the hood, and climbed into the SUV.

Pharaoh looked in the rearview mirror and noticed he had somewhat of a pumpkin head. He cranked up the SUV and skirted off. He was mad as hell, his intentions were to grab Tez, and go look for the dick suckas. He decided not to sweat the clowns. He thought about his shipment and meeting Eric the next day. He got out carrying the food. Tez opened the door, and laughed when he saw Pharaoh's face.

"Damn my man, you got knocked the fuck out," laughed Tez. Pharaoh wasn't salty at the remark, he joined in laughter.

"Ain't shit," he said.

"What happened? Do you need to suit up my nigga?" asked Tez.

"Nah, t's cool. Them hoe ass jump outs got down on me up at "Fat Burgers," said Pharaoh handing Tez his burger and fries.

"Shit they can get it too," said Tez.

"I know, but not right now. We got entirely too much on the floor, and besides that little shit comes with the game."

"I still say we suit up and go find them fish pussy asses," laughed Tez.

"I see you made the news again," said Pharaoh.

"Oh, you know I do what I can, when I can do it," said Tez sarcastically.

"Well check this out. I went down to the county and seen Ollie."

"Word! What he talking 'bout?" asked Tez.

"Shit, he hanging in there like a champ. But dig, he says that he can bcat his case if it weren't for Tamara and Kellie," said Pharaoh.

"Who is Tamara and Kellie?"

"Tamara is the white bitch at the bank, and Kellie is ole' girl I sent you to get my car from. They must have I.D.'d you as being my friend, and linked Ollie with me and you."

"Shit where they live at? I'll have 'em missing by morning," said Tez pulling out his 40 caliber.

"Calm down Rambo, both of them hocs live in the suburbs, so we gon' have to be careful."

"All you gotta do is tell me their address, and it's been done.

Let me worry about the details," said Tez.

"A'ight killer," joked Pharaoh.

Pharaoh tried to eat his burger and fries, but his jaw was killing him. He put an ice pack on his face, and stretched across Tez's couch. Tez didn't touch his food. He was excited to have another job. He sprinted to his bedroom and quickly suited up. He returned to the living room, and stopped in front of the television.

"How I look?" he asked Pharaoh modeling in his kill-drobe.

"Like a nigga 'bout to go straight to jail," said Pharaoh.

"You know better than that. Nigga I'll hold court in the street before they take me."

"Be safe my nigga," said Pharaoh closing his eyes.

It was getting dark outside on the warm spring day. Tez let back the sunroof on his Cadillac, and fired up a blunt. He drove west smoking his L trying to get right for the occasion. He turned right on Greenfield, and headed into the suburbs of Southfield, Michigan. He pulled into the parking lot of the Northland Condominiums and killed his headlights as he bent the corner of the complex. Tez didn't actually have a plan. He didn't even know if Kellie was at home. 'Now how the fuck am I going to get inside?' he asked himself. No sooner than he made the statement, an older couple pulled up and parked. Tez scrambled to pull the Mack-90 from under the passenger seat. He tucked the rifle under his hoodie and exited the vehicle. He trailed the couple up to the door. The older man opened the lobby door, and held it open for his wife. Tez attempted to enter behind them. The man jerked the door, "who are you here to see?"

Tez had his keys in his hand and raised them for the older gentleman to see. "I live here apartment seven," said Tez. The older man who happened to be black looked at Tez in disbelief.

His wife spoke up, "George leave the young man alone."

George, whom the woman referred to, reluctantly let the handle go.

Tez thanked the woman, and headed for the stairs. He reached Kellie's door, before knocking he looked around to see if the old man was coming. There wasn't a soul in sight. Tez knocked three times on the door.

"Who is it?" asked an approaching voice.

"Juan, baby hurry up and open the door."

Kellie didn't hear anything past Juan. She unlocked the door, then swung it open. Her face was lit up ear to ear with a huge smile. Her expression dropped when her eyes realized it was not Juan. By this time Tez had the Mack-90 pointed in her face. "Bitch don't scream," he ordered as he shoved Kellie back into the apartment. He closed the door behind him. Kellie was wearing some skin tight pajamas, with no panties. Tez examined her like a deranged rapist. He shook his head at the thought of raping her.

"What do you want?" asked Kellie frantically.

"You know the business you rat bitch." Tez slapped Kellie to the ground with the barrel of the Mack-90. He reached down and grabbed her arm. "Get up bitch. It ain't over!" he yelled. He cornered her and began striking her with the butt of the rifle.

Kellie screamed at the top of her lungs. Tez wanted to torture her and finish beating her before killing her, but he was in an aprtment complex,. He knew someone had to hear Kellie screaming. "You getting off light bitch," he said as he grabbed two large pillows off the couch. He sat them on top of Kellie. She was lying on the floor in a pool of blood. He put the pillows on top of her head, and pulled out his 40 cal. He shot seven times into the pillows, muffling the sound. He removed the pillows, and was satisfied with the red holes that covered Kellic's face. Tez stood to his feet and looked down on Kellie's dead body. He rolled her over on her stomach, the kicked her in the ass. "You rat bitch…," he said, the turned to leave.

    Tez made it to his car without incident. He pulled off constantly checking the rearview to make sure no one caught his tag. He headed back east, but remained in the suburbs. A squad car from Oak Park, Michigan pulled out of an all night coffee shop, and tailed Tez, he had made his mind up. As soon as they hit the lights he was going to punch it. The squad car tailed Tez for what seemed like forever. Tez was wearing his seat belt, doing the speed limit, and his tags were straight. He was, however, driving while black (DWB.) The squad car followed Tez a few more streets, then turned off. "Ya'll bitches betta turn off," said Tez looking in the rearview mirror.

    Tez pulled into Tamara's trailer park. He parked behind her car, blocking it in. He got out and walked up the three attached wooden stairs. He could see someone walking around inside. Lights were on in every room of the trailer. Tez opened the screen and started to knock. He hesitated because he wasn't sure Tamara would fall for the same trick Kellie did.

    Tez stepped back and kicked the door open. Tamara was sitting on the couch talking on the phone, when her front door swung violently open. She scremed at the sight of Tez. "Tamara are you okay?' asked a voice on the other end. Tez snatched the cordless phone from Tamara and hung it up. She balled up on the edge of the couch, with her hands shielding her face.

"Please don't kill me," she pleaded. Tez was standing over her with his 40 cal. pointed at her head.

"They made me tell, I swear!" pleaded Tamara.

"They made me kill you, I swear!" said Tez mocking Tamara's white voice.

"Boom! Boom!" Tez put his signature gun shot wounds on Tamara's dead body. The phone rang, Tez turned and looked at it. He reached down and answered on the fourth ring.

"Hello" he answered.

"Tamara, Tamara are you okay?" asked a woman's voice.

"Tamara is no longer with us," said Tez.

The woman on the phone hung up. Tez looked at the phone and pushed *69, someone picked up.

"Bitch who you hanging up on?" asked Tez.

Chapter 13

Pharaoh woke up at the sound of his cellphone ringing. He had slept on Tez's couch. Tez was passed out on the loveseat across from Pharaoh. Pharaoh reached over to the coffee table and picked his cell phone up. He saw the name Eric on the screen. Pharaoh jumped to his feet. "Ah..shit," he said in pain. His body was aching from the ass whoopin' the police put on him the day before.

"Hello" he answered.

"Juan, it's me Eric. I just made it into the city, where would you like to meet?"

"Same spot. Do you remember how to get there?"

"Run it down for me again."

Pharaoh gave Eric directions, then rushed into the bathroom. He washed his face, which was even more swollen than last night. "It ain't that bad," Pharaoh lied to himself. He walked back into the living room and tapped Tez on the leg.

"Wake up my manz," said Pharaoh.

"What?" growled Tez, as he rolled from right to left, then wiped his face. "I'm up."

"Get up and let me out."

"My man you getting all this money, you need to get you a crib," said Tez getting to his feet.

"Yeah, well a couple more flips, and that's exactly what I'm going to do."

"Did you take care of that?" asked Pharaoh as he stopped and turned at the door.

"A dead mothafucka can't tell shit," answered Tez.

"Both of em'?"

"Yeah...man."

"I'mma start calling you Terminator," laughed Pharaoh.

Pharaoh waited for Eric in the rear of "Randazzo's." While he waited he called his uncle Killer B., Dee, Tone, Mike, and Chris. Each wanted what they had bought the last run. Pharaoh scrolled through his phone and stopped on Sasha's name. He pushed the call button and waited patiently as the phone rang five times. No answer, Sasha's voicemail picked up. "Hey mommie it's me Juan. I was just calling to let you know I should be back in Phoenix in a couple of days. I miss you, I'll try calling you later, bye."

Pharaoh could see the smoke of the eighteen-wheeler, and hear it's engine. It sounded like music to his ears. He jumped out of the SUV and greeted Eric as he pulled around the corner. Eric put the truck in park, leaving the engine running. He climbed down from his seat, and went straight to work. He opened the back hatch, while Pharaoh pulled the SUV up to the rear of the truck.

"I got here as fast as I could," said Eric moving a mile per minute.

"You good, I just got here about five minutes ago," said Pharaoh.

Pharaoh helped Eric unload the weed and place it in the SUV. Within five minutes they were done. He handed Eric an envelope, "That's twenty grand, I hope to see you soon."

"Man, you're moving this, aren't you?" asked Eric.

"It's really selling itself," said Pharaoh climbing into his rental.

He drove to his mother's house using his usual back streets. Pharaoh wore his seat belt, and played all three mirrors. He relaxed as he pulled into the driveway of his mom's house. No cars were at the house. It was just after one o'clock in the afternoon. Pharaoh had missed his mom by twenty minutes. She was a registered nurse at Hutzel

Hospital and worked afternoons. He backed the SUV up to the patio and began unloading one hundred pounds. He carried them inside, and locked them in this bedroom. He raided the fridge, hoping to find some leftovers. He was in luck; Mom Dukes had cooked some fried chicken, fried cabbage, and Jiffy corn bread. Pharaoh warmed his food up, and made some grape Kool-aid. He quickly devoured his food, and was ready to hit the streets. He grabbed a pen out of the coffee cup sitting on the counter. He searched around for a sheet of paper, but settled on a napkin. He wrote:

Hey Ma,

I pray everything is well with you. I apologize for not calling, but I assure you I'm okay. The chicken and cabbage was on point as always. I left two hun'd under your pillow.

Love,
Pharaoh

"I done came up, put my life on the line, soaked the game up, now it's my time to shine." The lyrics of Jay-Z and Memphis Bleek blasted through the Bose speaker of the Cadillac truck. Pharaoh was pushing it up Gratiot on his way to holler at Tone. Pharaoh talked to himself all the way there ignoring the loud music. "I'ma flip this. Grab three hun'd pounds, and copp me a Range and an apartment. Valdez should let me get three hun'd of em' for an even hun'd thousand," Pharaoh said, planning out his next move. He turned the corner of Helen, and punched it. He let down the front windows to let some air in, because the weed was extra strong from the temperature outside. He pulled in the driveway of Tone's spot. Tone was standing on the porch fresh out of weed. He had missed thousands in customers. "What up boy?" said Tone as he approached the SUV. "Damn what happened to you?" he asked looking at

Pharaoh's face.

"Jump outs got down on me last night. Ain't shit, you ready?"

"Yeah man I been calling you all day. This bitch been banging! Somebody killed them nigga's Jimmy and Curt. All their custos been coming through here," said Tone.

"Word!" smiled Pharaoh. He reached in the backseat and grabbed a large bag. He handed it to Tone. Tone in return handed him an enormous stack of small assorted bills.

"That's twenty five pounds," said Pharaoh.

"That's five G's from the last run," said Tone.

"A'ight my nigga, I'm up, be safe out here."

"Yep. You too," said Tone.

Pharaoh backed out the driveway and smashed off. He bent the corner of Jimmy and Curt's block, and rode past the house. There was still yellow crime scene tape around the railing of the porch. Pharaoh continued on his drops, stopping by his uncle Killer B.'s house.

"Nephew," said Killer B. as he opened the door.

"Nephew, my ass. Nigga you got my money?" snapped Pharaoh.

"Yeah nigga I got ya'll ends."

"Well, let me get me my manz." Killer B. pulled out five one hundred dollar bills, and handed them to Pharaoh. Pharaoh held them up to the light.

"Nigga, I wouldn't give you no counterfeit."

"Shit, I don't know what a nigga would do nowdays, it's hard out here," joked Pharaoh.

"What kind of deal you gon' give me?" asked Killer B. looking at the bag in Pharaoh's hand.

"The same deal I gave you last time."

"Nephew, you killing me."

"Come on man I got moves to make, you want this shit or not?" asked Pharaoh.

"Yeah, man. Boy, you drive a hard bargain. If yo' tight ass

ain't rich by now," said Killer B. handing Pharaoh a brown paper bag full of money.

"Yeah, well I learned from the best, You!."

"Do I have to count this?" asked Pharaoh looking into the bag.

"When you gon' learn to trust old unck, huh?"

"When niggas get they forty acres and a mule," answered Pharaoh as he headed for the door.

"I should be done with this by tomorrow," said Killer B..

"A'ight, hit me up when you finish."

Pharaoh went to holler at Chris. He dumped fifty pounds on Chris, and he needed fifty more a.s.a.p. Pharaoh shot to the North end and dropped ten pounds on Mike. He too wanted to double his order. Pharaoh punched it back to the Eastside. He stopped at Al's Barber Shop and sold Dee his two pounds. He was content with just his two elbows.

"When you gon' come get a hair cut?" asked Dee looking at Pharaoh's hair.

"Man soon as I can get a break. I've been running."

"I'm not gon' hold you. Be smooth out here."

"A'ight," said Pharaoh pulling back into traffic. He shot back to his mom's house to retrieve sixty pounds, fifty for Chris and ten for Mike. As he counted out the pounds, his cellphone rang.

"My manz I need some more," said Tone.

"You out?"

"Damn near, I only got four left."

"I'm on my way."

Pharaoh packed the remaining one hundred pounds into the SUV and headed out. He shot back to the North end and sold Mike his ten pounds, then worked his way back East. By the time he reached Tone, he was out. Pharaoh collected the twenty-five thousand and handed Tone the last forty pounds.

"Man this bitch cranking," said Pharaoh amazed by the long

line of cars in front of Tone's spot.

"This shit be gone by morning," said Tone.

"Well let me get up out of here," said Pharaoh trying to figure out a way to get more weed.

He pulled out of the driveway after waiting five minutes for an opening. He flipped open his cellphone and scrolled down to Valdez.

"Hello," answered Valdez.

"Hey Val, it's me Juan."

"Juan, how's it going?"

"I'm good."

"I just got off the phone with Eric."

"Yeah, he just left a couple hours ago. I need to see you like as soon as possible," said Pharaoh.

"Already?"

"Already."

"Well how soon can you be on a plane? asked Valdez.

"I guess tonight."

"I'll have a car waiting for you."

"See you then," said Pharaoh looking at the clock on the dash board. He rode around and bought a hundred thousand dollars worth of money orders, then went to see Tez before leaving.

"Hey dig, I gotta catch a flight back to AZ tonight."

"What the fuck I'm supposed to do?" asked Tez.

"Shit chill, have some fun, get some pussy, hell I don't know," said Pharaoh, as he handed Tez a bundle of money.

"What's this?" asked Tez.

"That's ten thousand. I'm 'bout to go re-up. When I get back we gon' stunt out." Pharaoh went in the bathroom, and stashed fifty thousand inside a secret compartment located in the linen closet. "My man, I should be back in a few days," said Pharaoh as he headed for the door.

Tez sat on the couch pouting like a bored ten year old. He wanted to go with Pharaoh, but he knew Pharaoh would more than likely have said no. He pulled out his money and began counting it, then jumped to his feet. "Fuck this," he said, stuffing his money into his pants pockets. He walked into his bedroom and picked up his 40 cal. that sat on the night stand. He tucked it into his waist, then went to his closet and grabbed his bulletproof vest. He suited up for no particular reason, but left the Mack-90 behind.

Tez got in his Cadillac and rode around smoking blunt after blunt. He drove East on 7 Mile Road and noticed that Al's Barber Shop was packed. It was after closing, so that meant they were shooting dice. Tez parked in front of B.B.'s Diner across from Al's, then got out. He crossed the street in slow motion. He was on cloud nine. E-Major looked at the video monitor when the buzzer sounded. He recognized Tez and buzzed him in. "What's up boy?" asked E-Major locking the door behind Tez. E-Major was one of the many playas who went to Al's to shoot craps on Friday nights. He was a little older than Tez.

"Ain't shit. What they doing in the back?" asked Tez.

"Shooting big! You smelling good, smell like Gan."

"Yeah, I'm allergic to regular weed," laughed Tez.

"Come on, let's see if we can't win a couple thousand," said E-Major leading Tez into the back room.

There were wall to wall, old sweaty men, smoking cigars in the back room. There were only four men under the age of forty. Tez, E-Major, and two off -brand West side niggas. "Shoot that money," said Al as he waited for a fader. He had a pile of hundred dollar bills laying on the pool table. He was sweating, his sleeves were rolled up, and he was on a roll. Al was 74, but moved like he was 20.

"Shoot that money, any part of it," he snapped.

"I got you for a grand," said one of the West side nigga's. No soon as he said it, Al shot the dice.

"Seven and a winner," said the house man.

"Shoot that money," said Al.

"I like em' for a thousand," said Tez.

"Bet" said the second West side nigga.

"Eleven and a winner," said the house man.

"Shoot that money, I need a fader not a friend," popped Al.

"Bet back?" asked Tez.

"It's a bet," said the West side nigga.

Al rolled an eight.

"Bet another thousand he straight make it," said Tez.

"It's a bet."

"Eight and a winner," said the house man.

"Bet back my man?" asked Tez.

"Nigga bet five thousand he miss," said the West side nigga.

"Bet it." Al caught a ten.

"Bet something he don't bar it," said West side.

"Bet five thousand," said Tez.

"Bet!" said West side quickly closing the bet.

"Ten and a winner," said the house man. The West side nigga got mad and threw the money all across the pool table. Tez didn't bother to pick the money up. He attempted to walk around the table, but E-Major stopped him. "Man, we all suppose to be players. Chill that shit out," said Mo'. Tez wasn't trying to hear about none of that. He pulled out his 40 cal., and waved it from right to left.

"All you soft ass mothafucka's get naked," he said.

"Come on Tez man, what would Pharaoh say?" asked Mo'.

"Shut yo' bitch ass up. Ya'll Pharaoh's people, not mine. Now, bitches, strip." "Boom!" Tez let off a round into the ceiling to let everyone know he was serious.

      He grabbed Mo's briefcase which sat on the floor. He threw it up on the pool table, then clicked open. "You," said Tez pointing the 40 cal. at the house man. "Search everybody and put everything in the brief case. I don't want no jewelry, just money," said Tez. "Boom!" He let off another round. The naked men stood there shaking in fear. "Bitch ass nigga, hurry the fuck up," he ordered. After filling the briefcase, Tez clicked it shut and backed out of the room, still holding the men at bay. He crossed the street almost getting hit by a car. "Bitch!" he screamed at the driver of a Ford Expedition. Tez jumped in his Caddy and skirted off.

Chapter 14

Pharaoh was driven to the warehouse by the same concierge service in a Lincoln Towne car. Inside it was all business as usual, Mexicans were everywhere. Pharaoh walked over to the storage room and pushed it open. Valdez was going over some paper with another Mexican gentleman, talking in Spanish . Pharaoh waited for the two to finish whatever illegal transaction they were conducting.

"Juan!" said Valdez, closing the door behind the man he was talking to.

"I got a hundred thousand," Pharaoh said, sitting the briefcase on the table.

"Good," said Valdez as he feasted his greedy eyes on the money orders.

"I was hoping I could get three hun'd pounds," said Pharaoh.

"Sure, but what I want to do is front you an additional three hundred pounds," said Valdez. He walked over to the boxes and opened one of them. "That way Juan you don't have to keep running back and forth," Valdez continued.

"However you want to do it Val, I'm with it," said Pharaoh.

"You keep moving like this, you'll be a millionaire in no time," said Valdez.

"Yeah."

"When do you plan on going back to Detroit?" asked Valdez as he drove toward Pharaoh's apartment.

"I was hoping to leave tomorrow."

"Well, I'll have Eric set back out tomorrow. He should be back in a few hours," said Valdez, as he pulled into Pharaoh's apartment complex.

"Catch you later Val," said Pharaoh, as he got out of the car. He didn't bother going upstairs to his apartment. Pharaoh jumped in his Monte Carlo, and flipped out his cellphone. He drove while scrolling through his phone. He stopped on Sasha's name and pushed the call button. Sasha answered on the second ring.

"Hello."

"Hey mommie."

"Juan, where are you?"

"I was getting ready to ask you the same. I'm here in Phoenix."

"I'm at home."

"I'm on my way."

Pharaoh arrived at Sasha's apartment building and parked next to her Lexus. He got out and made his way up to the front entrance. He pushed her apartment buzzer, and Sasha let him in. She stood in the hallway with her apartment door ajar. She broke into a smile when Pharaoh turned the corner and walked towards her. He leaned forward and kissed Sasha on the forehead.

"What happened to your face?" she asked.

"I missed you," he said, looking Sasha in the eyes while holding her by the arms, ignoring her question.

"I missed you too Papi," she said, moving into the apartment. "Are you hungry?" she asked, locking the door.

"Nah, but I've got something else in mind," said Pharaoh, as he lifted Sasha up into his arms and carried her into the bedroom.

Pharoah laid her across the bed, then climbed on top of her, he ran his fingers through Sasha's hair as he passionately kissed her. She wrapped her legs around his ankles, and dug into Pharaoh's back with her nails. Pharaoh undressed Sasha, one article of clothing at a time, starting with her blouse. In between clothing he steadily kissed Sasha all over. She was breathing hard, as was Pharaoh. "I love you Papi," said Sasha. As Pharaoh slid the head of his dick inside Sasha's tight pussy, he sighed, "Ah, I love you too." Pharaoh slow stroked Sasha's left wall bringing her to her peak. Her left leg began shaking as Pharaoh continued to focus on her spot. Sasha pulled on Pharaoh's shoulders, trying to brace herself for an orgasm. "Ahh..Ah..Ah...," she moaned. Pharaoh continued to stroke, breaking into a sweat, he pulled out, and rolled her over on her stomach. Pharaoh gripped Sasha by her tiny waist with his left hand, using his right hand to insert himself in Sasha. "Shit.." said Pharaoh, as he began hitting Sasha from the back. Sasha turned around and looked Pharaoh in the eyes, with a slutty look on her face. The look in her eyes inflamed Pharaoh's passion. He was forced to break the stare as he began to ejaculate. "Fuck.. ah.. shit" screamed Pharaoh, holding his head back. He squeezed Sasha's ass cheeks, and rammed himself inside her, until draining every ounce of semen into her. Pharaoh fell over on his back staring up at the ceiling. He rubbed his chest, while thinking to himself 'damn, I just told her I love her.' It didn't feel like a lie, but it bothered Pharaoh because he had never told a woman he loved her and actually meant it. Sasha laid on Pharaoh's chest, playing with his nipple.

"How long will you be in town?" asked Sasha.

"I have to leave in the morning." There was a moment of silence. Pharaoh could feel tension starting to build. "Listen mommie, as soon as I get settled I want you to get on a plane, and come see me," he said.

"And when will that be?" asked Sasha.

"In a week or so, I'm in the process of finding an apartment. I want you to help me decorate it."

"So you don't have any plans on moving back to Phoenix?"

"Mommie, we already talked about this."

"Well, I want to talk about it again. I know you're involved with Valdez. Don't try and deny it either, cause my sister

Ambria has already told me," said Sasha.

"Since we're putting everything on the table, I might as well tell you the whole truth." .

"What do you mean the whole truth, Juan?"

"That's just it, my name isn't Juan." Sasha sat up and looked Pharaoh dead in the eyes.

"So what is your name?" she yelled.

"Mommie, calm down."

"Don't call me mommie. You're telling me I've been living a lie all this time?"

"Please listen," said Pharaoh, sitting up then taking Sasha into his arms. "Sasha, I didn't intentionally lie to you. I came to Phoenix because I was on the run. I told you my name was Juan because I had no idea one day you'd be the love of my life. You've got to believe me. There's nothing more I would like to do than to start over. Look at me mommie."

Sasha slowly turned and looked at Pharaoh. She was crying slightly. Pharaoh wiped her tears, then kissed her. "Hi, my name is Pharaoh, and who might you be?" he asked. Sasha started smiling, satisfied with Pharaoh's attempt.

"I'm Sasha."

"That's a pretty name. Well, listen Sasha, I was wondering if you'd like to join me for dinner?"

"I'd love to."

     Pharaoh climbed out of bed taking Sasha by the hand. He led her into the shower and made hot passionate love to her, then washed her from head to toe. They got dressed, and headed out to Sasha's favorite Chinese restaurant.

Chapter 15

Pharaoh had a long flight back to Detroit. The plane had a gas leak, and made an emergency landing at KCJ airport in Kansas City. The pilot announced the emergency landing over the intercom. It didn't seem serious, but the turbulence caused the passengers to panic. The stewardess walked the aisle trying to calm down the passengers. The plane shook violently, and the oxygen masks dropped down. That's when all hell broke loose. An older white woman jumped out of her seat and yelled, "I'm too young to die!" She ran full speed towards the back of the plane.

The guy sitting next to Pharaoh was rocking back and forth. He was a young black man, probably in his mid-twenties. He looked out the window, then turned to Pharaoh and said, "Man I'm on parole, I don't even supposed to be out of the state. They gon' violate me." Pharaoh looked at him, and thought to himself, 'nigga we 'bout to die.'

Pharaoh thought about everything he had on the floor. 'Man this ain't a good time to die,' he thought. He promised himself that if he lived, he would enjoy life to the fullest. He thought about Sasha and realized she was the one for him. "Please God let this plane land safely." No sooner than Pharaoh finished his brief prayer, the plane slammed on the runway and fish-tailed from right to left. The plane was in total chaos. Pharaoh braced himself, holding on to the seat in front of him. The plane didn't seem as though it was going to stop. It ran off the runway and onto the dirt road alongside the air strip. Dirt and smoke enveloped the plane as it smashed into the side of a garage. The plane's nose came out the opposite side of the garage and came to a screeching halt. Everyone aboard let out a deep sigh, as to say, "I'm alive!" "Thank you Lord," said Pharaoh.

Pharaoh waited inside the KCJ air terminal, while technicians worked on the plane. He called Sasha and told her to catch the next plane to Detroit. He waited for almost two hours, then the stewardess rounded everyone up who was aboard. People were reluctant to get back on the same plane. Pharaoh figured if the Lord willed him to die, then it would be. He boarded the plane, fastened his seat belt, and dosed off. He awoke at the sound of the plane landing. He looked out the window, and smiled at the sight of familiar ground. "Home sweet home," he said. He walked over to the rental car place across from the Metro air terminal and rented a Cadillac XLT SUV, similar to the last one he rented, except it was much larger.

It was 10:30 a.m. and Pharaoh looked a mess. He took I-94 until he reached 7 Mile Road. Pharaoh stopped in front of Al's Barber Shop and parked. He got out and rang the buzzer. Dee buzzed Pharaoh in. Once inside, Pharaoh could sense that something was wrong because no one greeted him. Mo' usually had a snappy comment and a smile for Pharaoh.

"What's up, Mo', Al, everybody?" said Pharaoh, looking around the barbershop at the still faces. No one said a word. Mo' put his clippers in the sterilizer and excused himself from the man he was cutting. He walked towards the back room, and motioned Pharaoh to follow.

"Let me holler at you P," he said. Everyone watched as Mo' and Pharaoh walked into the back room. Pharaoh pulled the door shut behind him and took a seat on a stool.

"What's up Mo', somebody die around here or something?"

"Not yet," answered Mo'.

"I'm at a loss, you mind telling me what's going on?"

"Your main man, Tez robbed everyone Friday."

"Nah, not my Tez," said Pharaoh, in disbelief.

"It was him. I know who Tez is."

"Was he wearing a mask?"

"No, he was initially gambling, some words were exchanged between him and some youngster from the West side. I tried to defuse the situation. Next thing I know, Tez pulls out a gun and tells everyone to strip."

"I'm sorry Mo, what did he take?"

"He made off with close to forty thousand."

"I got the money Mo, but please call off the goons."

"I'm going to overlook the ordeal, but only on the strength of you, under no circumstances do I ever want him back in the shop."

"I got you Mo. I'm 'bout to go get that forty thousand for you, I'll be right back," said Pharaoh, as she stormed out the door.

Everyone in the front watched as Pharaoh made his exit. He jumped in the SUV and peeled off. Tez lived four streets over from Al's. Pharaoh bent the corner of 7 Mile Road and Syracuse, and punched it. He ran two stop signs doing over 70 mph. He came to a screeching stop, then pulled into Tez's drive way. He jumped out leaving the truck running. He ran up Tez's stairs, and banged on the screen door with his fist. Tez was asleep on the couch when he heard the banging. He grabbed his 40 cal. off the coffee table, and rolled onto the floor. He crept to the front window and peeped out. Pharaoh saw the curtain move, and yelled.

"Nigga I see yo' ass, open the mothafuckin' door!"

"Damn," said Tez. He reluctantly opened the door. Pharaoh stormed in grabbing Tez by the collar and rammed him into the wall.

"What the fuck's wrong with you," asked Tez.

"Nigga, why the fuck you rob Al's?"

"Ah, man fuck them coward ass niggas."

Pharaoh picked Tez up and slammed him on his back. Tez quickly recuperated, and jumped to his feet. Tez pointed the gun in Pharaoh's face. "Shoot! Shoot nigga!" yelled Pharaoh. "Just like I thought," said Pharaoh as he lunged at Tez knocking the gun out of his hand. Tez caught Pharaoh with a Holifield uppercut, then a vicous three piece spicy. Pharaoh fell to the ground. He laid on his side with a line of blood trickling down his mouth. "Don't get it fucked boy! I'll still put these mickies on you," said Tez, as he stood over Pharaoh. Pharaoh rolled over and managed to stand up. Tez stepped back knowing that Pharaoh wasn't finished.

"Bitch!" yelled Pharaoh, as he swung right, then left. He caught Tez in the eye with a stiff jab. Tez stumbled back, then rushed Pharaoh into a corner. He choked Pharaoh, making him tap out. "When I let you go, you better not swing on me," said Tez. He slowly removed the death grip, and backed away. Pharaoh gained his composure, then stormed towards the bathroom. He opened the linen closet and reached up into the stash spot. He felt the bundle of money and grabbed it. Satisfied that it wasn't tampered with, he walked back into the front, his cellphone was on the floor ringing. He reached down and picked it up.

"Hello."

"Juan, I need to talk to you," said Chyna.

"Look, I'm in the middle of handling something, I'm a call you back," said Pharaoh and hung up before Chyna could say another word.

Tez was sitting on the couch, with his shirt off. "You ain't fucking with me no more my manz?" said Tez. Pharaoh didn't acknowledge him, he walked toward the door and opened it. He slammed the door behind him, and jumped into the SUV. Tez swung the door open and yelled at Pharaoh as he pulled off. "Well fuck you then!" Pharaoh shot back to Al's and dropped the forty thousand on Mo'.

He drove around trying to let off some steam, then went to his mom's house for the night.

Chapter 16

Sasha called Pharaoh from the Metro airport, to let him know she had arrived in Detroit. He rolled out of bed feeling groggy from his fight with Tez. It was 7:30 a.m. Pharaoh's mom was in the kitchen sitting at the table doing crossword puzzles, sipping green tea, and listening to jazz.

"Hey Ma," said Pharaoh, smiling from ear to ear as he entered the kitchen. His mother turned to Pharaoh, as he leaned down and kissed her on the cheek.

"Good morning sleepy head. Oh my God! What happened to your face?" she asked.

"Just a little squabble, I'm alright Ma," said Pharaoh.

"Did you kick their ass?"

"I think I lost that one, but that's life right." Pharaoh's mom got up and hugged her youngest son.

"Sit down Pharaoh, are you hungry?"

"Nah, I can't stay."

"You need to give those streets a break, and rest your bones."

"I've got to go pick my girlfriend up from the airport."

"Girlfriend? Um, I don't recall you bringing no one home to meet me."

"Well, I'll bring her by later. She might be the one."

"I'll be the judge of that."

"I'mma see you later," said Pharaoh as he kissed his mom before leaving.

"I love you," she said.

"Love you too."

Pharaoh pulled into the Metro and scanned the entrance. As he pulled to the curb, he spotted Sasha standing in the window. He illegally parked, put on his hazzards and jumped out. He sprinted towards the entrance, Sasha hadn't seen him. He crept up behind her, "you waiting on someone ma'am?" Sasha turned around, not recognizing Pharaoh's voice, "I'm waiting on my..." She realized it was Pharaoh and slapped him on the shoulder playfully.

"Papi, you're so silly," she said. Pharaoh kissed her, then reached down and picked up her two Burberry bags.

"Damn, what you do, bring all of Phoenix with you?" he joked.

"Hah. Hah. Hah."

"Did you enjoy your flight?" asked Pharaoh, as he and Sasha exited the terminal.

"It was okay, except one thing."

"What's that mommie?" asked Pharaoh, as he put her luggage in the hatch of the SUV.

"I'm allergic to coach."

"Is that right," laughed Pharaoh, as he opened Sasha's door. He walked around the truck and climbed in. He leaned over and kissed Sasha passionately. "It won't happen again mommie," said Pharaoh as he pulled away from the curb.

"So this is Detroit?" asked Sasha, as she looked out the passenger window.

"Yep" answered Pharaoh, examining her face for approval or disaprroval.

"So where are we going?"

"I want to take you to meet my mom."

"How do I look?" asked Sasha, as she flipped down the visor, and looked in the mirror.

"You look fine."

"Is she mean?"

"Of course not, mommie just be yourself, and she'll love you. I mean who couldn't love you?" asked Pharaoh, as he rubbed Sasha's hair trying to assure her.

Pharaoh pulled into his mom's driveway and cut the engine off. He turned and looked at Sasha and said, "Just relax mommie, come on." He walked around to open Sasha's door and they entered the house through the side door. His mom hadn't moved, she was still in her nook doing crossword puzzles and drinking tea. "Ma, I would like for you to meet my girlfriend, Sasha." Pharaoh's mom stood and extended her hand, and introduced herself. "I'm Pharaoh's mother. Everybody calls me Mom Dukes. Have a seat," she said, motioning Sasha to sit across from her.

"Pharaoh you didn't tell me she was this pretty."

"Yeah, well I'm going to take a quick shower. I'mma let you gals chat," said Pharaoh, heading for the bathroom.

Mom Dukes casually picked at Sasha, but she did what Pharaoh suggested, be herself. Mom Dukes was satisfied with Sasha's intentions, her mother's intuition told her that she had Pharaoh's best interest at heart. Pharaoh exited the bathroom fully dressed and ready to depart. He walked back into the kitchen, and went straight to the cookie jar. He grabbed several homemade chocolate chip soft batch cookies, and leaned against the counter eating. He watched as Sasha and his mother conversed. They made plans to go shopping before Sasha was to return to Phoenix.

"I hate to interrupt ya'll Home Shopping Network frenzy, but I'm starving. Can I treat my favorite two ladies to brunch?" asked Pharaoh.

"Aw, thank you baby, but I'm okay. You two go ahead with out me," said Mom Duke's.

"Are you sure Ma?"

"Yeah."

"I'll bring you a carry-out, Western Omelet."

"Sounds good!"

"You ready mommie?"

"Yes. It was nice meeting you, Mom Dukes," said Sasha, as she stood and grabbed her purse.

"The pleasure was all mine."

Pharaoh kissed his mom on the forehead, then headed towards the back door. Pharaoh opened Sasha's door, and told her that he forgot something inside. His mom's was waiting by the door when he opened it.

"So what do you think Ma?" asked Pharaoh.

"She's the one."

"Thanks Ma," said Pharaoh, as he cracked a smile.

"Be careful," said Mom Dukes as Pharaoh left. He climbed into the SUV smiling from ear to ear. He leaned over and kissed Sasha, started the truck, then backed out of the driveway. He drove while holding Sasha's hand.

"Do you think she likes me?"

"Of course, I told you she would." Pharaoh was cut off by the sound of his cellphone ringing. He looked at the screen, it was Tone.

"What up doe?" he answered.

"Hey, I need to holler at you."

"You done?"

"I got like ten left."

"That should hold you until tomorrow, but um, I'ma come get that thirty."

"Come through."

"In a minute," said Pharaoh, as he hung up the phone. He checked his voicemail and it was full.   Pharaoh first stopped by Tone's spot to pick up the thirty thousand dollars he had for him. Pharaoh pulled into the driveway, and got out. He crossed the grass, and walked up the stairs. Tone had already unlocked the door, and opened it by the time Pharaoh reached the porch. He handed Pharaoh a large brown grocery bag.

"Here you go my nigga. Damn who that in the car?" asked Tone, kneeling down to get a better look.

"That's the wifey," Pharaoh said proudly.

"Man, she killing shit."

"Look, I'm 'bout to get up out of here. I'mma holla at you tomorrow," said Pharaoh, giving Tone a play.

"A'ight, one," said Tone.

Pharaoh and Sasha had brunch at the "National Coney Island." He ordered his favorite, a Western Omelet with cheese and hash browns. Sasha ordered biscuits and gravy, and fried potato wedges. They sampled each other's food, Pharaoh hated biscuits and gravy, but he endured it to please Sasha.

"I know you want to do some shopping," said Pharaoh.

"Yeah," answered Sasha, smiling like a little school girl.

"I'm going to let you and my mom go shop until ya'll drop, I've got to go see about this apartment," said Pharaoh.

They finished their food, and ordered his mom's food, then left. He dropped Sasha off at his mother's house, and gave her a few thousand. "Buy me some Polo shirts," he said, as he kissed Sasha goodbye. He flipped open his cellphone and browsed through the numbers while he drove. He stopped on his cousin Shannon's number and pushed the call button.

"Hello" answered Shannon.

"What up, Cuz?"

"Nothing much, what's good with you."

"Shit, are you busy?"

"Nah, why. What's up?"

"I want you to ride out to Kay Jewelers with me."

"Who you buying jewelry for boy?"

"My girlfriend, Sasha."

"It must be serious, 'cause I ain't never known you to spend a quarter on a bitch," joked Shannon.

"I'm on my way to get you."

"I'll be here."

Pharaoh picked Shannon up from her home on East 7 Mile and Barlow. She lived in a ranch style home, two car garage, four bedrooms, finished basement, and marble floors. Shannon was a few years older than Pharaoh. She was an inspiration for Pharaoh, because she was on top of her game, Shannon was a hair stylist and a fashion expert. They drove out into the deep suburbs of West Bloomfield, MI until they reached the elite Kay Jewelers. Pharaoh and Shannon browsed the many glass casings.

"What exactly are you looking for?"

"A ring."

"What kind of ring?"

"An engagement ring."

"Um, bitch must have some fire head," laughed Shannon.

"I'm serious Shann." A sales rep approached Shannon and Pharaoh.

"May I help you?" asked the middle aged white woman.

"It's about damn time. Shit we only been in here ten minutes," snapped Shannon. The white woman batted her eyes with a look of confusion.

"How much are you looking to spend?" Shannon asked Pharaoh.

"Twenty-five thousand at the most."

"Bitch must have had that wet, wet," laughed Shannon.

"You got major jokes today, huh?" asked Pharaoh.

"We'd like to look at some engagement rings," said Shannon, talking to the sales rep. The woman ushered Pharaoh and Shannon to a glass case. She went behind the counter and removed several trays of different rings.

"I want something set in platinum."

"Okay," said the sales rep as she put all the gold rings back into the case. Shannon picked up a 3 ct. diamond ring set in platinum. She tried it on as if it were for her.

"This is it," she said, modeling the ring.

"What's the ticket on it?" asked Pharaoh. Shannon took the ring off, and looked at the price tag. "Twenty three thousand."

"Have her wrap it up," said Pharaoh.

"We'll take it," said Shannon.

"Will that be cash or credit." Shannon turned to Pharaoh for the answer.

"Cash ma'am," answered Pharaoh. The sales rep put the rest of the rings back in the case and went to ring up the purchase.

"Hey look, Shann, I know you can show for twenty-three stacks, right?" asked Pharaoh.

"Of course."

"Good, 'cause I'm not trying to get indicted," Pharaoh said as he handed Shannon the money. The clerk returned and Shannon counted out twenty-three thousand dollars, plus sales tax. By law, the woman had to contact the IRS and give them Shannon's information. All the transactions made Pharaoh nervous, so he left and sat in the truck. An hour later, Shannon came walking out with a Kay Jewelers bag in her hand. Pharaoh, relieved that everything had panned out, he sat up and started the truck.

"Here you go," said Shannon, as she climbed in the truck and handed Pharaoh the bag.

"Thanks Shann."

"You're welcome. So, who's planning your wedding?"

"Are you up for it?"

"You gon' let me plan your wedding?" Shannon asked, flattered.

"Fo' show, I couldn't think of anyone more qualified."

Pharaoh dropped Shannon back off at her house, then drove downtown. He pulled in front of "City Slickers" off Gratiot Avenue. It had been a while since Pharaoh had bought dress clothes, but he wanted to look clean for the evening. He was greeted by an older man who was working the floor when he entered the store.

"Can I help you sir?" asked the sales rep.

"Uh, yeah," Pharaoh answered. He didn't know exactly what it was he was looking for.

"What exactly are you looking for?" asked the rep.

"See that's the thing, I don't know."

"What's the occasion?"

"Marriage proposal."

"Oh boy, come with me. I'mma hook you up nice," said the rep, grabbing Pharaoh by the shoulders, and leading him toward a rack of shoes. "See it all starts with the shoes, then you put together your suit accordingly," said the rep. He pulled a black big block gator shoe off a rack and handed it to Pharaoh.

"You like?" he asked.

"Yeah. Wow!" said Pharaoh, looking at the price tag inside the shoe.

"Eleven hun'd," he said.

"If you gon' do it, baby, you gotta do it right. Don't cheat yourself, treat yourself," said the rep.

"You really selling these mothafuckas, ain't you? laughed Pharaoh.

"I'm just saying, from player to player."

"Let me try 'em on in a size eleven and a half."

"I'll be right back," said the rep, as he sped off into the back room.

Pharaoh browsed around looking at the large selection of gators, ostrich shoes, boots, and sandals. The sales rep came flyng back into the store lobby, carrying a Maury's shoe box. He kneeled down beside Pharaoh, and removed the shoes from the box. He jumped to his feet, and ran behind the cash register. He removed a pair of socks from a drawer, then rushed back to Pharaoh. "Here put these on," he said, handing Pharaoh the dress socks. Pharaoh took his shoes and socks off, then slipped into the silk socks. The sales rep handed Pharaoh the right shoe, then the left one and ushered Pharaoh in front of a floor mirror.

"Righteous," said the sales rep, as he stood behind Pharaoh

with his hands on his shoulders.

"Let me get these," said Pharaoh, as he turned and boxed the shoes. The sales rep took the box from Pharaoh, then raced for the cash register.

"Cash or credit?" he asked on his way behind the counter.

"Cash," answered Pharaoh, as he pulled out his money, and began counting.

"What about the suit?" asked Pharaoh.

"My man, Billy, next door is gon' hook you up," said the sales rep, as he punched the buttons on the register a mile per minute.

Pharaoh paid the sales rep, then walked through a joint door which connected "City Slicker's" and "Broadway," a clothing store where all major players, pimps, hustlers, and gangsters went to get suited. An older gray-haired gentleman approached Pharaoh as he walked through the door.

"You must be Billy," said Pharaoh.

"One and only." Billy reached down and took the shoes out of Pharaoh's hand. He opened the box, and looked at the shoes. "Follow me," he said. He escorted Pharaoh to his private office, where he showed Pharaoh numerous different materials, patterns, and cuts. Pharaoh didn't know what to choose. "All this shit is fly, but I don't want nothing tight," said Pharaoh.

"I got you, young blood," said Billy. He walked Pharaoh over to a stool, and sized him. "How soon do you need this suit?" asked Billy.

"I was hoping by the time I leave this store."

"Son this ain't Men's Warehouse! We tailor suits, nothing is sold off a rack or dummies back."

"Well, when can you have the suit ready?" asked Pharaoh.

Billy looked at his watch before answering. "It usually takes us one week to make a suit." Pharaoh cut Billy off, sensing the bullshit.

"How much man?"

"Two thousand and I'll have the suit ready in an hour."

"A'ight old school," said Pharaoh, as he counted out two grand, then handed it to Billy.

Billy hunched his back with greed in his beady eyes and counted the money hastily. Pharaoh decided to go visit Ollie, seeing as though he was downtown and had an hour to waste.

The county jail was within walking distance, so Pharaoh left his rental parked in front of "City Slickers." He was told by the corporal working the front desk that he couldn't visit Ollie because it wasn't his visiting day. A crispy hundred bill quickly made it Ollie's visiting day. Pharaoh took the elevator up to the sixth floor on the old side of the county jail. He was buzzed in by none other than the female deputy he encountered on his last visit. She grunted and snatched the visitor's pass from Pharaoh through the bars separating them. Pharaoh refrained from cussing her out, because she could have pressed the issue about Ollie's visiting day. She read the pass, then turned on her heels. After twenty minutes or so, Ollie was escorted to the visiting booth.

"What up doe?" he asked as the bars shut behind him.

"Ain't nothing my baby, what's good? asked Pharaoh.

"Man, my lawyer filed a motion for dismissal. He says that them rat bitches were found dead."

"What's understood, don't need to be said," smiled Pharaoh.

"Man I can't wait to go to court."

"When is your next court date?"

"'Bout a month and some change."

"You know niggas done came up hard. When you touch, I'mma have a Benz sitting outside the courthouse for you," said Pharaoh.

"You doing it like that? What about Tez?"

"Man, me and that nigga fell out yesterday."

"Word. What happened?"

"Just say Tez is on some other shit nowadays. My nigga I'm bout to ask my girlfriend to marry me."

"Who is your girlfriend?"

"This chick I met while Tez and I were in Arizona."

"She bad?"

"No question. Nigga she Latin."

"Good luck my nigga," smiled Ollie.

"Time!" yelled the deputy.

"Man that bitch be on bullshit," said Ollie, as he turned and looked at the deputy.

"Can't yo' ass hear? I said time!" she yelled.

"I'mma get at you later my manz, be smooth," said Pharaoh.

"One," Ollie and Pharaoh said as they put their fists on the glass.

Pharaoh looked at his watch as he walked back to "Broadway." It was just after four o'clock, and Pharaoh had a lot to do before picking Sasha up from his mom's house. As he walked in the store, Billy was wrapping his suit up in a "Broadway" suit cover. He handed Pharaoh the suit, along with a receipt. "I threw in some socks, a tie, handkerchief, and a shirt," said Billy. Pharaoh thought to himself, 'for two grand, you'd think all that would be included.'

"Thanks Billy," he said, as he made his departure. Pharaoh stopped at a florist shop on Grand River and Gratiot. He purchased a dozen roses, half red and the other half white. He also purchased a card, and paid the clerk to scribe a few lines of game. Pharaoh flipped open his cell phone as he drove east on Gratiot. He called information and asked for the number to "Krystal Imams," a high priced restaurant in downtown Detroit off the water.

Pharaoh made reservations for two at eight o'clock. As he drove towards his mom's house, his cellphone went off. Pharaoh picked it up and looked at the screen. It was

Tez. "I'm not fucking with that clown right now," he mumbled as his his voicemail picked up. Pharoah pulled into his mom's driveway, and noticed that her car wasn't there. He parked the SUV, and reached in the backseat for his suit and shoes. He rushed inside the house to discover a note from his mom:

Hey son, Sasha and I are out doing some shopping, we'll be back shortly. -Love Mama

Pharoah rushed in the bathroom, and took a quick five minute shower. He was in his bedroom getting dressed, when he heard his mother's voice. She and Sasha just walked in the house.

"Pharaoh," she yelled through the kitchen.

"I'm, in my room Ma. I'll be out in a second."

Pharoah finished getting dressed, then sprayed some of his favorite cologne on. He walked into the kitchen suited and booted. Sasha looked up in awe. "Wow! Papi, who died?" she asked with a smile.

Pharoah's mom turned around in her seat. She jumped up, then ran towards her bedroom. She came running back into the kitchen sliding to a stop with her digital camera in hand. "Come on Sasha, let me snap a few pictures of you all," said Mom Dukes. Sasha and Pharaoh posed for the camera, until the memory card got full.

"Ya'll look so good!" said Mom Dukes.

"Thank you Ma," said Pharaoh.

Sasha was wearing an elegant sundress, so she didn't have to change clothes.

"What's the occasion Papi?"

"I made dinner reservations at eight. We should get going," answered Pharaoh.

"Ya'll kids have fun," said Mom Dukes, as she walked Pharaoh and Sasha to the door.

"See you tomorrow Ma," said Pharaoh, as he climbed into the SUV.

Pharaoh and Sasha arrived at the restaurant just before eight. They valet parked, and made their way inside. They were greeted by a midle-aged white man at the front door.

"Reservations?" he asked.

"Dickson," answered Pharaoh.

"Ah, yes, right this way sir," said the maitre d, as he escorted Pharaoh and Sasha to their table. Pharaoh pulled Sasha's chair out for her. "Thank you, Papi. This is nice," said Sasha, looking around at the crystal light fixtures, and waitresses carrying silver trays. A waitress appeared soon as Pharaoh took his seat.

"How are we doing this evening," said the waitress.

"Oh, just fine," said Pharaoh. The waitress handed Sasha, then Pharaoh menus.

"I'll be back shortly to take your orders." Pharaoh studied his menu, not knowing what half the dishes were, let alone how to pronounce them.

"This looks good," said Sasha.

"What's that mommie?"

"This lobster tail."

"Sounds good," said Pharaoh, sitting his menu on the table.

"Are we ready to order?" asked the waitress, as she approached the table.

"Uh, yes, we'll have two lobster tails, and a chef salad," answered Pharaoh.

"Very well," said the waitress, as she scribbled down their orders.

"And what would you like to drink?"

"A bottle of your best red wine." The waitress turned on her heels, and went to fill their orders.

Pharaoh reached over the table and grabbed both of Sasha's hands. He rubbed the backs of her hands with his thumbs, while looking into her eyes. They enjoyed the jazz provided by the "Kenny G," who expertly played the saxophone.

Pharaoh excused himself as if he had to use the men's room. He located the maitre'd, and paid him fifty dollars to round down to his rental and retrieve the roses he forgot in the back seat. When Pharaoh returned to the table, the waitress was placing their food and wine on the table.
"Anything else sir?"
"No thank you, we're good," answered Pharaoh.

As Sasha and Pharaoh enjoyed their meal, the maitre'd approached their table with the flowers in hand, he handed them to Sasha. She smiled, then read the card attached:

"To the love of my life. The source of my happiness. With you, life has meaning. I wish to spend the duration of my life with you...."

Before Sasha could look up, Pharaoh was already down on one knee. She put her hands over her face, and became teary eyed. Everyone in the restaurant turned in silence, as Pharaoh gathered his spill. He looked up at Sasha, while holding her left hand, and said,
"Sasha Perez, you mean the world to me. These past few months have made me realize that life's worth living, and I want to live it with you. Sasha, will you marry me?" asked Pharaoh.
"Yes! Yes, Papi!" screamed Sasha, jumping into Pharaoh's arms. They kissed passionately, while everyone in the restaurant stood and clapped. Someone was kind enough to send the couple a bottle of champagne. Sasha and Pharaoh had dessert and enjoyed the remainder of "Kenny G's" set.

Pharaoh and Sasha drove across Jefferson Avenue to the GM Renaissance building. They booked a suite and took the elevator up to the fourth floor. "I'll be right back, I'mma go freshen up a bit," said Sasha, as she raced for the bathroom, happily. Pharaoh closed the door behind him, then walked into the bedroom. He took off his shoes, undid his tie, and took off his shirt, and flopped down on the bed. He pulled his cellphone out of his suit jacket. He had it turned off during dinner with Sasha, and the voicemail was beyond full. He scrolled through the names of the callers, all but one was from Chyna. Pharaoh looked up to see if Sasha was coming. He heard water running.

"Are you okay in there?"

"I'll be out in a minute Papi." Pharaoh pushed the call button, and the phone began ringing.

"Hello" answered Chyna, with a funky attitude.

"What's up, you blowing my phone up like somebody died."

"We need to talk."

"Look, I don't think I'mma be seeing you again."

"The hell you ain't. Nigga I'm pregnant!" yelled Chyna.

"How I know it's mine," asked Pharaoh.

"Cause yo' ass was busting all in me, that's how!"

"I'mma come see you tomorrow," said Pharaoh, in a hurry to get off the phone. He hung up the phone, turned it off, then tossed it on the nightstand beside the bed. Sasha came out of the bathroom and stopped in the doorway striking a seductive pose. She was wearing a matching bra and panty set.

"What's wrong Papi, you look like you just seen a ghost?" said Sasha, as she walked towards the bed.

"Nothing, mommie. You look wonderful," said Pharaoh switching the subject.

He inched his way to the edge of the bed and took Sasha into his arms. She pushed him back on the bed, then climbed on top of him. Sasha started kissing Pharaoh's chest, and worked her way down to his stomach. She unbuckled his belt, and helped him out of his pants, then boxers. Pharaoh stood at attention. Sasha grabbed his dick and began jacking it, while talking in Spanish. Pharaoh grabbed her head and pushed her face down on his dick.

Sasha sucked up and down using no hands. Pharaoh could feel himself about to have an orgasm, so he pulled Sasha up. He rolled her over on her back then slid her panties off. He wrapped her left leg around his waist, while he stood. He took her right leg and stretched it up taking her toes into his mouth. Pharaoh inserted himself slowly. Sasha squirmed in satisfaction as he began to deep stroke her. He sucked and licked each toe equally, while looking down into Sasha's eyes.   She couldn't take it, she tried desperately to sit up, but Pharaoh used his free hand to hold her down by the stomach.   He took Sasha's squirming hands and rubbed them on his chest.   "Papi!" she screamed, as she shot a large clot of semen on Pharaoh stomach. Pharaoh sped up as he could feel himself about to cum again.   He took Sasha's legs and pinned them up against her shoulders, so he could feel her bottom. Sasha pulled Pharaoh deeper into her, as she could feel the head of his dick grow larger. "Ah...ah...ah..." sighed Pharaoh, as he let off an ounce of net in Sasha.   He continued to stroke her until they fell asleep.

Chapter 17

Pharaoh woke up early. He had trouble sleeping because he couldn't stop thinking about Chyna and the possibility of him being a father. Pharaoh and Sasha had breakfast in bed, and then checked out. It was nine o'clock in the morning, and Pharaoh wanted to visit a few potential apartments. He circled downtown Detroit, looking at the various high rises. His first stop was the Woodward Towers. Pharaoh didn't bother to inspect the apartment, because the bum infested exterior turned him off. He drove south until he reached the River View Apartments. Pharaoh and Sasha were pleased with the building's surroundings. It was located next to the Joe Louis Arena and Cobo Hall. Pharaoh pulled into the security gates, and parked. He and Sasha were amazed by the atmosphere. As they entered the lobby, it seemed more like a health club than an apartment building. There was a visible gym on the ground floor and tenants could be seen through large bay windows running on treadmills, riding exercise bikes, lifting weights, etc.

Pharaoh and Sasha approached the lobby desk and received a warm welcome from the receptionist.

"Good morning, and welcome to the "River View. How may I help you?" the petite ,young black woman asked.

"I would like to take a look at the available penthouse," answered Pharaoh.

"Just one moment sir," said the receptionist, as she picked up the phone and dialed out. A few words were exchanged, then the receptionist hung up the receiver. "The manager will be with you shortly. Please feel free to help yourself to our complimentary continental breakfast."

There was a large spread of fresh donuts, muffins, bagels, coffee, tea, etc. While Pharaoh and Sasha fixed themselves orange juice and bagels the manager appeared and the receptionist pointed in their direction. The manager approached Pharaoh and Sasha and introduced himself. He escorted them onto an awaiting elevator and pushed floor twenty-five, they filed off the elevator into a secluded hallway. The manager pulled out a huge key ring, and searched through the keys until finding the right one. He unlocked the door, then pushed it open allowing Sasha and Pharaoh to enter first. It was a three bedroom penthouse, equipped with plush wall-to-wall cream carpet. The walls were freshly painted. The entire penthouse was surrounded with huge bay windows, giving a beautiful view of the Detroit River.

"We'll take it," said Pharaoh.

The manager excused himself, so he could go draw up a lease agreement. The apartment cost two grand per month, with a six month lease and an option at the end to extend. Pharaoh called his mother, and asked her to take Sasha shopping for furniture. He also told her that he proposed to Sasha and that she accepted. Pharaoh's cell phone rang, it was his driver, Eric. Pharaoh immediately answered, trying not to miss his call.

"Hello".

"Juan, it's me Eric. I'm about an hour away from Detroit, same place?"

"Yeah, same place," answered Pharaoh as he hung up.

"Listen mommie, I've got to make a few runs. I need for you to stay here and take care of the lease. My mom is coming to take you furniture shopping. I'll see you a little later on," said Pharaoh as he gave Sasha the money for the lease, and furniture.

"Be careful Papi."

Pharaoh kissed Sasha before leaving. He rushed out

of the apartment building, jumped in his rental, and sped off. He drove to a U-Haul rental place on East 7 Mile and Van Dyke. The SUV he was in wasn't large enough to lug six hundred pounds. Pharaoh rented a medium sized U-Haul truck, leaving his rental in the parking lot. As he drove to "Randazzo's," the meeting place, Pharaoh called Tone, Chris, Killer B., and Mike to see what everyone was trying to cop. He knew Dee only wanted two pounds. Eric pulled into the back of the warehouse, and began unloading the truck like clock-work. Pharaoh tossed pound after pound into the back of the U-Haul, until they finished. Eric was expecting to get paid, but Pharaoh was all tapped out.

"Valdez fronted me these pounds, so I guess he's going to pay you when you get back,"

"We'll figure it out," Eric said as he climbed into his truck pissed.

Pharaoh jumped into the U-Haul and sped off laughing. He went to his mother's house to stash the excess weed, then made his drops. Pharaoh dropped the U-Haul back off at the rental place, and jumped in his rental. He flipped open his cellphone and called Chyna.

"Hello."

"Where you at?" asked Pharaoh, as he drove east on 7 Mile Road.

"I'm at work."

"I'm on my way, come outside," said Pharaoh, as he hung up. Heturned left on Outer Drive and 7 Mile Road, and pulled into the parking lot of ""007"." Chyna was standing in the doorway, she saw Pharaoh pull up and headed for the truck.

"So what you ducking a bitch," she said, closing the door after climbing into the SUV.

"Let's cut to the chase, here," said Pharaoh, handing Chyna a stack of hundred dollar bills.

"What's this for?"

"It's a thousand dollars, five hundred for an abortion, and five hundred for any inconvenience."

"Nigga I'm not having no abortion!" Chyna screamed, throwing the money in Pharaoh's face.,

"So what you gon' keep a baby I don't want?"

"Ya' ass should've thought about that."

"How much money do yo' tack head want?"

"Nigga fuck you," said Chyna, as she reached for the door handle, Pharoah grabbed her arm. Chyna tried to snatch away, but he had a death grip on her.

"Look, calm the fuck down. I think it's fucked up you just gon' keep the baby, I mean you're a stripper, but none the less, I'mma man up. I'm going to be there for you all through the pregnancy, but when you drop that bad, we gettin' a blood test. Deal?" asked Pharaoh.

"That sounds fair," said Chyna.

Pharaoh picked up the scattered hundred dollar bills, then handed them to Chyna. This time she accepted, and tucked them away in her bra. "I got to get going. I'mma come check on you tomorrow." Chyna opened the passenger door, and got out of the truck. Pharaoh watched as she made it safely into the club. He skirted off mad as hell. "Fuck!" he yelled, slamming his hands on the dashboard repeatedly. Pharaoh rode around for two hours thinking about his new life, and how much things had and would change. He needed to talk to someone, but him and Tez were beefing and his only other friend was behind bars. "Fuck it," he said, turning the corner of Syracuse. He pulled into Tez's driveway and hit the horn. Pharoah decided to be the bigger man, even though Tez was in the wrong. Tez peeped out of the window, then rushed for the front door. He came outside wearing no shirt, with a bottle of Remy Martin in his hand. Tez opened the passenger door and climbed into the truck.

"What up doe?" asked Tez, as if the fight had never

happened.

"Ain't shit man."

"What's wrong my nigga?"

"Man, I just got engaged last nigh."

"Word! Congratulations, but to who?"

"Sasha."

"So, what you down about?"

"You remember ole' girl I met at "007", the short girl?"

"Yeah, Chyna right."

"Yeah, my man, why this bitch just tell me she was pregnant."

"You bust in her?"

"Yeah," answered Pharaoh, as he leaned back in his seat in disgust.

"I'm in love with a stripper," Tez teased, singing the song by "T-Pain."

"Man this shit is serious."

"Tell the bitch to get an abortion."

"Bitch said she's keeping it."

"You want me to kill the bitch?" asked Tez.

"I thought about it, but nah."

"So, what you gon' do?"

"I told the bitch I'mma take care of it. I've got to find out a way to tell Sasha."

"I wouldn't tell her shit," laughed Tez.

"But what's up with you? You done chilled out?"

"I'm good. Who's next to get slumped?"

"Shit we good right now. All you got to do is chill."

"So what I'm suppose to do, sit in the house all day?" asked Tez.

"Nah, ain't nobody down in Southwest since you killed Mel. Why don't you set up shop down there," suggested Pharaoh.

"When?" asked Tez.

"Right now. Go put a shirt on, and follow me to my mom's

crib so I can give you some work," said Pharaoh, as he started the SUV.

Chapter 18

Three weeks later....

"All rise for the honorable Judge John C. O'Meara," said the court marshall. The judge entered the courtroom through his chambers, and took his seat. He was an old Irish-American, probably eighty years of age. He was one cough away from having a heart attack. "Thank you," he said, parking his wrinkled self in his plush leather chair. "You may be seated," said the marshall.

Ollie sat at the defense table with his lawyer William Swor, an Arab from Dearborn. He was famous for beating the first terrorist case tried in the U.S. post 9/11. Ollie scanned the court room to see who all showed up for support. In attendance were his mother, sister Shaunte, and a few other relatives. He was hoping to see Pharaoh and Tez, but they weren't present. "What are we doing today?" asked the judge, as he fumbled through some papers in frot of him. The prosecutor stood up, she was Chinese, her name was Francis Carlson. The media referred to her as "send em' up state Carlson," because she had never lost a case.

"Today your honor, we're here to hear the defendant's motion for dismissal."

"On what grounds?" asked the judge.

"Lack of evidence," said Ollie's attorney, as he stood.

"Ms. Carlson?" said the judge.

"The government's star witnesses were found mysteriously murdered a few weeks ago," said the prosecutor.

"With all do respect your honor, and to the victims, I don't believe that has anything to do with my client, and his freedom," said Ollie's lawyer.

"I beg to differ," mumbled the prosecutor.

"Ms. Carlson, this is no place for assumptions. Now, what other evidence do you have to support your case?" asked the judge.

"A bunch of theories, no facts," yelled Ollie's mouthpiece.

"Thank you Mr. Swor, but I was speaking to Ms. Carlson."

"Well, your honor, the government believes that the defendant is guilty of bank robbery, fleeing from police, and the use of a firearm to commit a violent crime. The government is seeking the use of the two former witnesses' statements as evidence," answered Carlson.

"Your honor, my client has a constitutional right to face all accusers, that would violate his 6th amendment, right to confrontation clause," said Ollie's lawyer.

"So, Ms. Carlson, back to my original question. What other evidence do you have to support your case?" The prosecutor couldn't come up with a rebuttal. "I see," said the judge.

The judge looked down at Ollie, more like snared at him, "this is the part of the law I'm not in agreement with, but it's the law. I have no choice, but to dismiss the case on the grounds of a lack of evidence. There's no need to waste tax dollars on a trial, only to be overturned by the Sixth Circuit. You are fee to go," said the judge reluctantly, slamming down his gavel. Ollie jumped up and bear-hugged his lawyer. "You the fuckin' truth," he said as he kissed Mr. Swor on the forehead.

Pharaoh was parked outside the courthouse across the street. He was listening to the radio, when he saw his friend walking down the steps. Pharaoh smiled from ear to ear, he rolled the windows down, and bust a u-turn on Lafayette Blvd. Ollie and his family stopped to see who it was inside the late model Mercedes 600 SL. Pharaoh leaned over the passenger seat, and turned down the radio.

"Need a ride nephew?" .

"Ah, my nigga! What it do baby?" yelled Ollie. Pharaoh got out of the car and handed Ollie the keys.

"This all you my nigga, good to see you home," said Pharaoh. Ollie was at a loss for words. He took the keys, and walked around the car in awe. "Get in my nigga, it's your," said Pharaoh. "I'mma take 'em shopping and get something to eat," said Pharaoh talking to Ollie's mom. He jumped in the passenger seat while Ollie took the wheel.

"I can't believe I'm out, my nigga. I ain't never think I was gon' make it out that bitch," said Ollie, as he punched the 600 SL down Gratiot.

"Well you here now my nigga, and we on," said Pharaoh.

"On with what?"

"With that popcorn."

"What the fuck is popcorn?"

"Weed, nigga I got a plug, so holla. Here!" said Pharaoh, as he handed Ollie a brown paper bag full of money.

"Man, ya'll niggas done came up. Where Tez at?"

"Shit, he probably down in Southwest. He done took that area."

"So what you want me to do?" asked Ollie.

"Not shit, just enjoy life for a while," said Pharaoh, then turned up the radio.

The past three weeks Pharaoh had flipped over two thousand pounds. Valdez stepped his shipments up to a thousand pounds per week and dropped the price to three hundred per pound. Pharaoh leased three triple black 01' 600 SL's from Reuben his broker, one for him, Tez, and Ollie. He plushed out his apartment and leased one identical across the hall for Ollie. Sasha went back to Phoenix to break the news to her family. So far, Pharaoh had kept his word on being there for Chyna during her pregnancy. She was twelve weeks and the doctor said it was too early to tell if it were a boy or girl. Pharaoh had planned a surprise coming home party for Ollie. Ollie's mom, family, and Tez were all in on it, they were at the "Good Life Lounge" waiting on Pharaoh and Ollie to come from shopping. "Surprise!" everyone yelled, as Ollie and Pharaoh entered the lounge. Ollie turned around and smiled at Pharaoh, as to say 'you got me.' Tez rushed Ollie at the door, giving him a huge bear-hug. He lifted Ollie off his feet, then spun around in a circle.

"Look at you my nigga. You done got big as shit," said Tez, putting Ollie down.

"Man, ya'll done went all out for ya' boy," smiled Ollie.

Everyone greeted Ollie with the usual phony smile, and 'how you doings.' Pharaoh led Ollie into a V.I.P. booth where two brick house red bones were seated. Pharaoh introduced Ollie to the young ladies, and turned on his heels, leaving Ollie with the women. Pharaoh bought the bar, all drinks were on him. It was pretty much a private party, except for a few straglers. Everyone was enjoying themselves, Pharaoh, Ollie, and the two red bones were ball-rooming. The drinks were plentiful, and the soul food provided by Mom Dukes was on point. The D.J. cut the music and everyone focused their attention towards the bar. Two men were in each other's grill selling death. One man was holding a bottle of Dom while he blindsided the other man as he continued to wolf. The bouncers quickly defused the situation, by throwing both men into the parking lot.

Ollie and Pharaoh rushed off the dance floor to see what had taken place. Ollie's sister informed them that the bouncers had thrown Tez and the other guy out of the club. Pharaoh and Ollie ran for the front door, as they pushed it open they heard several gunshots. Pharaoh was the first to exit the club, so he witnessed Tez slaughter the other man. He shot the man in the chest seven times, sending him flying backwards, the man fell back in slow motion, then slammed into the pavement. Tez stood over him and finished him off, then threw up the symbol of 7 Mile with his free hand. Pharaoh pushed Ollie back into the club, and told him not to let anyone out until he could get Tez in the car.

"Nigga come on!" yelled Pharaoh, through the rolled down window of his 600 SL. Tez who was still in a daze, turned and looked. He gathered his senses, then ran around the car and jumped in. Pharaoh casually pulled out of the club and into traffic.

"Man, what the fuck is wrong with you?" asked Pharaoh.

"Fuck that bitch ass nigga. He tried to jump tough in front of his little bitch," said Tez.

"Dog you done fucked up ya' manz coming home party. Look at you, nigga, you sloppy drunk," said Pharaoh, shaking his head.

Chapter 19

Six months later....

Pharaoh and Sasha were asleep at their penthouse in downtown Detroit, it was four o'clock in the morning. Pharaoh was awakened by the loud sound of his cellphone ringing on the night stand. He reached over still half asleep, he felt around in the dark until grabbing the phone. His intention was to turn the phone off, he thought that he had, like he always did before going to bed. Something told him to answer it.

"Hello" answered Pharaoh, in a groggy voice.

"Juan, this is Kimkeysha."

"Who?"

"Chyna's friend, listen Chyna just went into labor. We're down at St. John's Hospital on Moross and Mack," said Kimkeysha.

"I'm on my way." Pharaoh jumped out of bed, awakening Sasha.

She rolled over and asked, "where you going Papi at this hour?"

"I got to go bail Tez out of jail," answered Pharaoh, as he rushed out of the door while getting dressed.

"Be careful!" yelled Sasha.

Pharaoh pulled into the parking lot of St. John's Hospital up to the emergency room door. He jumped out of his car and ran inside. He was told by the nurse at the desk that Chyna had just delivered the baby. She escorted Pharaoh up to Chyna's hospital room. He stopped at the entrance of the room at the sight of Chyna holding the bundle of joy, she had given birth to a six pound eight ounce baby boy. She looked up and smiled as Pharaoh approached her bed. The nurse asked if he would like to hold the baby. She made Pharaoh wash his hands, and put on a gown, shoes, hat and face mask. The nurse handed Pharaoh the baby. He stood next to Chyna rocking back and forth, looking down at the little boy.

"Hey little man," said Pharaoh, as he cracked a smile.

"What is his name?" asked the nurse, holding the birth certificate.

"Pharaoh Andre' Dickson, Jr.," Pharaoh happily said.

"I knew yo' mothafuckin' name wasn't no damn Juan!" snapped Chyna.

"Be cool woman," said Pharaoh, as he walked around the room talking to his son. Chyna was fuming, so she tried to throw anything out there that could possibly upset Pharaoh.

"Nigga, don't get ya' hopes up too high. You still ain't had no blood test yet," said Chyna.

Pharaoh ignored Chyna, making her even hotter. He had every intention on getting a blood test, as soon as the baby was released from the hospital. Pharaoh spent the night at the hospital, hoping that they would release Chyna and the baby in the morning. He slept in a chair next to Chyna, while Pharaoh Jr. was in an observation tank. Pharaoh woke up several times during the course of the night to check on lil' Pharaoh. He would walk out of Chyna's room, and look through the observations glass. He was afraid that somehow they might mix his son up with someone else's kid. Pharaoh called Tez, but he didn't answer his phone. Ollie came down to the hospital to show his support. Ollie stopped at the gift shop, and bought cigars that read "It's a boy."

The sun started to rise, and Pharaoh didn't want Sasha worrying. He asked the doctor if Chyna and the baby could leave. The doctor wanted them to stay for at least twenty-four hours, for observational reasons. Pharaoh kissed Chyna on the forehead, while she was in a deep sleep. He sent Ollie back to the gift shop to buy some flowers and a card. He opened it and wrote: *"I had to take care of some business, call me when you're released."*

Pharaoh left the hospital driving slowly back to his apartment. He was having mixed feelings. 'What should I do?' Pharaoh thought. He contemplated breaking off his engagement with Sasha, but he didn't love Chyna, this he was certain of. Sasha on the other hand, Pharaoh loved sincerely, it was Sasha he wanted to spend his life with. 'How did I let this happen?' he asked himself as he reluctantly pulled into the security gates of his apartment complex. Pharaoh dragged out of the car, and into the building. He took the elevator up to the 25th floor. When the door opened, he just stood there, the elevator was about to close, but Pharaoh grabbed it and got off. He stood at his apartment door, trying to gather the nerve to tell Sasha the truth. "Ah," sighed Pharaoh, letting out a deep breath, as he entered the apartment. He walked into the bedroom, where Sasha sat up in bed watching some Spanish soap opera. He began taking off his shoes, then his clothes. Pharaoh climbed in bed under the comforter.

"Is Tez okay?"

"He's fine. Mommie I have something to tell you," said Pharaoh, as he grabbed Sasha's hand.

"What is it Papi?" asked Sasha, turning to face him. Pharaoh looked into Sasha's deep green eyes and choked.

"I love you mommie, that's all," he said, then kissed Sasha.

"I love you too Papi." Pharaoh rolled over and went to sleep.

Chapter 20

After three blood tests, by three separate clinics, Pharaoh was satisfied that lil' Pharaoh was his son. He still hadn't found the courage to tell Sasha, as a result he was living a double life. Chyna wouldn't stop working at "007" because Pharaoh wouldn't commit to a relationship. Chyna started throwing temper tantrums, and threatening Pharaoh that he wouldn't see his son again.

It was June 1, 2002. One week before Pharaoh and Sasha's wedding. Tez, Pharaoh's best man, flew Ollie, Donald, Pharaoh's older brother, Killer B.,Tone, and all the women who worked at "007", out to Vegas first class for Pharaoh's bachelor party. Tez booked a presidential suite at the Bellagio. Pharaoh was under the impression that they were going to a fight, Roy Jones Jr. vs. some bum. Pharaoh and company sat ring-side. They watched two pre-matches by two overrated, never before heard of champions, both featherweight, but in different divisions, both fights ended by rule of judges. Pharaoh, Tez, Ollie, Killer B., Tone, and Donald made small wagers amongst themselves, and with several floor bookies.

"And now for the moment we've all been waiting for. Ladies and gentlemen, the main event," roared the announcer, as he stood center-ring, dressed in a black suit. Some unknown bum made a quiet entrance. He stepped into the ring, did a little foot shuffle, then bounced off into his corner. Pharaoh and company pointed and laughed at the short, stocky, bald-headed black man. "Clown ass nigga, you 'bout to get knocked out!" yelled Tez as he stood to his feet, and put his hand to his mouth to echo the sound. As

Tez took his seat, the lights in the arena went out. Some basement made rap song sounded through the arena, then a spotlight appeared. It followed a hooded Roy Jones, Jr. and his entourage. Ollie, Tez, and Pharaoh started to giving each other dap as Roy climbed into the ring. Roy did his patented slide, two-step, then a hurl of uppercuts. The announcer exited the ring. The referee explained the rules and the fighter's touched gloves. The bell sounded and the fighters met in center ring. Roy Jones, Jr. landed a fierce ten piece on his opponent, sending him face first to the ground. The referee sent Roy to his corner and counted the bum out.

"Ah, man that's it," said Tez, as he stood back up. "You's a bum for real Roy. You ain't never fought nobody. When you gon' give my manz Benard Hopkins a title shot?" yelled Tez.

"You's a nut," said Pharaoh laughing, talking to Tez.

"You the best bum I know Roy, fuck what he talking about," yelled Ollie, holding up the numerous tickets indicating him a winner. All the men joined in laughter at Ollie's comment.

Pharaoh and Tez did some gambling, while the others went their separate ways. Pharaoh won twenty thousand shooting craps, Tez had lost that, and some. He had one too many shots of Remy Martin. "This some bullshit. Them dice are fuckin' loaded!" yelled Tez, as he reached across the table in an attempt to pick up the dice. The pit boss motioned two plain clothes officers, and they collared Tez up. They escorted him off the main floor into a near by eatery. Pharaoh was trailing Tez as the cops escorted him away.

"He's just drunk," pleaded Pharaoh. "Please let me take him up to the room."

"Make sure he doesn't come out his room until he's sober. If we catch him on the floors tonight, he's going to jail," said one of the officers. With that Pharaoh put his arm around Tez and walked him to an elevator.

"Man, nigga can't go nowhere with yo' ass," said Pharaoh, as he walked Tez onto the elevator. They exited the elevator, and walked down the hall to their suite. Pharaoh pulled out his room key, put it in the cylinder, then pushed the door open. The lights were off, not a sign of anyone. Pharaoh pulled Tez into the room and shut the door, he flipped on the light switch and turned around. Everyone yelled, "surprise!" Ollie, Killer B., Donald, Tone, and twenty-five young ladies filled the suite. Tez slapped Pharaoh on the shoulder

"nigga, now tell me I didn't get you." Tez had set the whole thing up, he paid the pit boss and two officers for their small roles.

"Yeah, you got that one off," laughed Pharaoh.

The women were completely naked, with the exception of stilettos and garter belts. There were thirty-one flavors of ass in attendance, something for everyone's preference. Tez escorted Pharaoh to a plush leather office chair, which sat dead center of the suite. Pharaoh took a seat, receiving multiple lap dances. Ollie was passing out cigars, and a bottle of Dom P. Tez was on the couch in a sandwich with two red bones, he was leaned over sucking one of the lady's titties, and fingering her at the same time. The other woman was rubbing Tez's back and kissing his nape. Killer B. was seated on the loveseat getting head from a petite, caramel complexioned girl. Tone was lying on the floor on top of this thick white broad with blonde hair. Pharaoh's brother, Donald, was sitting on the couch with Tez and the two females. Pharaoh absorbed everyone's situation, and was pleased with his own four girls as they surrounded him taking turns giving him head.

Pharaoh grabbed one of the girls by the waist and lifted her on top of his dick. The girl was fucking Pharaoh's brains out, when out of nowhere, she was hit in the head with a Dom P. bottle. The thick glass, mixed with blood flew in Pharaoh's face. The music came to a stop instantly. Pharaoh managed to lift the girl up off him and stood up. Chyna was on the girl's ass, like a crackhead on his last hit. She pounded the poor, thick girl's head against the granite floor. Pharaoh reached down, prying Chyna off the girl. He dragged her out on the balcony, and slammed the screen behind them.

"What the fuck is yo' problem? Better yet, what the fuck are you doing here?" demanded Pharaoh.

"I should be asking you the same thing. Who are you getting married to?" yelled Chyna.

"Look bitch, that is of none of your concern. We aren't together, in no way shape, form, or fashion. Get that through your fuckin' head!" yelled Pharaoh.

"Fuck you nigga," said Chyna, as she attempted to walk past Pharaoh. He stepped in front of her, and gritted his teeth.

"What, you gon' hit me?" asked Chyna, stopping in her tracks. Pharaoh took a deep breath, and exhaled.

"Bitch I wouldn't give you the satisfaction," he said stepping aside to let Chyna pass. Pharaoh walked over to the balcony and leaned over it, looking down on Vegas. Tez made his way to the balcony, after watching Chyna storm out of the suite.

"You good my manz?" asked Tez as he approached Pharaoh.

"How that bitch get out here?" asked Pharaoh.

"My bad my nigga," said Tez.

"Man..." said Pharaoh, leaving Tez out on the balcony.

Chapter 21

It was June 7th, 2002, the day Sasha and Pharaoh decided to get married. Sasha wanted to get married back home, so Pharaoh's cousin planned the wedding. It was being held in the garden of Sasha's parents' estate. Toro, Sasha's father, blessed Pharaoh into the family and gave him a platinum masterpiece Rolex watch. Pharaoh stood beside the altar wearing a white tailor made suit courtesy of Billy at Broadways'. He wore a pink bow tie, and a pair of matching gators. Tez, along with Ollie, Donald, Pharaoh's brother and Joey, Sasha's brother, stood behind Pharaoh wearing identical suits as Pharaoh's. Toro escorted Sasha down the aisle of the garden. She wore a pearl white dress that exposed her shoulders and back. Her hair was pulled up into a bun. Shannon decorated Sasha's veil with assorted gems.

Everyone turned around in their seats as Sasha made her way to the altar. Pharaoh was at a loss for words as Toro handed Sasha over to him. She looked up at him with her lustful green eyes, and smiled, together they turned toward the Catholic priest. The priest in turn waited for everyone to be seated, then proceeded. "Dearly beloved, we're gathered here today, to join this couple in holy matrimony…"

Sasha and Pharaoh exchanged vows: "Papi, I vow to love, honor, and cherish you, to be the best possible wife I can be. I vow my heart, soul, mind and body to you and only you. Papi, I vow my all," said Sasha.

Pharaoh hadn't written any specific vows. He figured if he could start off strong, and close strong, everything would be good. "I vow to always put you above and beyond anything the world could possibly offer. I promise to be a friend, companion, confidant, and the best possible husband I can be to you. I vow to share life with you, the ups and downs. I vow to be honest, and trustworthy. Sasha it is you I vow to spend the rest of my life with," Pharoah concluded.

"Very well. Do you Sasha Perez take this man to be your lawfully wedded husband, to love, honor, and cherish through sickness and health 'til death do you part?" asked the priest.

"I do," answered Sasha.

"And do you Pharaoh Dickson take this woman to be your lawfully wedded wife, to love, honor, and cherish through sickness and health 'tio death do you part?" asked the priest.

"I do," answered Pharaoh.

"Rings please." Sasha's sister Ambria handed her Pharaoh's ring. Tez patted his pockets in search of Sasha's ring.

"I put it in my inside pocket," whispered Tez, to the impatient Pharaoh.

"I'll be right back," he said, running out of the garden into the house. He came flying back down the aisle out of breath. Tez extended the ring to Pharaoh, who snatched it, and rolled is eyes.

"Place the rings on each other's hand," ordered the priest. Pharaoh put Sasha's ring on first, then Sasha placed Pharaoh's band on his finger.

"By the powers vested in me, I now pronounce you husband and wife. You may kiss the bride." Pharaoh lifted Sasha's veil, then passionately kissed her. Everyone stood and applauded as they walked out of the garden as husband and wife.

The reception was held in the ballroom of the estate. Pharaoh and Sasha sat at a large table, joined by Tez and Ambria. Everyone enjoyed the enormous spread. Sasha's father, Toro, went all out on the catering. There was everything from seafood, to Mexican, to soul food. Maids ushered the many aisles waiting on people. Champagne was like water, so many bottles were being popped, it sounded like the 4th of July. Tez stood up and tapped his dinner fork on his glass. "May I have everyone's attention please," asked Tez. Everyone stopped and gave their undivided attention to him. "I'd like to make a toast" he said, holding his glass high in the air full of bubbly. "I'd like to first and foremost congratulate the bride and groom on their new marriage. I wish you a life time of happiness together. To my manz, my ace, my nigga! I love you like a brother, and if anyone I know deserves to be happy, bro it's you. Here's to you," Tez, said before he downed his glass.

Everyone raised their glasses, then drained them. A few others gave toasts, then came the gifts. Ollie gave Pharaoh and Sasha his & her Cartier watches. Tez gave them a $20,000.00 gift certificate to 'Detrich Furs.' The best gift of all came from Sasha's father. He bought the couple a mansion two streets over from his, and a brand new 'Bentley Arnage.' After the toasts and gifts, Sasha and Pharaoh cut their cake. They took the first slice, and fed it to each other, then took to the dance floor and slow-danced, as everyone watched and took pictures. More champagne flowed as the evening turned to night. Sasha's family began to leave as the party started to dwindle. Pharaoh's family was driven by several limousines to his and Sasha's new mansion. Ollie and Tez hooked up with Rachael and Lisa, while Pharaoh and Sasha set out for their honeymoon in Barbados.

Chapter 22

After Pharaoh and Sasha returned from their honeymoon in Barbados, he went back to work in Detroit, while she flew to Phoenix to decorate their new mansion. Pharaoh was grateful for the gift, but he felt it was Toro's way of keeping them in Phoenix. Pharaoh rolled with the flow because he didn't want to lose his connect with the family, he missed his son more than anything. He vowed that once he had met his quota, he was going to tell Sasha, and deal with the consequences, when and if there were some. No sooner than Pharaoh's plane landed at the Metro Airport in Detroit, his cellphone rang. He looked at the screen of the phone as he exited the plane. It was his driver Eric.

"E," what's up baby?"

"I'm 'bout an hour away," said Eric.

"See you in a few,"

Pharaoh took a cab back into the city and had the driver drop him off at the U-haul rental place. Pharaoh rented a mid-sized truck and headed for the warehouse to meet Eric. He pulled around back and parked in his regular spot. Forty-five minutes had passed and Pharaoh was beginning to worr, he looked at his watch several times, then flipped open his cellphone. He scrolled down to Eric's name, and pushed the call button. As the phone began to ring, Eric turned the corner in the semi. He pulled up next to the U-haul, put the truck in park, and jumped out. Pharaoh backed the U-haul up to the hatch of the semi, then climbed out and began loading pound after pound.

"I was beginning to think the worst," said Pharaoh.

"Nah, two fucking trains, can you believe that, two!" yelled Eric, as he moved like a nigga on the run.

Pharaoh finished packing the U-haul, and pulled the sliding door down. He and Eric slapped fives and both men climbed into their trucks, and pulled off in opposite directions. Pharaoh called Tone, Chris, Killer B., and Mike. They all were desperately glad to hear he was back, and he had the work. Pharaoh dropped off the excess weed at his mom's house, then made his rounds. His last stop was Tez's house. He pulled the U-haul into the backyard and jumped out leaving the truck running. He knocked on the back door. Tez peeped out the kitchen window, then opened the door. Pharaoh walked back to the U-haul and opened the back door. He turned and looked at Tez who was standing on the back porch, with his shirt off.

"My manz, help me carry this shit in," said Pharaoh, referring to the one hundred pounds of weed. Tez started scratching his head, and Pharaoh peeped the bullshit coming.

"See what had happened was," said Tez, as Pharaoh cut him off.

"Save it my manz, you got one more time, and boy I swear," said Pharaoh, as he headed up the basement steps.

"How was the honeymoon?" asked Tez, in an attempt to change the subject.

"It was a'ight, but it's back to the basics. Nigga you need to tighten up. You mean to tell me, you ain't got none of the money?" asked Pharaoh.

"See, what happened was," said Tez.

Pharaoh threw his hands up in the air, as to say I give up. He pushed opened the back door, and walked out. He hopped in the still running U-haul, and backed out of the driveway. Pharaoh flipped open his cellphone and pushed call on Chyna's name. The phone rang several times, no answer. Pharaoh looked at his phone then hung it up. He pulled into Chyna's apartment complex, and parked in the visitors parking space, because both of Chyna's parking spots were occupied. He parked the U-haul, then walked up to the lobby entrance. He pushed Chyna's apartment number. Seconds later her voice came over the intercom.

"Who is it?" she asked, in a funky tone of voice.

"I did call, but you wouldn't answer yo' damn phone. Girl, open the door."

"If I didn't answer, that means I wasn't trying to be bothered."

"So you gon' play these childish ass games?"

"What the fuck do you want? How come you ain't at home with your wifey?"

"Look bitch, I just want to see my son."

"I've got company."

"That's cool, I'm not tripping on that lil' shit. I'mma take my son to spend the night with me."

"You aint 'bout to have my son around no bitch!" yelled Chyna.

"First off her name is Sasha. Secondly, she's in Phoenix at our new mansion. Are you gon' give me my son or what?"

Chyna hung up the intercom. Pharaoh stood there in the lobby for a few seconds, then Chyna buzzed him in. He walked up two flights of stairs, then turned right on Chyna's floor. She was standing in the door with Pharaoh Jr. fully dressed. He approached the apartment and smiled at the sight of his son and reached down to pick him up. "Hey lil' man. Daddy missed you," said Pharaoh. He looked up and acknowledged Chyna, who had her ass on her shoulders. "I'll bring him back tomorrow around two o'clock," said Pharaoh.

"Yeah, whatever," she said, slamming the door in Pharaoh's face. He turned and walked down the hallway playing with lil' Pharaoh Jr. They drove to his apartment where he and Jr. played and ate candy until they fell asleep.

The next morning Pharaoh cooked blueberry pancakes, scrambled eggs, and beef sausages for breakfast. He and Jr. laid on the living room floor and watched Cartoon Network.

"You know daddy loves you right," said Pharaoh, as he rubbed his son's jet back wavy hair. Jr. couldn't talk yet, but he looked up at his dad and smiled. They finished off their breakfast, then took a bath. Pharaoh cracked open his safe and took out five thousand. "You know what this is?" he asked Pharaoh Jr. as he sat on the bed. Pharaoh picked him up and sat him on his lap, and showed his son how to count money. He then dressed and took Jr. to Chucky E. Cheese. They played every game in the place, using over two hundred dollars worth of tokens. They ate pizza and watched Chucky, the mouse, put on his performance. Pharaoh bought Jr. several toys from the ticket counter, along with a huge bag of assorted candy. There was a mall attached to Chucky E. Cheese, so Pharaoh took Jr. shopping. He spent close to three thousand dollars on clothes and toys. It had been a long, but fun day.

It was a quarter to two, and Pharaoh told Chyna he would have Jr. home by two. He pulled in Chyna'a apartment complex at exactly two o'clock. "Well lil' man, I had a blast, we should do this again sometime," said Pharaoh, looking at Jr. who was eating some candy.

"Let's get in here before yo' crazy moma have a fit," said Pharaoh, as he got out of the car, and walked around to get Jr. Pharaoh tried to call Chyna's cell phone, but got her voicemail. He carried Jr. into the lobby and pushed Chyna's apartment number. A man's voice could be heard in the background as Chyna answered.

"What...?" she answered, dragging out the word.

"Open the door."

"Nigga fuck you. Ya' wanna play daddy, then I'mma let you play daddy."

"What the fuck is you talking about?"

"Let me spell it out for ya' ass, seeing as though you's slow. I'm done playing mommie, so take your little crumb snatcher home to ya' wife, and let her play mommie," said Chyna, as she hung up the intercom.

"Chyna! Chyna!" yelled Pharaoh.

He tried buzzing her apartment several times, but to no avail. Pharaoh waited in the lobby for hours hoping Chyna would open the door, or someone would either come or leave. Nothing, Pharaoh finally walked back to his car, and put his son inside. He turned back to see if Chyna had come down, but no sign of her. He drove back to his apartment and he and Jr. sat on the couch. Pharaoh told himself that Chyna would get over it, whatever it was and she'd come running for Jr. after a few days. A few days was all Pharaoh had before he had to be back in Phoenix. He promised Sasha that he would be spending more time with her.

Chapter 23

Three days had passed, and Chyna still hadn't tried to contact Pharaoh, his flight was scheduled to leave in two hours, so he broke the ice and called Chyna. Her phone just rang, and rang. Pharaoh hung up and tried calling again, nothing. He clicked off and flopped down on the couch next to Jr. "Why me?" he asked looking up at the ceiling. He thought about every possible soul he knew that he could ask to watch Jr. Pharaoh's options were slim to none, he didn't want to take him over to his mother's house because he still hadn't told Mom Dukes about Jr. Pharaoh tried to call Chyna one last time. "Fuck it," he reached down and picked up Jr. and headed for the door. Pharaoh decided to take Jr. to Phoenix with him. The entire flight he tried to come up with a logical explanation, he could tell Sasha. Pharaoh Sr. and Jr. arrived in Phoenix five minutes after six in the evening. Sasha was waiting inside the terminal and spotted Pharaoh, as he walked through a sliding door with Jr. in his arms.

"Over here Papi," said Sasha, as she waved Pharaoh over. Pharaoh let out a long sigh, then walked in Sasha's direction. "Who's the handsome little fella?" said Sasha, as she smiled and played with Jr.'s fingers.

"Oh, this is my nephew, Donald's son. His name is Donald Jr., but I just call him Jr.."

"I didn't know Donald had any kids," said Sasha.

"Yeah, him and the mother are separated. He had to go out of town, so I told him I'd watch 'em."

Sasha drove them home to the new mansion, courtesy of Toro. Pharaoh entered in astonishment. Sasha had laid the eight bedroom, four bath, four car garage, white colonial out.   Wall-to-wall white marble floors filled the mansion, the kitchen countertops were matching white marble, the furniture had been imported from France. Sasha's theme was white, except for the bedroom, which was laced will satin lavender sheets and pillows. There was a plasma television in every room, including the bathrooms and kitchen. Pharaoh toured the house as if he was a complete stranger. He walked out back and was nearly blinded by the sparkling clear, in-ground swimming pool. Beside it was a man-made waterfall, which overlooked the mountains and the dry desert. Pharaoh entered the two bedroom pool house, and flopped down on the couch. Sasha, who was playing with Jr., was waiting for Pharaoh's approval.

"So, do you like it Papi?"

"I love it mommie, I just can't believe that it's ours."

"Well, believe it," said Sasha, as she leaned over and kissed Pharaoh. "Not in front of Jr.," she laughed.

"Ah, when he gets older, he'll understand," said Pharaoh, as he continued to try to get Sasha in the mood.

　　Pharaoh relaxed at home with Sasha and Jr. for a week. She asked Pharaoh when Donald was expecting him and Jr. back in Detroit. Truth be told, Pharaoh had fallen in love with his new life in Arizona, he didn't want to have to go back to Detroit, and face reality.

　　Meanwhile, back in Detroit, Tez and Ollie hooked up and went to "007"." It was early in the day and they were bored. Tez's philosophy was, why be bored, when you can go fuck with a whore. He ran this same line on Ollie just minutes before pulling into the parking lot of his second home. Tez valet parked his 600 SL, and he and Ollie made a grand entrance. Tez stopped at the front door once inside the club; he folded his arms and cocked his head to the side, taking on a B-Boy stance. The DJ announced Tez as Nino

Brown. A couple of strippers approached Tez and Ollie, then ushered them to a booth. "If you ain't fucking, I ain't fucking with you," announced Tez, pulling out a bankroll, spreading it across the table. One of the girls reached for a fifty dollar bill. Tez grabbed her hand and twisted it. "Bitch, you ain't earned nothing yet, that's what's wrong with you bitches, ya'll always want something for nothin'," said Tez.

"Let her go!" ordered Chyna, as she approached the scene.

"And just who the fuck you supposed to be, mighty morphan mothafuckin' Power Ranger?" asked Tez, looking up at Chyna. One of the bouncers defused the situation, but Chyna stood their waiting to take Tez and Ollie's order.

"What you sorry ass niggas having?" asked Chyna.

"Hold on baby girl, we ain't come here for all that," said Ollie.

"You're old girl from the bachelor party, what's your name, Dina?" asked Tez, as he realized he had met Chyna before.

"Chyna!" she snapped.

"Well, look Chyna, I don't know what you and my manz got going, but leave me out of it. Now, I want two double shots of Remy Martin and give my manz here what he wants."

Tez stared at Chyna's frame with one thing on his mind. She turned and walked away after filling Ollie's order. Tez watched her closely as she stood at the bar while the barmaid poured their drinks.

"You done ran the hoes off, my man," said Ollie.

"Um" mumbled Tez. He was still in his trance, staring at Chyna.

Tez's eyes hadn't left Chyna's body since she approached the booth. The barmaid sat Ollie and Tez's drinks on the counter, Chyna picked them up and headed for the booth. Her eyes locked with Tez's, she could see the desire and lust beaming from his eyes. Her first instict was to ask Tez, what the fuck he was staring at, but she played it cool by smiling at Tez as she leaned over, putting their drinks on the table. "Hey Ollie, go grab some hoes," he said. Tez didn't have to tell Ollie twice. He slid out of the booth and walked over to the stage where two girls put on a show.

"Let's cut to the chase, I'm trying to see you. I don't care nothing about you and Pharaoh," said Tez, talking to Chyna. Chyna played coy for a second.

"What do you think he'll say?" pointing to Ollie.

"He ain't even got to know, that's why I sent him away." Tez reached over the table and grabbed the ink pen Chyna had in her hand. "Here, just call me whenever you're ready," said Tez as he wrote his number on a napkin and handed it to Chyna.

Chyna tucked the napkin in her apron, smiled, then turned on her heels. She walked away enticingly; throwing her ass like it was going out of style. She was plotting her revenge on Pharaoh, and Tez had played right into her hand. Ollie came back to the booth empty-handed.

"Where the hoes at?" Tez asked.

"Ah, man fuck them boot mouth bitches. They on bullshit."

"Nah nigga, you just ain't got no game," laughed Tez.

It was two o'clock in the morning and the DJ announced last round. The club was about to close, Tez and Ollie had been at there all day. They spent over five thousand between the two of them. Ollie was at the bar trying to get him and Tez a last round of Remy Martin. Chyna approached Tez and whispered in his ear.

"Where are you going from here?"

"Drop my manz off, then I'm to the crib."

"I was hoping we could hook up tonight," suggested Chyna, as she played with her belly button ring.

"Most definitely, as a matter of fact, I'm 'bout to drop him off right now. I guess you can call me when you're ready," said Tez, standing to his feet.

"Sounds like a plan," said Chyna, as she rubbed Tez from his chest down to his dick, then turned to leave. Ollie returned to the booth with the drinks. He noticed Tez was standing.

"What's wrong my nigga?"

"Ain't shit, let's be up," answered Tez, taking his drink and downing it.

Tez raced to drop Ollie off at his apartment. He didn't say anything the entire way there. After dropping Ollie off, Tez took the Lodge Freeway back east. As he drove, his cellphone rang. He looked at the screen and didn't recognize the number. He pushed the talk button anyway.

"Hello."

"Where you at?"

"Who is dis?"

"Oh you meet that many hoes a day?"

Tez was at a loss 'cause he couldn't place the voice.

"Nigga it's me, Chyna."

"Oh, my bad. Baby you got to forgive me, I'm perbing like E..mothafuckin'."

"Um hum..."

"But uh, what's the deal. You trying to see me or you in for the night."

"I'm in for the night, but you're more than welcome to come keep me company."

"I'm on my way. Where you live at?"

Chyna gave Tez directions, and talked to him until he reached her apartment complex. Tez parked next to Chyna's Chrysler Sebring, then made his way to the lobby door. Chyna had walked down from her apartment. She stood in the vestibule wearing a Winnie the Pooh night gown, and matching slippers. Her thick calves, and thighs were showing. Tez opened the door and examined Chyna from head to toe.

"You look comfortable," he said.

"Come on," said Chyna, grabbing Tez by the hand and leading him up to her apartment.

When Chyna turned around to lead the way Tez made a tight faced expression because she wasn't wearing any panties. Her ass seemed to have a mind of it's own as she walked. Chyna pushed open her apartment door, letting Tez enter first. Tez stood with his back to Chyna as she locked the door. "Damn," he said, turning around.

Chyna had slipped her nightgown over her head and it rested on the floor beside her slippers. Tez wasted no time, he fully accepted the invitation. He pushed Chyna up against the front door, took both of her hands and raised them above her head as he kissed her perfect C cup titties. Chyna managed to free her hands and slid from under Tez's body. She walked into the living room and posed on the couch in a doggy style position. She arched her back, and teased Tez with her bedroom eyes, while he raced to undress. Tez made it down to his birthday suit, slipped on a condom, then climbed on the couch. Tez gripped Chyna's ass with one hand, while inserting himself with the other. He sighed in satisfaction, as he began to stroke her from the back. Chyna's pussy became extremely moist and it only made Tez stroke faster. He now palmed both of her ass cheeks, spreading them apart, Tez couldn't dig all the way in her because of the height difference. He kneeled down further and moved his hands up to Chyna's small waist. Chyna's ass looked like Jello, as it slapped up against Tez's pelvis. Satified that Tez was lost in her magical box, she turned her head toward the entertainment system. She smiled, then waved her right hand at a video camera hidden in the entertainment system. Tez had worked up a sweat. He pulled his dick out of Chyna, and stood up. He removed the condom, and began jacking his dick. He made Chyna sit up on the couch, while he worked himself to satisfaction. Tez grabbed Chyna's hair, as he ejaculated all over her face. She grabbed Tez's dick, put it in her mouth and sucked him soft, as Tez squirmed from the satisfaction. Tez quickly worked himself back up, with the help of Chyna. They went for round two, then three, while Chyna caught every moment on camera.

Chapter 24

Pharaoh and Jr. arrived back in Detroit on a Thursday afternoon. It was pouring down raining, the sky was pitch black, and every so often lightning would fill the sky. Pharaoh drove slowly through the semi traffic. He pointed up at the sky to the lightning. Jr. smiled at the bright bolts of lightning. "I wonder if yo' crazy moma has calmed down," said Pharaoh, as he scrolled through his cellphone. He stopped on Chyna's number and pushed the call button. Two rings, and she answered.

"Hello."

"I'm 'bout to bring Jr. home, or are you still on your bullshit?" asked Pharaoh.

"I'm cool."

"So is that a yes, or a no?"

"Nigga, just bring my son home," she said, slamming the phone in Pharaoh's ear.

"You betta not grow up to be like yo' mommy," said Pharaoh as he rubbed Jr.'s head.

He pulled into Chyna's complex, parked in her vacant spot and got out. He walked around to the passenger side and got Jr. He carried Jr. up to the lobby, and pushed Chyna's apartment number, without answering, Chyna buzzed them up. Pharaoh made it up to the apartment, and she was standing in the door wearing her Winnie the Pooh gown, and slippers. Chyna reached for Jr. and took him into her arms. She bounced up and down saying, "Mommie missed you, yes I did." Pharaoh just stood there. Chyna looked up at him, "what are you waiting on? You ain't coming in."

"Daddy gon' see you later lil' man," said Pharaoh, as he leaned over and kissed Jr. goodbye. Chyna ran back into the apartment, sitting Jr. on the couch. She grabbed the videotape of her and Tez getting' physical. She kissed it and ran out into the hallway. She caught Pharaoh walking down the stairs.

"You might want to watch this," Chyna handed Pharaoh the tape. He looked at both sides, it had no label.

"What's this?"

"A rude awakening," said Chyna as she turned and headed back up the stairs.

Pharaoh tucked the tape in his glove box. He drove to his mom's house while making calls. Tone, Killer B., Mike, Chris, and Tez were out of weed. Pharaoh packed the trunk and backseat of his 600 SL full of weed. He made his rounds, stopping at Tez's last. He pulled into Tez's driveway and hit the horn. Pharaoh was waiting for Tez to peep out the window before getting out. Tez heard the horn, and crawled to the front door. He looked through the peephole at Pharaoh still sitting in his car. Tez's cellphone started ringing. He pulled the phone off the clip on his hip and looked at it. "Damn," he said. It was Pharaoh calling. He knew nine times out of ten Tez was home because his 600 SL was parked in the backyard. Tez reluctantly answered.

"Hello," he answered, trying to sound as if he just woke up.

"Nigga, come open the door," said Pharaoh.

Pharaoh reached over into the glove box and grabbed the tape Chyna had given him. He popped the trunk and started carrying Tez's hundred pounds into the house. After finishing up with Tez's load, Pharaoh flopped down on the couch. He tossed the tape on the coffee table, and let out a sigh. Tez disappeared into the back of the house. He came back into the living room carrying a plastic grocery bag and tossed it on Pharaoh's lap.

"What's this, what...Tez paying his tab?" joked Pharaoh.

"Hah.. Hah.. Ha...," said Tez.

"Nah, seriously how much is this short?"

"It's all there," said Tez, reaching down to the coffee table. Tez picked up his car keys, then the video tape. "What's this?"

"Some tape my baby mama gave me. It's probably of my son taking his first steps," answered Pharaoh.

"Well, look I'm 'bout to shoot a few moves," said Tez.

"A'ight I'ma chill and count this money. Here," said Pharaoh tossing Tez his car keys.

"I got you blocked in."

Tez was in a rush to leave. He felt uneasy around Pharaoh because he had slept with Chyna. He loaded the weed into his trunk, backed Pharaoh's car out, then pulled out in his own 600 SL. Pharaoh raided Tez's fridge. He made his favorite, wing-dings and French fries. Pharaoh got some hot sauce and ranch dressing from the cabinet, and two ice cold Fruitopia's out of the fridge and walked into the living room. He put the tape into the VCR and turned on the television. He doctored his food up, and waited for the tape to begin playing. Pharaoh ate his wing-dings and fries, as Chyna's pretty brown round appeared on the screen. "Okay," he said, sitting up at attention. Chyna was on all fours on the couch. Pharaoh was enjoying what he was seeing, until the ass of a charcoal black man blocked the camera.

Pharaoh thought Chyna's silly ass made a sex tape with her new man. He continued to watch, as the man in the video climbed onto the couch, inserting his penis inside of Chyna's pussy. The man's identity still couldn't be made out, Pharaoh could only see his chest, and legs. Once Tez slouched down further, so he could dig deeper into Chyna, his face flashed across the screen. Pharaoh dropped the wing-ding he was chewing, and stared in disbelief. He watched as Tez stroked Chyna to death. She took the cake when she smiled and waved at the camera. Pharaoh stood up and ejected the tape. He gathered all his money, and left.

Chapter 25

Valdez raced back and forth inside the warehouse, located on the outskirts of Phoenix. For him and the men inside, it was just another day of receiving and shipping marijuana. He hollered orders in Spanish to the many workers. He was occupied with weighing the marijuana, and packing it. Loud industrial fans made it impossible for one to hear, unless a person was hollering, or was standing right beside you.

The INS, and Phoenix Taskforce executed a search warrant on the warehouse. They filed in wearing bulletproof vests, helmets, and carrying assault rifles. "Freeze!" ordered a DEA agent in Spanish over a bullhorn. The workers, all whom were Mexican, dropped what they were doing, and bolted for the back door and dock. They were sandwiched in by more agents waiting out back. The workers and Valdez were all placed in handcuffs, and transported downtown to the Federal building in Phoenix. The feds seized phony passports, social security cards, credit cards, computer systems used to manufacture fake I.D. cards, four eighteen-wheeler's, scales, and over ten thousand pounds of marijuana. None of the workers could speak English. The INS agents conversed with them, trying to disclose their identities. All of them, including Valdez, were illegal immigrants. The DEA agents gave each man a chance to supposedly help himself. The workers all kept their mouths shut out of fear. If they told, they wouldn't be able to stay in the country, so they thought.

When the agents called Valdez into the interrogation room, he volunteered everything. "I will tell you everything, please just don't deport me back to Mexico," he pleaded.

"Who are you working for?" asked one of the DEA agents.

"My father-in-law, his name is Toro."

"And what's Toro's last name?"

"Perez."

"Where does Toro Perez live?"

"Him and my mother-in-law live on Florida Ave. in an estate. I don't know the address off hand, but I can show you or draw a map."

"What's Toro's phone number?"

"His home number is 917-****, and his office number at "The Zone" is 921-****."

"What's "The Zone?"

"It's a bar & grill that Toro opened about a year ago."

"So who's Toro's boss?"

"To my knowledge there is no other higher. Toro works with other Mexican cartels from Mexico, when our crops are low, but he's his own boss."

"Describe Toro."

"He's about 5'5", 120 pounds, gray hair, mustache, about 65 years old."

"Who else is involved in your cartel?"

"Well there's four under-bosses. Each of us supply a number of major cities, particularly Mid-west."

"Who are the other three bosses?"

"Joey, Toro's oldest son, Skip and Veto, they aren't blood related. Joey supplies all of Ohio and Indiana. Skip supplies Chicago and Wisconsin. And Veto supplies Minnesota and Nebraska. I have Detroit, and the surrounding areas."

"Who are you dealing with?"

"Pharaoh, he's my wife's sister's husband. He's from Detroit. I have pictures of him and his street team at my home from his wedding. I'm supposed to drop him off a thousand pounds next week. He just received a shipment yesterday," said Valdez.

"What's Pharaoh's phone number?" asked the DEA agent.

"His cell number is (313) 623-****. He drives a black on black Mercedes Benz 600 SL. He's about 6'2", 190 pounds, black, low cut, black hair. Uh... What else?" said Valdez, trying to provide as much information as possible.

"How do you transport the marijuana to Detroit?"

"By an eighteen-wheeler."

"Who's the driver?"

"Pharaoh's driver name is Eric. He's white, about 5'9", 165 pounds, blue eyes, long blonde hair, young, probably thirty."

"Where can we find Eric?"

"His cell number is 927-****. If I call him and say I need him to meet me at the warehouse, he'll come flying. He drives a red Ford S10, late model."

"Who else are you selling to?" asked the DEA agent.

Valdez went on providing all the information he could. He gave up everything and everyone. He pleaded with the agents not to deport him back to Mexico, and vowed to assist them in their investigation. The agents let Valdez go on a personal bond. They also let all his workers go back to the warehouse. The feds wanted Valdez to continue on shipping and receiving until they could catch everyone involved on all ends. They kept the bust out of the media, and returned everything that was seized.

The DEA agents in Phoenix contacted the Detroit office, and relayed their investigation to the agents working the field. The DEA agents ran Pharaoh's name through their database, and found nothing on record. His phone wasn't registered in his name, neither was his car, or apartment. The agents had Valdez place a call to Pharaoh so they could possibly trace it.

"Hello," answered Pharaoh, turning down the radio in his

car.

"Hey, this is Val."

"Oh, what's up Val?"

"Just checking on you, that's all. Listen, you've been doing extremely well these past six months. I'm going to add an additional thousand on your next load, so you can take a vacation with Toro and the rest of us to Mexico."

"That sounds great. Are the wives coming?" asked Pharaoh.

"No, just the men. We need our time to unwind too," said Valdez, trying to stall until the feds traced the call.

"Well right after Eric touches me next week, I plan on catching a flight back to Phoenix," said Pharaoh.

"Got it," whispered one of the DEA agents.

"Alright, I'mma let you go, see you soon," said Valdez.

"A'ight Val."

　　　Pharaoh had a Nextel phone. The feds were able to trace his whereabouts because his cellphone had a chip inside that was somewhat of a tracking device. The feds contacted Nextel Corp., and had them use the satellite closest to Detroit to pinpoint the location of the phone. Once the location of Pharaoh's cellphone was disclosed, the DEA put two field agents on surveillance. Agents Nate Browski, and Jeff Stephens were assigned to the investigation. They were both ten year veterans with the DEA, they'd been partners their entire careers. Both were hard nose agents, who wore plain clothes and drove unmarked Chevy Luminas. "There it is," said agent Browski, talking to his partner. He was pointing at Pharaoh's 600 SL parked in front of Al's Barber Shop. Agent Stephens radioed the dispatcher at the DEA headquarters and relayed their findings. He ran the plate number and it came back to a Jerome Williams, address Orchard Lake, MI. Pharaoh was sitting inside his car talking to Dee. He had just gotten his hair cut, and was now politicking with Dee on some prices.

"Shit, what you let me get 'em for if I cop ten or better?" asked Dee.

"For you," laughed Pharaoh. "I'll let you get 'em for nine hun'd."

"That's a bet. I'mma get up with you tomorrow," said Dee.

"A'ight be smooth," said Pharaoh, starting the car.

Dee gave Pharaoh some dap, then exited the vehicle. Pharaoh looked in his rearview mirror to check traffic. It was clear, so he pulled out and headed east on 7 Mile Road. Agents Browski and Stephens had parked several cars behind Pharaoh. They pulled out behind Pharaoh and tailed him from a distance. Pharaoh turned right on Gratiot Ave. and drove south.

"Don't those new foreign model cars have, what you call it, samn, uh that fucking 'On Star' shit?" asked Agent Stephens.

"I believe so. Let me see," said Agent Browski.

He radioed dispatch and asked to check whether or not Pharaoh's Benz in fact had On Star, or something similar. Agents Browski and Stephens waited patiently for the dispatcher to come over the radio. They continued to follow Pharaoh on Gratiot. Agent Stephens, who was in the passenger seat, jotted down every intricate detail in a spiral notepad.

"Sir, are you there?" asked the female dispatcher.

"Yes, the vehicle has a low jack system. It comes stock with all the late model Mercedes Benz. The name of the company is 'Power Trak,' the telephone number is (800) 521-****," said the dispatcher.

"Thank you," said Agent Browski.

Agent Stephens had written down every word. He contacted the company and had them activate the electronic voice system in the car. Every word Pharaoh said would be recorded. Pharaoh turned left on Helen St. and drove down three blocks. He pulled into the driveway of Tone's spot.

He was already in the window, when Pharaoh pulled up and met Pharaoh at the front door.

"What up doe my baby?" asked Tone, as he opened the screen door, and stepped out onto the porch.

"You got somebody here to watch the house?" asked Pharaoh.

"Yeah, why what's up?"

"Bend a few corners with me," said Pharaoh, as he walked back to his car and got in.

Tone hollered inside to one of his workers to let them know he would be right back. He pulled the door closed, and sprinted down the stairs. He cut across the grass, and got in the passenger side. Pharaoh backed out of the driveway, and headed south. He turned on Grand River until he reached Jefferson Ave. Pharaoh and Tone got caught by a red light, there was no music playing, only silence. Tone broke the ice, "what's up baby, you a'ight?" Pharaoh let out a long sigh. He wasn't sure if he wanted to go through with his initial plan. He weighed the pros and cons of the situation. He became furious at the image stuck in his mind of Chyna smiling at the camera while Tez blew her back out.

"Look, I need for you to murk somebody."

"All you got to do is point, you know that my nigga," said Tone.

Pharaoh drove across Jefferson as the light turned green. He coasted across the Belle Isle Bridge. The sun was out, and so were the freaks. A mustang full of white girls honked their horn, then flashed Pharaoh and Tone. They were probably some teenaged suburbs brats, who often came to the Isle to mingle with black men. They had the top down on the burnt orange Cobra Mustang.

"Catch them hoes, my man!" said Tone, as he watched the Mustang turn into an orange dot.

"Fuck them skanks, you know Tez, right?" asked Pharaoh.

"Yo' manz, Tez?"

"Yeah, that's who I need you to murk," said Pharaoh.

"Damn, I ain't know you was talking about him."

"Is that a problem?"

"I mean nah, as long as you won't have any regrets."

Pharaoh didn't say anything for a moment. He knew that would be almost impossible, but he was prepared to live with it.

"I need you to murk the nigga next week after I leave. I'm going out of town for a minute," said Pharaoh.

"You sure about this?" asked Tone.

"Yeah man!" hollered Pharaoh. "Look, the nigga ain't the same, he on strictly bullshit. I want to kill him my mothafuckin' self, but it would hurt me too much, you feel me?" asked Pharaoh.

"I feel you my nigga."

"Soon as you murk the nigga, you can have his spot down in southwest. The nigga dumping over a hun'd elbows a week down there," said Pharaoh.

"That's a bet, but how you want me to do the nigga?" asked Tone.

"However you feel fit," answered Pharaoh.

Pharaoh and Tone drove around Belle Isle several times. Tone accepted the hit, and switched the subject, trying to lighten the mood. He and Pharaoh caught up with the young white girls in the droptop Cobra Mustang.

Chapter 26

One week later...

Pharaoh was up and at 'em early. Like clockwork, he drove to the U-haul rental place, and rented a mid-sized truck. He made his calls to Tone, Killer B., Chris, Mike and Tez. They all made their orders; Pharaoh told them it was going down today. They all knew what that meant, the weed would arrive in Detroit sometime that day. As Pharaoh drove east on 7 Mile Road his cellphone rang, it was Ollie.

"What up doe?"

"We still on for today?" asked Ollie, referring to the weed shipment.

"Yeah, as far as I know my guy should be here in a few hours. Where you at?"

"Shit, I'm out in Adrian, Michigan."

"Who the fuck you know out there?"

"I'm out here fucking with this nigga name Los."

"How'd you meet him?"

"Shit, I just get on the E-way and came up on any exit. You never know who you'll meet, unless you get out here and travel."

"I feel you my nigga, hold on," said Pharaoh, his phone was beeping. He clicked over and answered. "Hello."

"Pharaoh this is Kimkeysha. You need to get down to St. John's Hospital, lil' Pharaoh swallowed some Drano."

Pharaoh hung up on Kimkeysha and Ollie both. He punched the U-haul down 7 Mile, running red lights like he was Johnny Law. Pharaoh pulled the large truck into the visitor's parking lot of St. John's Hospital, double-parked and jumped out. He ran into the emergency entrance doors, coming to a sliding stop at the front desk.

"Pharaoh Dickson, what room is Pharaoh Dickson in?" he demanded.

"Sir just calm down," said the desk nurse, as she typed the name into the computer.

"He's in room 20, third floor."

Before the desk nurse could finish her sentence, Pharaoh bolted for the elevator. He pounded on several elevator buttons and watched as they inched down to the ground floor. "Ding!" sounded the opening doors of an elevator behind Pharaoh. There was an older white man in a wheel chair, with an I.V. hooked into his arm. He was being pushed by a male white nurse. "Why don't you hurry the fuck up!" yelled Pharaoh, as the nurse carefully pushed the old white man off the elevator. Another elevator beside the one Pharaoh was standing in front of was opened. Pharaoh entered the empty car, and pushed floor three. He exited the elevator reading the door signs. He turned right and sprinted down the hall to a packed room. Two doctors, two Social Workers, Kimkeysha, one nurse, and Chyna stood in the room. Chyna was at Jr.'s bedside holding his little hand. All eyes turned on Pharaoh as he entered the room. The sight of Jr. laid up in the bed with tubes running up his nostrils made Pharaoh lose it.

"You stupid bitch!" he yelled, making his way towards Chyna. The two Social Workers, one male and one female stepped in to interviene. They grabbed Pharaoh by the waist, and pushed him out into the hallway.

"Sir, sir, please just calm down," pleaded the male Social Worker.

"Yes," answered Pharaoh.

"Well, I'm with the Department of Social Services. Your son swallowed some Drano. It was a very small quantity, so he should be just fine, are you and the mother together?"

"No."

"Well sir, I'm going to be honest, this is considered to be negligence."

"So what are you saying, ya'll here to take my son?"

"There will be a full investigation done, and if you can prove to a judge that you're a responsible parent, you'll be granted custody."

"I already have custody, he's my fuckin' son!"

"When Pharaoh is released from the hospital, he'll be released into the custody of the Department of Social Services. And when you appear in court, you'll have your chance to convince the judge."

"Like hell," said Pharaoh, cutting the social worker off.

Pharaoh called one of the doctors out into the hallway and asked if Jr. would indeed be alright. The doctor assured him that Pharaoh Jr. was going to be just fine. With that, Pharaoh began to relax. He walked down to the gift shop and bought everything in sight, from teddy bears to candy. As Pharaoh waited out in the hallway for the doctors to give him the go-ahead to visit Jr., his cell phone rang.

"Hello," answered Pharaoh.

"Hey, it's me Eric. I'm 'bout an hour away."

"Ah, shit, a'ight, listen I'ma send my manz Tez," Pharoah told him.

"I don't know about that. How come you can't make it?"

"Family problems."

"Alright, I guess I don't have a choice," said Eric.

Pharaoh hung up and quickly tried to figure out who he could send to meet Eric. He called Ollie back to see if he had left Adrian yet. He hadn't, he was still farting around with some off brand. Pharaoh called Tone, but he couldn't do it either because he was the only one at the spot. "Fuck it," said Pharaoh, as he swalled his pride. He dialed Tez's number. He had been keeping his distance from Tez, only accepting his calls so he wouldn't suspect anything.

"Say something," answered Tez on the first ring.

"Hey dig, my man, I need you to come down to St. John's."

"What up?" asked Tez, sitting up on the couch.

"Jr. done swallowed some Drano, he cool though. I need you to come get this U-haul and meet my man Eric in the back of Randazzo's. He'll be there in about an hour."

"I'm on my way," said Tez.

Twenty minutes later Tez exited the elevator on the third floor. He stopped an older female black nurse in the hallway and asked her to point him to room 207. "Thank you," said Tez, as he made a right, and headed down a long hallway. He stopped in front of Jr.'s room and tapped on the door. Pharaoh was at Jr.'s side rubbing his head, when he heard the knock.

"Who is it?" asked Pharaoh.

"Tez."

Pharaoh kissed Jr. on the forehead, then went into the hallway.

"What up doe? Is he alright?"

"Yeah, he cool, but they talking about taking him."

"Who?" asked Tez, reaching for his 40 cal. in his waistband.

"Be cool," said Pharaoh, grabbing Tez and pushing him back.

"Social Services, they stupid, if they believe I'm having that."

"What you gon' do?" asked Tez.

"I tell you what I ain't gon' do. I'm not 'bout to let them take Jr. nowhere. I'mma take him to Phoenix."

"You know I got your back." Pharaoh almost snapped at Tez's phony words, instead, he decided to end the discussion.

"O yeah, here you go," said Pharaoh, reaching into his pants pocket, handing Tez the keys to the U-haul.

"You already talked to old boy, he knows that I'll be meeting him instead of you?" asked Tez.

"Yeah, everything is cool. Let me get your car. I'll meet you at yo' house later."

"A'ight. Be smooth, my nigga," said Tez, giving Pharaoh the keys to his 600 SL.

Pharaoh went back in Jr.'s hospital room. He stood at his side rubbing his hair and talking to him. Chyna and Kimkeysha went down to the cafeteria, so Pharaoh could be alone with Jr. Pharaoh had planned that once the sun went down, he would unplug the tubes from Jr. and carry him down to the parking lot. The two social workers left strick instructions for the hospital not to release Jr. Pharaoh, however, had other plans.

Chapter 27

Tez pulled into the rear of Randazzo's warehouse, Eric was parked facing the U-haul. Seeing the U-haul approaching, he jumped down from the cab, and waved Tez to the back of the truck.

"Back it in!" yelled Eric. Tez backed the U-haul up to the back of the trailer, then got out leaving the U-haul running. Eric extended his hand and introduced himself. "I'm, Eric, you must be Tez."

"One and only," said Tez.

"Good, let's get to work," said Eric, as he unlocked the trailer.

Tez turned his back to open the hatch of the U-haul. When he turned around the trailer doors swung open. "Freeze DEA!" yelled several agents, as they jumped from the trailer with AR-15's. Tez turned to run, but Suburbans and Luminas pulled in from both directions. "Get down on the ground, now!" yelled an approaching agent. Tez stood there spinning around in a circle, he shook his head and accepted defeat. He was about to ly down but he wasn't moving fast enough for the paranoid DEA agents. "Boom!" Tez fell face first on the pavement, his body lay motionless. One of the agents quickly rushed forward and cuffed Tez, then rolled him over to his side. "Ah," sighed Tez. The agent shot Tez with a bean bag in his back. "You're alright," said one of the agents. He helped Tez to his feet, then frisked him. The agent removed the 40 cal. from Tez's waist and ushered Tez over to an awaiting triple black Suburban "Watch your head," said the agent, putting Tez in the backseat. There were two white male agents sitting in

the front seats, wearing bulletproof vests, and DEA jackets.
"My name is Special Agent Thomas and this is my partner,
Special Agent Kemp. Do you know your rights?" asked the
driver.

"Yeah, and I'd like to exercise them," said Tez.

"You can play hard ass all you want, but you need to start
thinking about your future," said Agent Thomas.

"I want my lawyer."

"You're going to need ten lawyers, with all the charges your
facing. Look, we now you're not the head guy. We know
this, we want Pharaoh."

"Am I going to jail or what?" asked Tez.

"That depends on you. We want you to help us take down
Pharaoh. It's just a matter of time before he falls anyway,
why fall with him?"

"Man I don't know what the fuck ya'll talking about. Ya'll
got the right plan, just the wrong man. I ain't nobody's
snitch," said Tez.

"Oh no, well listen to this hard ass," said Agent Kemp, as he
pushed the play button on the tape deck.

>   *"Fuck them skanks, You know Tez right?" said*
> *Pharaoh. Tez recognized the voice instantly, it was*
> *Pharaoh.. "Yo' manz Tez?" said Tone. "Yeah, that's who I*
> *need you to murk," said Pharaoh.*

The words were like a knife in Tez's stomach. He
couldn't understand why, had Pharaoh found out about him
and Chyna. Even if he had, was it that serious? Tez asked
himself a series of questions. Most of Pharaoh and Tone's
conversation fell on deaf ears, he held his head down, but he
managed to hear.

>   *"You sure about this?" asked Tone. "Yeah man!"*
> *hollered Pharaoh. "Look, the nigga ain't the same, he on*
> *strictly bullshit. I want to kill him my mothafuckin' self, but*
> *it would hurt me too much, you feel me?"* Agent Kemp
stopped the tape, and stared back at the now delirious Tez.

"Where you get that from?" asked Tez.

"Your buddy's Mercedes has a low jack system. It allows us to record anything said inside the vehicle," said Agent Kemp. "I don't know what you've done to make Pharaoh want to kill you, but, like I said you need to start thinking about yourself," said Agent Kemp.

"You're facing a lot of time here," added Agent Thomas.

"What do I have to do?" asked Tez. Agents Thomas and Kemp gave each other that look The one that said conviction. Agent Thomas started up the Suburban and pulled off. Agent Kemp reached over the seat and uncuffed Tez.

"You smoke?' asked Agent Kemp.

"Yeah, weed. You got any?" asked Tez. Agent Kemp laughed.

"Nah, how 'bout some food. You hungry?"

"I'm good." Agent Thomas turned down Syracuse, Tez's street. He drove three blocks and pulled into Tez's driveway. Tez was looking crazy in the face.

"How long ya'll been on us?" asked Tez.

"You'd be surprised," answered Agent Thomas, as he cut the engine. He turned and looked at Tez.

"Here's the deal, Pharaoh, or anyone else for that matter, knows you've been arrested. What we're going to do is go inside and get as much clothes as you need."

"For what?" asked Tez.

"You can't stay here. Once word gets out that your cooperating, Pharaoh just might send someone to kill you," said Agent Kemp.

"Ha, I'm the real--," said Tez, cutting his statement short. "Look, I'm not worried about none of that."

"But we are. A dead witness is no good in the court of law. It's either that or you can go sit downtown in the musty county jail," said Agent Kemp.

Tez decided to take the first option. The feds were

going to put him in the Witness Protection Program. They filed a complaint against Tez, in case he tried to run. They needed him to cooperate, so they could charge Pharaoh and everyone else with conspiracy. All they had was Valdez's word, and in the feds it takes the word of two or more people to create a conspiracy. If Tez didn't cooperate, all the feds could charge him with was intent to buy over a one thousand pounds, which still carried at least fifteen calendars. Tez gave up everything. He implicated Ollie, Killer B., Tone, Dee, Mike, and Chris, pulling them all into the conspiracy. He figured if he was going to be labeled a snitch, he might as well spare none.

Chapter 28

Agents Kemp and Thomas prepped Tez in a interrogation room, on the tenth floor of the downtown Detroit Federal Court Building. Tez had to testify in front of the grand jury, so a judge could sign warrants for everyone on the conspiracy arrest. All of the questions were pre-meditated; the grand jury members walked Tez through the five minute interview/testimony. Judge Townsend signed the arrest warrants for Ollie, Tone, Killer B., Chris, Mike, and Dee. They were all simultaneously arrested, and taken downtown to the court building. They all sat in a cold holding cell, waiting to be fingerprinted, then interrogated.

"Ain't you Pharaoh's uncle?" asked Ollie, talking to Killer B.

"Yeah, you look familiar," said Killer B.

"Ollie, I met you last summer at the car show on Mack."

"Yeah, yeah that's right," said Killer B., remembering.

"Ya'll know lil' Pharaoh?" asked Chris.

"Yeah, that's my right hand," answered Ollie.

"Ain't that a coincidence, we all know Pharaoh," said Tone.

Chris, Ollie, Killer B., and Tone all looked at Dee.

"I know P too, I'm his barber," said Dee.

"What they say they got you on?" asked Ollie, talking to Dee.

"Conspiracy to distribute marijuana," answered Dee.

"Me too," everyone said in unison.

"McGrady!" yelled a marshal, then clicked open the cell door. McGrady was Tone's last name. He pushed open the cell door, and walked out. He was handcuffed with a belly chain and ankle braclets.

"Where I'm going?" asked Tone.

"Some fine gentlemen want to have a word with you," answered the marshal. Tone was put on an awaiting elevator, and sent up to the tenth floor. Tone exited the elevator, taking tiny steps because the anklets were digging into his skin.

"Can't you loosen these shits," said Tone, looking down at his feet. He stopped walking. The marshal grabbed him by the, "we're almost there." The marshal pulled Tone into an interrogation room, inside awaited Agents Thomas and Kemp.

"Thank you," said Agent Thomas, as he stood greeting the marshal. He closed the door and pulled Tone's chair out for him.

"I'll stand, this shouldn't take long," said Tone.

"Another hard ass huh," said Agent Kemp.

"I'm Special Agent Thomas, and this is my partner Special Agent Kemp. We're assigned agents working your case. First off, do you understand your rights?"

"I know I have a right to an attorney, as well as a phone call, I wish to use both of them," said Tone.

"Johnny Cochran couldn't beat the charges you're up against," laughed Kemp.

"Yeah, whatever, is this all ya'll want?" asked Tone.

"As of now, you're only being charged with conspiracy. It's up to you whether or not you'll face any additional charges," said Thomas.

"Man what the fuck are you talking about?" asked Tone.

"Sound familiar?" asked Agent Kemp, pressing the play button on a small recorder sitting on the table.

"How you want me to do the nigga?" was the queston that filled the small room. Those were Tone's very own words. He took a seat, as Agent Kemp smiled, and hit the stop button.

"You see, my friend, you've accepted a murder-for-hire,

that's life!" yelled Thomas, slamming his hand on the table.
The word, *life* hit hard like a bullet from an AK-47.

"The murder-for-hire charge is still up in the air. You need to start making some wise decisions, like as of yesterday," said Agent Kemp.

"How do I know I can trust ya'll?" asked Tone.

"You really don't have a choice, but we've never screwed anyone who didn't screw us. So, what's it going to be, life or freedom?" asked Kemp.

"Man, what ya'll wanna know?" asked Tone.

Agent Kemp popped his felt-tipped ink pen open and began writing every word Tone said. Agent Thomas was doing all the questioning. Tone had flipped, so did Mike, Chris, Killer B., and Dee. Ollie was the only one who stuck to the code, he denied any involvement, and pleaded Pharaoh's innocence as well. They were all fingerprinted and put back in the holding tank, waiting on the marshals to take them over to the county jail. They would be formally arraigned the following morning and have a brief bond hearing. While they waited in the holding tank, they conversed about the individual interrogations. They all lied about not agreeing to cooperate, except Ollie.

"I told them bitches to eat a fat baby's dick," Killer B lied.

"Man, I hope my wife called my lawyer," said Chris.

"Yeah, that's what's up," said Tone.

Chapter 29

The sun went down and Pharaoh was still at the hospital at Jr.'s bedside. He looked at the clock on the wall; it was ten minutes after seven. Pharaoh then looked at his cellphone to check if he had any missed calls, none. 'I wonder if Tez is taking care of business,' thought Pharaoh, he dialed Tez's number, then pushed the talk button. The phone just rang, rang, and rang, he hung up and tried again, same result. "I knew I shouldn't have had that crash dummie do nothing," Pharaoh said as he reached down and gently removed the tube from Jr.'s nose. "Come on lil' man, it's time to break camp."

Lil' Pharaoh was asleep and Pharaoh Sr. moved with precision. He wrapped Jr. up in a small blanket and put him over his shoulder. Pharaoh peeped out of the room into the hallway, no one was in sight. 'Now or never,' thought Pharaoh, as he dashed right into the hallway. He speed walked down the hall clutching Jr. in his arms for dear life. "Hey! Hey you, stop!" yelled the voice of an approaching nurse.

Pharaoh took the stairs, jumping down three and four at a time. He made it to the ground floor and quickly scanned the area for an exit. He was forced to exit through the emergency entrance. As Pharaoh made his way through the emergency waiting area, the telephone at the security guard's desk rang. He kept on moving, making it to the exit doors, as they slid open the guard slammed the receiver down, "hey you, stop!" Pharaoh bolted through the parking lot. He hit the alarm button on Tez's Benz, the horn sounded and the headlights flashed. Pharaoh ran full speed for the 600 SL, with the guard gaining on him. Pharaoh made it to the driver's side, and opened the door. Before he could sit Jr. in the car, two U.S. Marhals brandished their weapons and identified themselves. The security guard came running, joining the scene, he explained that Pharaoh had taken Jr. from the hospital.

"Pharaoh Dickson, we have a warrant for your arrest," said one of the huge U.S. Marshals.

"For what?" asked Pharaoh, still clutching Jr. in his arms.

"Conspiracy, and a list of other charges," answered the marshal. Pharaoh stood there in shock. The hospital guard attempted to reach for Jr., but Pharaoh jerked away.

"You're not taking my son anywhere!" yelled Pharaoh. Chyna and Kimkeysha came running out of the hospital. Chyna was screaming and crying.

"Pharaoh give me my son!"

"Mr. Dickson, please hand over the child, there's no need for anyone to get hurt here," said the marshal, as he and his partner held Pharaoh at bay.

Kimkeysha disregarded the entire ordeal, and walked up to Pharaoh, she reached for Jr. "it's going to be alright Pharaoh, I'll make sure lil' P is safe." Pharaoh reluctantly released Jr. who was now awake and crying. One of the marshals moved in and cuffed Pharaoh, and then searched him. Pharaoh was in a daze, his eyes didn't leave his son's. He watched from the back of the unmarked Lumina, as Kimkeysha, accompanied Chyna and the guard, carrying Jr. back inside the hospital. After putting Pharaoh in the back of the car, the marshals pulled out of the hospital parking lot.

"Marshal Bowers to dispatch."

"Go ahead Marshal."

"Yes, we have Pharaoh Dickson in custody, We're headed southbound on Moross, on our way to the Federal Building."

"Copy."

Pharaoh was punched drunk. He sat slouched down in the back seat, staring out the window. His mind was racing a thousand miles per hour. It still hadn't registered that he had been arrested. He was still thinking about the welfare of his son. "You're kind of young, aren't you Mr. Dickson?" asked the marshal who was driving, his question fell on deaf ears. The marshal looked in the rearview mirror at Pharaoh. He started to repeat his question, but decided not to bother. The marshal had seen that look Pharaoh was wearing far too many times in his career. He knew Pharaoh wasn't on earth at the moment. The marshal nudged his partner, then motioned his head at Pharaoh. His partner turned and took a glance at Pharaoh and shared a laugh with his partner at Pharaoh's expense. The marshal turned on Lafayette Blvd. in downtown Detroit. He sped along the pothole covered street until reaching the back entrance of the Federal Building. The marshal working control noticed the nose of the Lumina, and pushed the garage door button. The door flew up to the ceiling, and the marshal dipped down into the garage like it was the 'Bat Cave,' the door came flying shut behind the Lumina. The marshal pulled into a cramped parking space, and cut the engine. The garage was used primarily for judges' parking and transporting prisoners. Another marshal checked both his partners in with the marshal inside the control booth. They then popped the trunk of the Lumina and placed their bulletproof vests inside. The driver opened the back door where Pharaoh sat slumped down, He hadn't noticed any of the marshals' prior actions. The fluorescent lights which filled the garage, nearly blinded him. "Let's go Mr. Dickson," ordered the marshal in a moderate tone. He grabbed Pharaoh's arm and helped him out of the car. The marshal held Pharaoh by the handcuffs as he ushered him up a concrete ramp and onto an awaiting elevator. It was a quiet ride up to the tenth floor. The doors opened and Pharaoh, along with the two marshals, stepped out onto the marble floor. The hallway was empty. It was ten minutes after eight; everyone was long gone, with the exception of Special Agents Thomas and Kemp. The marshals escorted Pharaoh into the interrogation room, where Agents Kemp and Thomas were waiting.

"Thank you" said Agent Thomas, talking to the marshals. Agent Thomas took the cuffs off Pharaoh and pulled a chair out for him.

"Please, have a seat," said Agent Kemp.

"I'm Agent Thomas, and this is my partner Agent Kemp. We're the leading agents assigned to your case. Do you understand your rights?"

Pharaoh sat in the blue office chair, staring Agent Thomas in the face with a blank expression. Agent Thomas waited for a response, but to no avail. He tried to lighten the mood,

"Are you hungry, I'm famished?" asked Agent Thomas, picking up the telephone. "Yeah, this is Agent Thomas, please send three club sandwiches, three Coke's and chips up to the tenth floor. "Thank You."

"So Pharaoh, are you going to help yourself, or are you going to be the only one doing hard time?" asked Agent Kemp. Pharaoh shifted his cold stare to Agent Kemp, but said nothing. This was his way of picking their brains. He figured the more he ignored them, the more they would talk. "Let's see conspiracy to distribute marijuana, violation of interstate commerce, conspiracy to commit murder, shall I go on?" asked Agent Kemp, growing obviously impatient with Pharaoh's nonchalant attitude.

Agent Kemp slammed his fist down on the table, Pharaoh just let out a long sigh

"That's alright, you don't have to talk. All of your buddies, including your uncle, have already rolled over," said Agent

Kemp. A knot formed in Pharaoh's throat, as he wondered exactly how much the Deds knew. 'Where was Tez?' Pharaoh thought. Agent Kemp studied Pharaoh to see if his words had any affect on him. Pharaoh, well aware of Agent Kemp's motive, showed no sign of nervousness. A knock at the door broke the tension in the room. Agent Thomas answered the door, it was the U.S. Marshal he called for the food. "Thank you," said Agent Thomas, as he carried the food over to the table. He sat Pharaoh's sandwich, chips, and Coke in front of him. Pharaoh didn't budge; he didn't have an appetite. Agents Kemp, and Thomas stuffed their faces, in between bites, they gave their thesis on drug dealers and the conviction rate of the federal system.

"If you don't roll, there's always somebody else who will. Why do you think the government has a 98 percent conviction rate? Because someone always rolls over," said Agent Thomas, answering his own question.

"Your friend Tez is in witness protection right now, out on the streets, while you're on your way to the four star Wayne County Jail," laughed Agent Kemp.

"Yeah, and Tone, Mike, Dee, and your uncle Killer B., oh yeah, and Chris, they all rolled on you. You need to start doing some serious talking," said Agent Thomas, finishing his club sandwich.

"Are you going to eat that?" asked Agent Kemp.

Pharaoh sat there and absorbed everything they were saying. He deemed it all to be lies.

"You can play hard ass all you want, but I guarantee you'll come running trying to cooperate before it's all said and done." said Agent Kemp, as he placed his card on the table and slid it to Pharaoh.

"We're not going to waste anymore time on your thick skull. When you're ready to roll, give us a call," said Agent Thomas, as he picked up the telephone. "Yeah, he's ready to go," he said.

"You'll be arraigned in the morning, and have a bond hearing. I can almost guarantee you'll be denied bond," laughed Agent Kemp.

"Get up," ordered Agent Thomas, as he clicked the handcuffs in his hand.

Pharaoh stood to his feet and Agent Thomas placed the cuffs on him. Agents Thomas and Kemp walked Pharaoh back down the deserted hallway and onto an elevator where the two marshals stood waiting. "He has court in the morning in front of Judge Townsend," said Agent Thomas and handed Pharaoh over to the marshals. The door closed, leaving Agents Thomas and Kemp on the tenth floor. The elevator stopped in the garage, where Pharaoh was initially brought in. The marshals walked Pharaoh down the concrete ramp, and put him in the backseat of the unmarked Lumina. The driver walked to the control booth, and retrieved his and his partner's pistols. Pharaoh sat slumped down in the backseat feeling like his whole world had just come to an end. His mind was racing with thoughts of Jr. and all Agents Thomas and Kemp had said.

The driver pulled out of the garage, and turned left on Lafayette Blvd. He sped through traffic, trying to make every light. After five minutes of his reckless driving, he pulled up to the garage of the Wayne County Jail. The garage door opened and they drove in. It was a totally different scene from the garage at the Federal Building. There were garbage bags full of trash everywhere, and cigarette butts filled the parking area. The marshals went through the same protocol, checking in their weapons with the sheriff working in control. They then opened Pharaoh's door, and helped him out of the car. "Home sweet home," joked one of the marshals, as he escorted Pharaoh up to the sliding entrance door. The three waited briefly, then the door slid open. Pharaoh and the marshal entered the hallway leading to the jail's registry department. The stench of urine, musk, and a host of other unidentifiable odors rushed Pharaoh's nostrils. He balled his face up in attempt to stomach the smell. "What the hell is that smell?" asked Pharaoh, as the first door closed behind him. A second door slid open, the marshals had Pharaoh stand with his back to a wall while they handled the registry paperwork. A fat middle-aged black sheriff yelled through the glass. "Put all his personal property in this bag, and have him step around to cell three!"

The marshals frisked Pharaoh, placing his cellphone, keys, and Rolex watch in a plastic property bag. They uncuffed him then handed him a receipt for his property. One marshal pointed in the direction of the overcrowded cell. The bars slid open and Pharaoh wiggled himself inside. He stepped over two crackheads, one bum, and a dirty white boy, who were all asleep, despite the loud ruckus that surrounded them. Pharaoh walked over to the three telephones and picked up one of them. It didn't have a dial tone, so he tried the one next to it, same business. Pharaoh reached for the third phone, but the cord had been cut. He shook his head, then scanned the cell for a place to sit. 'On second thought, I'll stand,' Pharaoh thought, as he looked at the filth on the walls and benches. Bloody tissue clogged the sinks and toilets.

It was Pharaoh's first trip to the county jail. He had been arrested before, but he would always bond out from the police station. As Pharaoh stood in the center of the holding cell, trying not to brush up against anything, or anyone, he met eyes with a familiar face. "Pharaoh?" asked a young black guy, who was seated on a bench in the rear of the cell. "What up boy?" asked Pharaoh, as he stepped over the many bodies lying on the floor. He walked to the rear of the cell, and gave the young man a play, his name was Ralph, he was from Pharaoh's neighborhood.

"I just seen Ollie down here," said Ralph.

"Where he at?" asked Pharaoh, looking around the cell.

"He went upstairs a few minutes ago."

"What he say he was locked up for?"

"He was talking to like four niggas. They said they all on some weed conspiracy. Damn P, I ain't know ya'll was doing it like that. I mean, I seen ya'll when ya'll dropped triple 600's."

"Was one of their names "Killer B.?"

"I'm not fo' sho'."

"What about Tone, or did you see Tez?"

"Nah, I ain't seen Tez, but I did hear one of them say their name was Tone."

."How he look?"

"Light skinned nigga, 'bout my height." 'Yeah, that's Tone.' Pharaoh thought to himself.

"And you said it was four of them?" asked Pharaoh.

"Five, including Ollie."

Ralph rambled on and on, but Pharaoh went back into his zone. 'But how'? Pharaoh asked himself. 'How the fuck did the Feds jump on us, and where the fuck is Tez?' Pharaoh asked himself. Nothing was making sense. It felt like a bad dream, Pharaoh just knew he'd wake up any moment next to Sasha in his plushed mansion. Reality struck when Ralph tapped Pharaoh, bringing him back to Earth.

"You a'ight my nigga?" asked Ralph.

"Yeah, I'm good. What about you, what the fuck yo' young ass doing in jail?" asked Pharaoh, not that he really cared.

"Stolen car."

"Ah man, you out there still on that? When I get out you can come work for me," said Pharaoh.

"What's your bond?" asked Pharaoh.

"Thirty-five thousand, ten percent."

"That's it, nigga I got you, don't even trip."

"For real?" asked Ralph smiling.

"Nigga it's nothin' you just don't go stealing no cars. Matter of fact, I got a Caprice you can have."

"That black one you used to push."

"Yep, it's all yours. When they gon' let us use the phone?"

"Probably when we get upstairs, that's if we make it before ten o'clock," said Ralph.

No sooner than Ralph made that statement, the holding cell door opened. A huge white middle-aged corporal stood in the doorway with a stack of wristbands in his hand. "Listen up!" he yelled. The prisoners continued on with their conversations. The corporal ran his keys across the iron bars, "I'll wait until you're done talking, I've got all night." Everyone then gave their full attention to the corporal, because they knew he'd close the cell and make them wait forever to get upstairs. Once the corporal was satisfied with the noise level, he continued, "We're about to start processing you guys. The quicker we get this done, the quicker we can get ya'll fed and upstairs. When I call your last name, come forward and state your full name, date of birth, and social security number." The corporal began calling names, one by one the men filed through the tiny entrance. They were fingerprinted, photographed, and tagged with an identification wristband. Pharaoh and Ralph were among the last ones to be called.

They were shuffled from one holding cell to another, each with a different purpose. Once inside cell nine, Pharaoh inventoried his personal property, and deposited all his money into his inmate commissary account. Cell ten was for people who needed medical attention, or those on medication. Next, Pharaoh, along with nine other men, was escorted into the change out room. The white corporal was orchestrating the event, he ordered everyone to strip down into their birthday suits. Everyone stood there naked as a jay-bird, some covering their privates with their hands, while others stood free-balling. The smell that filled the area was horrible. Pharaoh looked down to the ground because he was standing in the second row. The guys in front of him had their asses were exposed to the men behind them. Pharaoh, trying to avoid the unpleasant sight, discovered something just as foul. On the floor sat a pair of once white underwear, they were now brown. A dirt ring surrounded the waistband, urine stains covered the front, and feces were caked in the ass of the underwear. The corporal ordered the group to raise their hands above their head, then to lift up their nut sacks. He ordered everyone to open their mouths, and say 'ah.' Finally, he ordered everyone to turn around, squat and cough.

Pharaoh had never felt so degraded in his entire life. The trustee sized everyone up by eye, and tossed them green 'Wayne County Jail' uniforms. Pharaoh quickly dressed, and ran over to the shower full of used shower shoes. He fumbled through the many assorted shoes and managed to match a pair up. After hanging his clothes in the property room, Pharaoh was handed a sack lunch and sent around to cell eleven. He and Ralph stood near the entrance of the cell, hoping to be one of the guys called first to go upstairs. Ralph was stuffing his face with a bologna and cheese sandwich, in between bites, he would take a swig of 'Kool-shot,' it was a flavored punch drink provided by the jail.

"You ain't gon' eat?" asked Ralph, looking at Pharaoh.

"I really don't have an appetite. Here," said Pharaoh, as he handed Ralph the bag.

Once everyone went through the change out process the sheriffs started taking groups of ten upstairs to quarantine. Luckily, Pharaoh and Ralph were among the first group, they were escorted to an awaiting elevator that also had a peculiar stench. They rode up to the twelfth floor and were put into another holding cell. The floor sergeant gave the men his house rules, as he called them, then performed another brief body search.

"This shit is crazy." said Pharaoh, talking to Ralph.

"Just wait until we get in quarantine," replied Ralph, like he'd been there several times before.

Ralph and Pharaoh were assigned to the same rock. They were handed bed rolls and a hygiene kit as they walked up the stairs. Once inside the rock, Pharaoh stood in the center as the door slammed behind them. There were no open bunks. It was a ten man cell, but there were now fourteen bodies, including Ralph and Pharaoh. Pharaoh sat his bed roll and hygiene kit on one of the stainless steel tables and scanned the room for two extra mattresses. "Hey my man," Pharaoh said, as he interrupted the conversation of two young men. The two men stopped talking, and gave Pharaoh a cold stare. They both were lying in their bunks facing each other. Neither one of the young men said a word. "Dig, me and my lil' manz need a mattress," said Pharaoh. Both young men were lying on double mattresses, they looked at each other, then returned to their conversation ignoring Pharaoh's request. He walked toward the one closest to him, before he could approach the young man, an older cat whom everyone called 'Old School' intervened. "Ya'll heard the man, get ya' asses up and give these brothers them damn mats!" ordered 'Old School.' The two young men mumbled under their breath as they got up from their comfortable nooks, and gave Pharaoh and Ralph the mattresses. "Good looking," said Pharaoh as he handed one of the mats to Ralph.

Pharaoh then raced over to the phone. He sterilized it to the best of his ability, improvising by using his shirt to wipe the receiver. It took him five minutes to figure out how to operate the phone, he dialed his home number in Phoenix, hoping to catch Sasha. The phone rang four times, and Sasha's beautiful voice came over the phone. Pharaoh felt relieved at the sound of his wife's voice. The operator took over, and explained the charges, and where the call was coming from. Before Sasha could accept the call, the phone went dead. "Hello, hello!" yelled Pharaoh as he pushed down on the lever trying to get a dial tone. The lights went out, and some one said, "they turned the phone off."

"What time they wake us up for court?" asked Pharaoh, talking to Ralph.

"Shit, like four in the morning."

"Good," said Pharaoh, as he looked around at the assorted faces.

The scene was almost identical to the registry holding cells, except, there weren't as many bodies. Heroin addicts laid stretched out on bare mattresses going through withdrawals. Pharaoh made his mattress into a recliner up against the wall; he and Ralph sat side by side, they talked about how they were arrested. Pharaoh did most of the talking. He told Ralph how life had been pretty good, up until a few hours ago. Ralph and Pharaoh stayed up all night reminiscing.

Chapter 30

Four o'clock the following morning, the voice of a sheriff came over the intercom posted on the wall. Pharaoh and Ralph had pulled an all nighter. "When I call your name, gather all your belongings and step to the door." said the sheriff. "Starr, Dickson, Dorn."

Pharaoh and Ralph wrapped their sheets up in their blankets. They rushed over to the sink, and quickly brushed their teeth. Pharaoh splashed some cold water on his face, then checked his waves, making sure they were intact. As Pharaoh checked his situation, the cell door opened. "Come on P," said Ralph, already out the door. Pharaoh snatched up his bed roll and darted out the door as it began to close. He walked to the end of a long line, which was wrapped around the entire quarantine section, at the back of the line he found a half sleep Tone and Mike.

"What up doe boy?" asked Tone, extending his hand giving Pharaoh dap.

"What it is?" asked Pharaoh, giving Mike dap.

"Who is this?" asked Tone, looking at Ralph. He was standing next to Pharaoh facing the three.

"Oh, this my lil' guy, Ralph. He cool," said Pharaoh.

"Man what the fuck is going on though?" asked Pharaoh.

"They talking about a conspiracy," said Mike.

"Yeah, that's what they told me too," said Tone.

"I mean, how the fuck they link all us together?" asked Pharaoh. Tone and Mike shrugged their shoulders and looked away.

The line started moving, as the sheriff's started taking groups of ten down to the registry. Pharaoh, Tone,

Mike, and Ralph all rode downstairs in the same elevator. They froze the game (stopped their conversation), until reaching cell two, the federal inmate holding cell. Pharaoh gave Ralph dap and told him he'd see him once they got back from court. Ralph had to go to cell eight, because he had a state case. Tone, Mike, and Pharaoh stood in a corner politicking on what they believed took place, and what they had to do to possibly beat the conspiracy.

"First we got to find out the source of their information," said Pharaoh, talking with his hands.

"It ain't nothing but some weed," said Mike.

"Yeah, but they claim to have me on some murder-for-hire bullshit," said Pharaoh. Tone became nervous by Pharaoh's statement.

"For real?" he said, playing dumb.

"Yeah man, it ain't shit though. I just want to find out how they got on us. Where Tez and Ollie at?" asked Pharaoh.

"I seen Ollie yesterday, he was in the holding tank with us, and two older cats. One of them said he was yo' uncle," said Mike. As Mike finished his statement, Ollie, Chris, and Killer B. walked in the cell. They all gave Pharaoh dap, while they greeted Dee who joined the pack.

"Man what the fuck's going on baby?" asked Dee.

"That's what everybody's trying to figure out," answered Pharaoh.

"Man, you know I just did ten, I'm not trying to go back for no garbage," said Dee.

"I feel you, I'm pretty sure none of us want to. We just can't panic," said Pharaoh. Everyone stood nodding in agreement. Ollie pulled Pharaoh to the side so they could talk alone.

"Where the fuck Tez at?" asked Ollie.

"I don't know. I sent the nigga to pick up the work, and that was the last time I seen, or heard from him."

"What you think they gon' do?" asked Ollie.

"Shit, we gon' have to wait and see how shit play out" answered Pharaoh, as he looked over at Tone, Killer B., Mike and Dee. Chris went over to one of the steel benches, and took a seat.

"We gon' be alright, hopefully we'll get bond," said Pharaoh, as he walked over to the bench, taking a seat next to Chris.

"What's up old man?" asked Pharaoh.

"I'm getting too old for this shit. The first case I caught I was with your father. I did seven years on that bid. Now I'm sitting here with Junior. I'm starting to think you niggas is janky," laughed Chris.

"You got jokes huh?" laughed Pharaoh.

"You got's to laugh, to keep from crying," replied Chris.

The group kicked the bo-bo's around for two hours. The day shift came on and things began rolling. The lights were turned on, and the cells were opened, cell by cell, the sheriffs fingerprinted each inmate. Pharaoh, and the click were allowed to change out into their street clothes. After the series of events, it was back to cell two, where the group waited an additional three hours.

"Man that's crazy how they wake a nigga up at four o'clock in the morning, just to come sit in this pissy ass cell," said Ollie, as he looked around the dirty cell.

"Yeah man, this shit is on some whole other shit" added Pharaoh.

Finally, two marshals, one white, one black showed up, they were carrying suitcases full of belly chains, hand cuffs and ankle bracelets. One by one, they called the group, along with a few others out. They rushed putting the chains, and cuffs on the inmates.

"Damn if ya'll moved that fast getting over here, the world might be a better place," said a young white guy as one of the marshals cuffed him up.

"You think?" asked the white marshal.

There were ten inmates total. The black marshal did a roll call, then escorted the men into a garage and placed them in an awaiting van. The white marshal drove the van over to the federal court building. He pulled the nose of the van up to the garage. The marshals went through their protocol of securing the side arms with control, then helped the men out of the van. They all walked up the concrete ramp, and crammed into the elevator. The men were uncuffed once they reached the third floor and sent to several holding cells. Pharaoh and Ollie were in cell three, while the others were scattered about.

"Man, it's cold as shit in here," said Pharaoh, putting his arms in his sleeves.

"Yeah, they got the air on two degrees," replied Ollie.

Pharaoh's court date was at two o'clock. He and Ollie kicked it, until lunch. The marshals fed them club sandwiches, cake, and a bag of plain potato chips. Pharaoh didn't pass on that sandwich as he did the night before; he punished the light meal, then chased it down with his Coke. Pharaoh then bundled back up in his shirt sleeves. He attempted to go to sleep, but between the cold and current events, he was unable to. The marshals started running people up to court. Pharaoh watched as Mike, Chris, Dee, then Killer B. all went to court. They all smiled and said kind words as they passed Pharaoh and Ollie's cell. None of the men returned to their cells. Pharaoh figured they were still in court. The marshal called Pharaoh and Ollie's last name. The cell door clicked open and they stepped out, they were handcuffed and put on an elevator. They got off on the sixth floor and were led down a long hallway to Judge Townsend's court room. The marshals put Pharaoh and Ollie in the jury box and uncuffed them.

Pharaoh scanned the court room and in attendance were his mom's and brother, Donald. Mom Dukes smiled and waved at her son. She mouthed the words," I called your lawyer, Richard Cunningham." Pharaoh gave her the thumbs up, then looked around for his lawyer. Mr. Cunningham had just entered the court room. He raced over to the jury box, and kneeled down.

"How are you doing Mr. Dickson, considering the circumstances?"

"It is what it is man. What do they actually have?" asked Pharaoh.

"I'm not certain. We'll have to wait for the discovery packet."

"So, do you think I'll get bond?"

"I'm going to be straight with you, I seriously doubt it, but I'll try my damnest."

"But I ain't never been in no serious trouble."

"I understand that, but these are some serious allegations you're facing. The government is going to say you're a danger to society because of the murder-for-hire charge."

"But I haven't been convicted of it."

"I know this, just like you know this, but the judge more than likely won't share our same view."

"Can you represent my manz, too?" asked Pharaoh, pointing at Ollie.

"No, it would be a conflict of interest, but I know someone."

"So when can I get, what you call it, the discovery so I can see what's really good?"

"I'm going to file a motion of discovery immediately, we'll more than likely receive it in a few weeks."

"So what I'm suppose to do, just sit and rot in that funky ass jail? Come on man, it's got to be something you can do."

"All rise!" said one of the court marshals, interrupting Pharaoh. Judge Richard P. Townsend entered the court room carrying several manila envelopes. He took his seat at the bench, and began sorting some papers. "You may be seated," said the marshal.

"Get me a bond," said Pharaoh, as his lawyer walked to the

prosecution side.

"What he talking 'bout?" asked Ollie.

"Not a bitch ass thing. Not nothin' I wanted to hear."

Court got underway. Pharaoh's docket number was called and his lawyer waved him over to the podium. The prosecutor plainly stated the charges against Pharaoh, and asked the court to deny bond. Mr. Cunningham did exceptionally well with his representation. He pointed back at Mom Duke's and Donald to show Pharaoh had family support. He stated that the defendant, Pharaoh had never been convicted of a felony. He went on and on, but to no avail. Judge Townsend, who was at least 70 years old, bald headed, except two strands of hair he had combed over into a bouffant. He looked down over his specs and promptly denied Pharaoh's bond. "Committed to the custody of the U.S. Marshal," was the only thing Pharaoh heard as he dropped his head. His attorney tried to assure him that in due time he'd get another bond hearing. Pharaoh wasn't trying to hear any of that. He waved Mr. Cunningham off as he headed back to the jury box.

Ollie was up next. He was represented by a court appointed attorney, who didn't even fight to get him bond. Ollie's whole arraignment and initial bond hearing only took five minutes, max. Pharaoh made hand signals to Mom Dukes asking her if she'd heard from Sasha or Tez. Mom Dukes shook her head no to both questions. She blew Pharaoh a kiss, as the marshals walked over and handcuffed him and Ollie. Pharaoh and Ollie were taken back to the third floor where they sat cuffed, waiting for the county sheriffs to take them back to the jail. There were five men waiting, Pharaoh, Ollie and three others. The county sheriff arrived and led the men onto an awaiting elevator. Pharaoh asked the sheriff about Tone, Mike, Chris, Dee, and Killer B.

"They all got out on bond," answered the sheriff.

Pharaoh and Ollie looked at each other in disbelief.

"How the fuck them nigga's get a bond, and not us?" asked Ollie.

"I'm saying. All them nigga's been to the joint at least once, and you mean to tell me I couldn't get bond," said Pharaoh.

"It's some shit in the game," said Ollie, as they stepped off the elevator into the garage.

The sheriff loaded the five men into the van, and drove them back to the Wayne County Jail. The musty stench hit Pharaoh in the face as he entered registry. He stood with his back to the wall, as the sheriff uncuffed the group. They were sent around to the change out room, where they were order to strip, and spread 'em.

"This some bullshit," said Pharaoh, to Ollie as they sat in cell eleven waiting to go upstairs.

"This how I was when I fell on that bank shit," said Ollie.

"Fuck it, ain't no sense for all of us being on lock. We gon' need niggas on the street," said Pharaoh.

"Yeah, 'cause having you out there handling business made it a whole lot easier on yo' boy," said Ollie. Pharaoh's last name was called in the first group of ten to go upstairs.

"A'ight my nigga be smooth. Call my mom's if you need to get word to me. I'mma pay for your attorney. If you hear from Tez, tell that nigga get at me," said Pharaoh, as he stood up.

"A'ight my nigga said Ollie, giving Pharaoh dap.

Pharaoh was handed a sack dinner and sent upstairs. Each step he took he dreaded, because it meant back in that detox cell, full of crackheads, and niggas telling whoppers about what they had on the street. Last night Pharaoh heard every new car named from an H2 Hummer, to a Bentley GT Coupe, he and Ralph laughed at the obvious lies. The niggas couldn't even make bond, and their hair told it all. Pharaoh and a young white boy were buzzed in the cell.

Ralph had already made it back, he smiled at the sight of his big homie.

"What they talkin' 'bout?" asked Ralph, as he met Pharaoh at the door.

"Bullshit, they denied my bond," answered Pharaoh, picking up the phone. He tried his best to sterilize the receiver, then began dialing his home number in Phoenix. On the second ring Sasha picked up.

"Hello," she said, as the operator took over. Sasha quickly accepted the charges.

"Papi, Papi. Where are you? Oh my God, I've been so worried."

"Slow down Mommie, slow down. I'm okay."

"Pharaoh where are you?"

"I'm at the Wayne County Jail, in downtown Detroit."

"I'm about to catch a flight!"

"Call my mom and let her know, so she can pick you up."

"Why are you in jail?"

"Well, the Feds indicted me on conspiracy charges. I went to court today, and they denied my bond."

"That's strange, because my father and brother were arrested on conspiracy charges."

"Really. When?"

"Yesterday, early in the morning."

"I might need you to get me another lawyer, 'cause my lawyer acting like he can't even get me bond."

"All you have to do is say the word Papi."

"You have one minute remaining," said the operator.

"Look Mommy, this phone is 'bout to hang up. I'm 'bout to call my mom, and let her know you're coming."

"I love you Papi."

"I love you too."

"See you soon," said Sasha, as the phone went dead. Pharaoh immediately began dialing Mom Dukes phone number.

"Hello," answered Donald on the third ring. He took forever to accept the charges, letting the recording play twice.

"This simple mothafucka" Pharaoh said.

"What up bro?" asked Donald.

"Ain't shit, where Ma at?"

"She right here, hold on, it's Pharaoh," Donald said, passing the phone to Mom Dukes.

"Hey baby."

"Hey, Ma, thanks for getting my lawyer."

"You welcome baby. I saw you and a gang of others on the news. Baby, who are all those folks?"

"I don't really feel comfortable talking over this phone."

"Oh, okay. How come that damn judge wouldn't give you bond?"

"Beats me, but uh, listen, Sasha is about to catch a flight, so she can be close to me. I told her to call you once she lands, so you can go get her from the airport?"

"I sure will baby. Do you need me to bring any money down there to put on your account?"

"Nah, I'm good. I need you to bond my lil' manz out for me."

"Who is he?"

"My little partner, his bond is thirty-five hundred. Hold on.

"Ralph, what's your last name?" asked Pharaoh, looking back at Ralph.

"It's Ralph Martin. His inmate number is 49285. You got that. Oh yeah, give him the black Caprice sitting in the backyard."

"Anything else baby?" asked Mom Dukes.

"Yeah, Ralph doesn't have a place to live, rent him an apartment."

"You have one minute remaining," said the operator.

"Okay, I'll help him find a place. When are you going to call back?"

"I'll give you a ring sometime tomorrow. I'mma try to get some rest, 'cause I haven't slept since I was arrested." The phone went dead. Pharaoh hung the phone up, and flopped down on his mattress.

"You a'ight my nigga?" asked Ralph, sitting beside Pharaoh.

"Yeah, my old bird 'bout to come bond you out. I told her to give you the Caprice, and she gon' help you find a spot to live."

"Square business?"

"Yeah man, I told you it's nothing."

"Good looking out. I gotcha, anything you need me to take care of, I'm on it," said Ralph.

"I might just hold you to that," said Pharaoh, as he looked up at the ceiling, lost in his racing thoughts.

Pharaoh fell asleep while Ralph talked his ear off, trying to convince him of his appreciation, and how loyal he would be. A few hours later Ralph's name was called over the intercom. The sheriff informed him that he had made bond and to gather all his personal property.

"Pharaoh, I'm out," said Ralph, as he shook Pharaoh's leg to wake him.

"Be smooth lil' nigga and get at me," said Pharaoh, giving Ralph dap, then falling back asleep.

Chapter 31

Two weeks had passed, and Pharaoh was still on ice at the Wayne County Jail. He was moved from quarantine, over to the old side of the jail, where he and Ollie ended up on the same ward, along with eight others. Everyday at mail call, Pharaoh would stand there anticipating his motion of discovery. It had yet to arrive, and it was killing him not knowing exactly what was going on. His lawyer hadn't been to see him, and he couldn't call anyone because his phone list hadn't been processed.

Ollie could tell that the ordeal was getting the best of Pharaoh. He tried to help him through the adversity, by playing spades and working out. A female sheriff who worked the morning shift brought in a newspaper article with Pharaoh and the rest of his conspirators' pictures; she handed it to Pharaoh with a smile, and stood at the bars while he read it. The article said Pharaoh was the kingpin of the marijuana operation based in Detroit, and that he was tied in with a Mexican cartel in Arizona. There were several additional pictures of Toro, Joey, and two other Mexicans, all beneath Pharaoh and his entourage. However, nothing was said about how the conspiracy came about, nor were there any pictures of Tez or Valdez. After reading the article, Pharaoh looked up at the sheriff, whom was still smiling in admiration.

"Do you mind if I keep this?" Pharaoh asked.

"Sure," answered the sheriff.

"How you say your name, Dudley?" asked Pharaoh, reading the name tag penned on her brown tight fitting sweater. Deputy Dudley was a petite red bone, about 5'6," long black hair, decent ass and titts, and a beautiful smile. Pharoah could tell that she was trying to choose him.

"Yeah, that's it. But you can call me Stacy, of course when no one is around."

"As you may know, I'm Pharoah. Thank you, I wish we could've met under better circumstances," said Pharoah, pointing to his green county outfit.

"It's cool, you look really familiar. Have you ever been to the 'Good Life Lounge'?"

"Yeah, a few times. I think the last time I was in there, was a few months ago. My manz coming home party was down there" said Pharoah, as he turned and pointed at Ollie, who was seated on a bench playing spades.

"That's where I saw you, I was at that party with my girl, Veronica."

"I didn't stay too long," said Pharoah.

"Yeah, two nuts got to fighting, and one of them ended up dead in the parking lot."

"For real, you sure?" asked Pharoah, playing dumb.

"Yeah, it was terrible. But anyway, I've got to make my rounds. We can kick it some more in between my rounds."

"A'ight Red," said Pharoah, as he watched Stacy turn and walk away.

"What she talking about my nigga?" asked Ollie, as Pharoah walked towards the bench.

Pharoah handed Ollie the newspaper article. Ollie began reading the clipping, and scanned down to the picture of Toro, and Joey.

"Who these Mexican mothafuckas?" asked Ollie.

"That's the plug," whispered Pharoah.

"Oh," said Ollie, as he continued to read the article. He laughed at Pharoah's picture, and commented about him being the kingpin of the operation. "They got you in herc like you mothafuckin' Ali Ba Ba," joked Ollie.

"They probably gon' try to give a nigga some time like I'm

Ali Ba Ba too while you bullshitting," said Pharaoh. Ollie's humor disappeared as he visualized the judge sentencing him to something outrageous, like four hundred months.

"Dickson!" yelled Sheriff Dudley.

"Yeah," answered Pharaoh.

"Visit."

Pharaoh jumped to his feet, and ran into his cell. He quickly washed his face, and patted his waves down in place. He cleaned his Cartier glasses, then made a hasty exit. Sheriff Dudley opened the cell door, and escorted Pharaoh to the visiting booth. "Have a good visit," she said, locking Pharaoh in the visitor booth.

"Hey Baby!" said Mom Dukes from behind the tiny visitor's glass.

"Hey Ma!" What you know good?" asked Pharaoh.

"Ah, nothing much. How are you holding up?"

"I'm fare for a square. Where's Sasha?"

"I don't know, she never called me, so I'm assuming she didn't come. I tried calling several times, but I kept getting ya'll voicemail."

"That's odd. She said she was coming. I can't call because my list hasn't been processed yet. That's why I haven't called you."

"When is your next court date baby?"

"Beats me. When you leave call my lawyer, and tell his muss mouth I said to come see about me a.s.a.p. and give him five grand for me."

"I already paid him."

"I know, but I need him to bring me that money when he comes to see me, so I can pay these guards to bring me in some food.

"Pharaoh don't get yourself in any more trouble."

"I'm not Ma, just please do that for me. They got me and Ollie on the same rock."

"That's good. I mean, considering the circumstances."

"Yeah...Ain't no telling how long I'll be down here, so when you get a chance, please send me some magazine subscriptions and books."

"What kind, baby?"

"Anything with some substance. Did you see the paper?"

"Yeah, they got you in there like some hardened criminal. This too shall pass baby, just be patient and have faith."

"I got something to tell you mama."

"What is it, Pharaoh?" asked Mom Dukes, with concern in her voice.

"I have a son."

"What? Where is he? How old is he?"

"He's almost one, and I believe Social Services has him. Me and his mother aren't on good terms. She's a shot girl at an exotic club, I met her while visiting the bar. It was a fling, but she contacted me and said that she was pregnant. I stood by her through her pregnancy, and when the baby was born I had three blood tests. They all came back positive."

"So you mean to tell me I have a grandson out there somewhere, and you didn't tell me? When were you going to tell me?"

"I don't know Ma, but I assure you I was going to."

"What's his name?"

"Pharaoh Dickson, Jr." Mom Dukes smiled, then returned to being angry with Pharaoh.

"That was really shitty Pharaoh. Nevertheless, if I have a grandbaby, you know I'm going to get him."

"Thanks Ma," Pharaoh said, exhaling, then smiling.

"What about Sasha, does she know about your little fling?"

"No, it all happened at the same time. When I asked Sasha to marry me, that's when Chyna started claiming to be pregnant."

"Don't you dare try to play the victim. If ya' ass hadn't been out cheating, you wouldn't be in this mess."

"Yes Ma," said Pharaoh, acknowledging his guilt.

"Visiting hours are now over. All officers please check your visiting areas, and send all visitors downstairs," said the voice of a sheriff over the jail's p.a. system.

"Well, I'mma get going. You take care, and give me a call whenever your phone is situated."

"Okay, love you Ma."

"Love you too baby," said Mom Dukes as she rubbed the tiny glass as if it were Pharaoh's face.

Sheriff Dudley unlocked the visitor's cell, and walked Pharaoh back to his ward. She led the way, as Pharaoh watched from behind; she purposely dropped her ring of keys. Pharaoh was lost in her provocative strut, when she bent down to pick up the keys, he kept walking. He bumped into her soft ass with his pelvis.

"Oh, excuse me," said Pharaoh, snapping back to reality.

"Um hum," said Sheriff Dudley, standing to her feet smiling.

"You have a good visit?" she asked, trying to break the tension.

"Oh! Yeah it was alright."

"That was your mom?"

"Yeah, that's my old bird."

"You look just like her," said Sheriff Dudley, as she let Pharaoh onto his ward.

"See you later alright."

"I look forward to it," said Sheriff Dudley, locking the cell door.

Chapter 32

Tez had been moved to Kalamazoo, Michigan by the DEA, for witness protection purposes. They let him keep his 600 SL and jewelry in attempt to pacify him. They had him stashed in a four bedroom ranch style home in a secluded, wooded area. His closest neighbor was two miles away. Tez was going crazy sitting in the house. He was playing 'NBA Live 02', when he thought about his arrangement with the government. 'I ain't say I wouldn't go back to the hood, and they ain't say I couldn't,' Tez thought.

He stood and tossed the joy stick on the coffee table. He turned the PlayStation 2 off, grabbed his car keys, and was out the door. Every night at eight o'clock, Tez had to call an eight hundred number to check in. It was to let the Feds know that he was safe. It was only two o'clock, so Tez had every bit of six hours before he had to check in. He punched his 600 SL down I-95, heading towards Detroit. Tez smiled as he crossed Eight Mile Road into the city of Detroit. He drove south on Mound Road until reaching Seven Mile Road. Tez turned right, and drove six blocks down to B.B.'s Diner. He parked and got out.

"Ahhh," Tez said, inhaling, then exhaling the air. He hit his alarm, then walked to the entrance of B.B.'s., all eyes were on Tez as he entered the Diner. No one spoke, they just stared. Tez ignored the crowd of gawkers; he walked over to the empty stool, and took a seat next to Dee.

"Hah" Tez laughed, holding his head back. "Don't worry Dee, I ain't gon' do nothing to you man."

Dee didn't respond, he wasn't worried about the

incident of Tez robbing Al's. He was wondering whether or not Tez knew about his cooperation with the DEA. Dee quickly paid for his meal, and excused himself, he high-tailed it across the street to Al's. Tez laughed at the sight of Dee scurrying across the street. He turned towards the door, as Kimkeysha and Chyna entered the diner. Chyna stopped and rolled her eyes at Tez, then walked over to the counter. Tez was sitting within arms length of Chyna, he grabbed her waist, and pulled her close to him.

"If I didn't know better, I'd say you was trying to act like you don't know a nigga," said Tez.

"Nigga get yo' greasy paws off me" said Chyna, jerking away.

"Ah, bitch, you wasn't saying that when I was beating that pussy up."

"Don't flatter yourself, I was acting--acting for the camera."

Tez became furious, as he realized now why Pharaoh wanted to kill him. Chyna had given Pharaoh the tape, that was the tape Pharaoh had at Tez's house. It was all starting to make sense, that's why Pharaoh had been acting funny. "Bitch!" yelled Tez, as he leaped from the stool. He shook Chyna vigorously, her head bobbed back and forth like a bobble head doll. Everyone in the diner watched the episode in shock. Kimkeysha tried to pry Tez's death grip, but was caught with an elbow to the nose, sending her falling to the ground with a face full of blood and a broken nose. "Bitch, you funky bitch!" Tez yelled, as he hit Chyna with a series of punches to the face. "Tez! Tez, that's enough!" yelled B.B. the owner. Tez satisfied for the moment with his work, backed off Chyna, then spit in her bloody face. B.B. and a waitress helped Chyna, and Kimkeysha clean up, while Tez took his seat as if nothing happened. "Can a nigga get some service around this mothafucka, shit nosy mothafuckas act like ya'll ain't never seen a bitch get whooped!" yelled Tez.

Chapter 33

Pharaoh and Ollie were having it their way. They were living like kings, considering the circumstances. Pharaoh's lawyer had been to visit him with the same story. He brought Pharaoh the five grand Mom Dukes had given him, and Pharoah used it to bribe the sheriffs working his floor. Like clockwork, he and Ollie had guards bringing in breakfast, lunch, and dinner. Sheriff Dudley brought Pharaoh a cellphone and two battery packs. At the end of her shift, he'd give her two of the packs to take home and charge. For the most part, Pharaoh stayed in his room making phone calls. Ollie would sit on the sink in the six by nine cell, while Pharaoh laid in bed.

"Man, ain't nobody answering their phone," said Pharaoh, as he scrolled through the names and numbers in his phone.

"You tried Tez number?" asked Ollie.

"A million times, his shit just rings and rings. His voicemail don't even come on. I know the nigga ain't locked up 'cause I had Mom Dukes call every jail in Michigan," said Pharaoh.

"That's crazy."

"Yeah, but what's even more crazy is my fuckin' wife is MIA," said Pharaoh, as he dialed Sasha's cell number.

"What's MIA?" asked Ollie.

"Missing in action" answered Pharaoh, as he listened to the phone ring. He had just about given up, when Sasha answered the phone.

"Hello."

"Mommie!" Pharaoh said excitedly, but it quickly turned to

anger.

"Where the hell have you been?" asked Pharaoh.

"Now all of a sudden you care."

"What the hell are you talking about, and where are you?"

"I'm at home in Phoenix. It's over Pharaoh, I hope they give your ass life!" yelled Sasha.

"What the fuck are you screaming about?"

"They showed me pictures, birth certificate, everything Pharaoh. How long did you expect to keep your little bastard of a son a secret from me, huh?" yelled Sasha, crying. Pharaoh wasn't about to admit to anything just yet. He had to at least see how much Sasha really knew.

"Who are you talking about, and what did they show you?"

"The DEA, they showed me pictures of you and your son. They showed me the birth certificate which you signed and copies of three separate blood tests, all which you signed, and you had the nerve to bring that little fucker in our home. Fuck you Pharaoh, it's over!" yelled Sasha, then hung up.

"Hello!, Hello!"

"Who was that my man?" asked Ollie.

"My wife, well my ex-wife," answered Pharaoh. He started to call Sasha back, but he could hear the conviction in her voice. It was over, just like that. 'Man, can life get any worse?' Pharaoh thought.

"Dickson!" yelled a female sheriff. It was mail call. Pharaoh was too stuck to move.

"I'll get it, my nigga," said Ollie, as he stood up, and exited the cell. He returned carrying a large white envelope that read 'Certified Mail,' it weighed every bit of three pounds. Ollie tossed it to Pharaoh, who sat up at the sight of the package. Pharaoh tore the envelope open, as if it was a Christmas present.

"What it say my nigga?" asked Ollie.

"Hold on," Pharaoh answered, as he read Tez's statement.

"This got to be some bullshit," said Pharaoh, handing Ollie

Tez's statement.

Pharaoh read everyone's statement. Killer B., Tone, Tez, Mike, and Dee had all agreed to cooperate, at least that's what it said in black and white. Pharaoh still refused to believe it, he thought that it was all a hoax by the government and DEA to get him to cooperate. He read Valdez's statement, and how the conspiracy came together. He handed each statement to Ollie after reading it.

"Do you believe this shit?"

"I mean, I don't want to believe it, but look at it. All these niggas are on the street, while we up in here. We're the only two who didn't make a statement," said Ollie.

"Yeah, it all looks good on paper, but I don't trust them slippery cracker jack ass mothafucka's. They think they got all the sense."

"I'm hearing you my nigga, but I don't think they could lie like this. This is perjury, if they're indeed lying," said Ollie.

"Well I'm not going to jump the gun," said Pharaoh, as he dialed his lawyer's cell number.

"Hello."

"Mr. Cunningham, it's me Pharaoh."

"What's up Pharaoh?"

"I just received my motion of discovery. I need to talk to you about it."

"Well I haven't read it. I just received mine as well. I plan on tackling it tonight. I'll be out to see you in a couple of days."

"A'ight man, make sure you do that," said Pharaoh, then hung up. Pharaoh tried calling Tez once more, but to no avail.

"Dickson!" yelled Sheriff Dudley.

"Nigga, she be on yo' dick, my man."

"Here," said Pharaoh, tossing Ollie the phone.

"What's up Ma!" asked Pharaoh, as he stood at the bars.

"I need you to help me clean up the hallway," said Sheriff

Dudley

"Hold on," said Pharaoh, as he ran back to his cell to get his shoes. "I'm fenna get some pussy. I'm fenna get some pussy," he whispered as he put his shoes on.

Ollie hadn't heard a word Pharaoh said. He was lost in a conversation with one of his hoodrats. Pharaoh slapped Ollie's leg as he exited the cell.

"You ready?" asked Sheriff Dudley, as she opened the cell door. Without answering, Pharaoh walked through the gate. He stood in the hallway looking back and forth.

"So what you need me to do?" asked Pharaoh, playing dumb.

"You know that's not why I called you out here. My partner is on lunch break, so we've got fifteen minutes."

She led him into the mop closet, and closed the door after looking up and down the hall. She pulled Pharaoh's pants down and pulled his already hardened dick through his boxer hole. She looked up at him while jacking his dick. Pharaoh grabbed her head and pulled it down on his dick. "Ah…" sighed Pharaoh, as Sheriff Dudley began stroking him. Pharaoh moaned and groaned in satisfaction, as she served him up. She pulled it out of her mouth and began jacking him.

"You want some pussy, don't you?"

"Yeah," Pharaoh whispered.

He turned over a mop bucket and sat on it. He watched as Sheriff Dudley quickly undressed. Pharaoh pulled her to him, then lifted her petite frame onto his dick. She clutched his shoulders as she snapped her pussy back and forth. Pharaoh palmed her yellow ass with both hands. He slid her up and down until reaching his climax. "Ah..ah shit!.." he said as he fucked Sheriff Dudley harder.

Chapter 34

Two days later Pharaoh was moved from the Wayne County Jail to Milan Federal Detention Center in Milan, Michigan. He tried everyting to stay at the county jail, but the marshals had orders to take him along with nine others to the hold over. Pharaoh left Ollie the cellphone and money so he could continue to do him. He didn't even know the Feds had a spot to hold people. The marshals packed everyone in the fifteen passenger van and hit the highway.

After forty-five minutes of listening to soft rock, and country music, they reached Milan a.k.a. 'Smiling Milan.' The marshals had warned all the newcomers, not to talk to anyone about their cases, past or present. They gave the group the run down on why the place had been nick named 'Smiling Milan,' they said it was because everyone walked around smiling all day, trying to gain information on someone else's case. Pharaoh took the information for what it was worth. He didn't have any plans on talking to anyone, except his lawyer.

Pharaoh was screened by a counselor and the facility's administrator. They asked him whether or not he was assisting the government, and if there was any reason he couldn't go to general population. 'A bunch of rat shit,' Pharaoh thought, as the two rattled on. He answered "no" to all of their questions, and in turn was sent to general population. There were two sides to Milan, the east side and west side. If there was some reason an inmate couldn't be around another inmate, they would send one to the east and the other to the west, it was called a separate-T. Pharaoh was sent to the East side. It was almost four o'clock, so all the inmates were locked in their cell for count. Pharaoh was led to his cell on the second tier by the unit officer. The east side held almost two hundred inmates; it was built identical to the west. There were three televisions mounted above a soda machine in the common area that was filled with tables where the inmates played cards, ate, and watched television. There were four phones, a small recreation yard attached to the unit, a religious room, a workout room, and a laundry room. For two hundred inmates, there was only one staff member working the unit, a total of ten people ran the entire facility. Milan was situated next door to Milan FCI Prison, so if there was ever a riot or major disturbance, the guards from the prison would help man the problem. The officer stopped at cell 210, and unlocked the door. "Damn!" Pharaoh yelled, at the smell of shit as he entered the cell. "Can't I wait til this shit airs out?"

"Nope," said the young redhead, freckle-faced, white officer, as he locked the cell behind Pharaoh. He put his shirt over his nose, as he mean-mugged his cellmate, who was rubbing his stomach and smiling.

"I'm Bobby, but everybody calls me Boo-Shay," he said extending his hand. Pharaoh realizing Boo-Shay hadn't washed his hands; extended his elbow to give him a play. He climbed on the top bunk, and smothered his face with a pillow attempting to block the smell. "What they call you?" asked Boo-Shay.

"My man, wait 'til that shit leaves the air, and we can kick it," Pharaoh said, then buried his face back in the pillow.

"Well, I'm from Inkster. You look like you're from Detroit. I can tell by them Cartier glasses, that's ya'll trademark," said Boo-Shay.

"Stand up count!" yelled the unit officer.

"You got to stand up, or they'll send you to the hole," advised Boo-Shay.

Pharaoh rolled off the bunk reluctantly and removed his tan khaki shirt from his nose. The smell of fresh feces still hung in the air, as Pharaoh stood beside the bunk bed. Two white officers peeped through the small glass on the cell door, and Boo-Shay took a seat on his bunk.

"Oh, you good now. We only got to stand up when they count." Without responding, Pharaoh climbed back in his bunk, Boo-Shay was very inquisitive.

"How old are you man?" asked Boo-Shay.

"Twenty-three," answered Pharaoh.

"This yo' first time being locked up?"

"Yeah."

"Facing a lot of time?"

"Shit, I don't kow."

"What they say you was charged with?"

"Attempted pimp, with a deadly bank roll."

"Who?"

"You related to 50 Cents my man?" asked Pharaoh.

"Nah, why you say that?"

"'Cause you got 21 questions."

"Ah, that's a good one," laughed Boo-Shay.

"I thought you was writing a book or something."

"You got jokes, huh? That's good though, you up on game. I was gon' tell you to watch yourself around here, 'cause this shit is something different," advised Boo-Shay.

Count had cleared, and the unit officer began unlocking the cells. Pharoah's cell clicked open, but he remained in bed because he had no urge to mingle with the sharks and snakes.

Boo-Shay grabbed his Nes Café coffee cup and radio, and was out the door. He ran down to the soda machine, and filled his cup with ice and Coke, then disappeared into a cell next to the laundry room. Four men sat inside the room, in silence, as they waited for a fifth man. Boo-Shay took a seat on the desktop, as the four men's leader entered the cell, his name was Burch El. He stood 5'10, 190 lbs, light brown skin, bald fade, and smart as a whip. Burch El had just been released from the state joint. Fresh off a fifteen year bid, he was busted for two kilos of crack cocaine, and a 9 mm. It was pretty much a wrap for him, but Burch El had other plans.

Also in attendance was Black. He was indeed black, all the way down to the core. The only thing white on Black was his t-shirt and socks, he stood about 5'9, 175 lbs., 360 degree waves, and sneaky as hell. He had been busted for conspiracy to distribute five hundred pounds of weed. He pled out to fifteen years, but Black was more than determined to beat out that date.

Bay was probably the oldest of the bunch. He had been to every prison in Michigan, but had no desire to tour the federal system. He was in on a string of bank robberies, crackhead snatch and grab jobs. With his criminal history, Bay was facing career criminal enhancement charges, which would land him in the ballpark area of life. He did all the group's typing, and legal work.

Last but not least, there was Nick. He was about 5'7, 150 lbs., mixed black and white, with plenty of money. Nick was the only one out the bunch who actually deserved to be in the feds. Boo-Shay was caught with an eight ball of crack cocaine, valued at $100, and a rusty 38. caliber with no firing pin. He too, was facing all day, because of his criminal history.

The group called themselves 'Let's tell Something Records.' It was all a game to them. They had theme songs to go with their infamous "record label," as they often referred to it. Every night, those who were signed to the record label, would sing one of their many hit songs. Their all time favorite was a remake of Keisha Cole's latest song. It went like this: *"I never knew what I was missing, 'til I started snitching...now I can't lose."* Everyone who was in agreement would sing in unison.

Burch El was the founder and CEO of 'Let's tell Something Records.' Having all five board members in attendance, he proceeded with the focus of the meeting. Every time there was a ride in, the group would gather and discuss their prospects. Four people came in on the bus, including Pharaoh, and Burch El wanted the low down. All five board members tried to keep their room available for new faces, such as Pharaoh because a new face meant new indictment, and a possible time cut.

"Where yo' celly from?" asked Burch El, directing his question to Boo-Shay. Bay sat on the edge of the bottom bunk with a pen and note pad, ready to write.

"I believe he's from Detroit," answered Boo-Shay.

"What he in on?" asked Burch El.

"I don't know yet, the nigga lightweight flashed on me, 'cause I was drilling him," answered Boo-Shay.

"That nigga is in here on a weed conspiracy. His name is Pharaoh Dickson, he's twenty-three, and from what I'm reading, he was the kingpin," said Nick, reading a news article about Pharaoh's case.

"Yeah?" said Burch El.

"Yep, it says here, that he's being charged with conspiracy to commit murder," said Nick.

"Well look, ya'll know the business. We gon' give him a fair chance to sign to the record label, if he don't sign we set fire to his ass. We gots to move quick cause the nigga might agree to cooperate in the future, then we don't get our proper chopper," advised Burch El.

Everyone nodded in agreement, while Bay jotted down almost everything. 'Proper Chopper' was the term the record label used to refer to a time cut. A 5kl.1, Rule 35, and 3553 (e), were motions filed by the government on behalf of the defendant, to reward him or her for their substantial assistance in the investigation of another.

"So Boo-Shay, see what all you can get out the nigga. Go in his shit, read his paperwork, mail, any and everything, pick that nigga like a booger. He got one week to make his mind up, or we jumping on his case," said Burch El.

What he meant by jump on his case was, the group would use any information they had about Pharaoh, they would use that information to fabricate a story, on how Pharaoh told them about his case, or they would make up a story about how two or more of them knew, and used to deal with Pharaoh on the street. By doing so they would creat a new conspiracy, and get their 'Proper Choppers.' The Feds dealt off hearsay, which allowed groups like this to operate. They weren't snitching, they were flat out lying on people and getting away with it. Now, they were moving to another target.

The group had jumped on this old guy named Gibson's case. He was busted with ten kilos of herion and was facing life. The record label tried to sign him, but he declined the offer. Bay, passed everyone their scripts about what they were expected to tell the government, and eventually a jury.

"You say that you were selling him two bricks a week, back in '89, up to '00," said Burch El, talking to Nick. "Black you say you were dealing with the nigga from '98 to '00. With ya'll two credible mothafuckas we got ourselves a conspiracy. The rest of us can just jump on the case afterwards," said Burch El.

"Then we get our proper chops, prop, prop, proper chops," laughed Boo-Shay, as he sang the lyrics. The group all laughed, and slapped fives, as they left the tiny cell. Pharaoh hadn't budged; he was still lying in bed staring up at the wall. He had no idea what he was up against.

Chapter 35

Pharaoh had slept for two days. In order to watch television, you had to have a radio, unless you were good at reading lips. The televisions ran off a satellite system, which was programmed to three separate radio stations. Boo-Shay had offered Pharaoh his radio on more than one occasion, but Pharaoh declined his offers. He was the type to always want his own, and had the patience to wait until he got his own.

It was eight o'clock in the morning, and all who had filled out a commissary slip were lined up outside of the religious room as the officer passed out the bags. Pharaoh was awakened by the loud talking coming from downstairs. He rolled off the bunk and looked out his cell door window. He quickly brushed his teeth and washed his face, then headed downstairs. All eyes were on him as he made his way to the end of the line. Pharaoh could hear people as they whispered loudly and pointed in his direction. The line inched forward, until finally Pharaoh's order came up. He signed his commissary receipt, and the officer handed him two enormous bags. Everyone watched as Pharaoh dragged the bags up to his cell. He laced up his new Reebok Classics, set his watch, and set all the local Detroit radio stations on his Sony radio. He had spent his monthly limit, he had damn near everything they sold. Boo-Shay conviently walked in as Pharaoh kneeled in front of his wall locker with goods every where.

"You did it real big uh?" asked Boo-Shay, smiling.

"Nah, man, this little shit ain't nothin', but for real, I don't think I'll have enough room," Pharoah said

"You can use my locker too, if you want," said Boo-Shay.

"A'ight bet that. You know how to cook this shit?" asked Pharaoh, picking up bags of rice, mackerel, and turkey log.

"That's what I does. Shit when you want me to cook it?"

"Soon as possible, here, cook these too," said Pharaoh, handing Boo-Shay a pizza kit. Boo-Shay grabbed everything he needed, and made his way to one of the microwaves.

"I see you boy, work young nigga, work," said Burch El, as he approached Boo-Shay at the microwave.

"After that nigga tastes this, he'll be open," said Boo-Shay.

"You crack on him about signing to the record label?"

"Not yet, the nigga been sleep the past two days, but I'mma see what it do tonight."

Pharaoh came walking down the stairs with his new get up on. He had his new Nes'Café coffee cup in his hand and walked over to the soda machine to fill it with Root Beer. Pharaoh could feel eyes piercing through his back. He turned around, and several people shifted their stare into another direction.

"Hey," said Boo-Shay, standing at the microwave. Pharaoh walked over to where Boo-Shay was working, and watched as he did his thing.

"What's the station to listen to the TV?" asked Pharoah.

"The first one is 88.1, second one 102.3, and the last one is 96.7," answered Boo-Shay.

"How long you been here?" asked Pharaoh, as he set the television stations into his radio.

"Bout two years."

"Two years!" Pharaoh repeated in shock.

"Yeah."

"Shit, I'd be damn if I sit up in here two years."

"I mean what can a nigga do?"

"I don't know, but uh, hold on!" Pharaoh said, as he raced over to the first television. He quickly pushed the pre-set button for station 96.7. There was a breaking story on the channel 4 news. Pharaoh raced over to the TV at the sight of Tez's picture. The news anchor said that a witness had come forward in the murder of James Johnson, a.k.a. Rolo. Tez was to be arrainged within seventy-two hours.

"You know dude?" asked Boo-Shay, who also ran over to see the story.

"Huh..oh, nah," answered Pharaoh.

Boo-Shay could tell that Pharaoh was clearly lying, but he didn't press the issue. Pharaoh became uneasy, and decided to go up to his cell. 'Man I hope these mothafuckas don't try to implicate me on no murder shit,' Pharaoh said to himself as he looked in the mirror mounted on the wall in his cell. Pharaoh turned his radio to 93.9, a smooth jazz and R&B station. He paced back and forth in the tiny cell, trying to calm his nerves. Boo-Shay opened the door with his foot because he had several bowls stacked on top of one another.

"You a'ight?" asked Boo-Shay, as he sat the food on the desk.

"Huh, oh yeah, I'm good," answered Pharaoh, as he snapped out of his trance. "This shit smells good," Pharaoh said as he bent over the food.

"Here you go."

"All this is for me?" asked Pharaoh.

"Yeah, ain't no sense in playing with it," Boo-Shay answered, digging into his pizza and fried rice.

"Damn, this shit taste like some carry-out." said Pharaoh, referring to the rice.

"Here, put some of this on it."

"Honey?" asked Pharaoh.

"Yeah, that's that work." Pharaoh and Boo-Shay pigged out. In between bites Boo-Shay quizzed Pharaoh to see if the time had begun to bother him.

"What they offer you?" asked Boo-Shay.

"Nothing yet. How 'bout you?"

"Shit they offered me three hundred and sixty months."
Pharaoh tried to add up how many years that was, but Boo-Shay gave him the answer.

"Nigga that's thirty calendars."

"What you do, kill somebody?"

"Not even close. They got me with an eight ball and a pistol."

"And they trying to bodyslam you like that, why?"

"The same reason they bodyslam everybody else. They want a nigga to tell something," said Boo-Shay, letting his words hang in the air. He was trying to get a feel as to whether or not Pharaoh was anti-snitch.

"So what you gon' do?" asked Pharaoh.

"What any nigga in his right mind would do."

"And what's that."

"Save your mothafuckin' self."

Pharaoh didn't respond, he had mixed emotions about the topic. Pharaoh was brought up under the code of the street. He was taught that you knew the job was hard when you took it, but everyone's values were different. He thought about the amount of time Boo-Shay was facing, and for what. He could only imagine how many months the government would throw at him.

"You think I'm a snitch, don't you?" asked Boo-Shay.

"I mean, do you. You've got to live with the consequences."

"I was just like you when I first caught my case. After watching niggas get sent off with life, and the niggas who told on them go home, shit, I quickly decided what team I wanted to be on. It'd be different if niggas was killing niggas for telling once they hit the street, but nah, niggas is embracing them. Me personally, I'd rather die on the street than in here anyway. Nigga gon' have to catch me in traffic."

Pharaoh sat back and listened to Boo-Shay's philosophy on snitching. He had some valid points, but Pharaoh peeped game. The nigga was only trying to justify being a rat.

"What you need to do on the real is come on home, and sign to the record label," said Boo-Shay.

"What you talking about?"

"You ain't heard. 'Let's tell Something Records'. Nigga, we got ten platinum plus hits. All we do is drop classics."

"What?" Pharaoh laughed.

"I'm serious. We specialize in motions, 5kl.1, 3553 (e), and my all time favorite, Rule 35 (b)."

"What the fuck is that?" asked Pharaoh.

"Oh, that's when you get your proper chopper!" said Boo-Shay, excited.

"And what's that?"

"A time cut. The judge gives you a separate time cut for every investigation you assist the government with."

"Man, you niggas is vicious," said Pharaoh, realizing just how serious snitching was.

"You'll come around, if not I'll send you some pictures of me, and some hoes at the club like this," said Boo-Shay, as he did a little dance pretending a woman's ass was in front of him.

"You's a nut," laughed Pharaoh. He rolled over and went to sleep.

Chapter 36

Pharaoh's attorney, Richard Cunningham, had finally visted him. He was escorted to the visiting room, and into another room where Mr. Cunningham sat, waiting, he stood and extended his hand as Pharaoh entered the room.

"Save the b.s. man where the hell have you been?" asked Pharaoh.

"Italy, me and the wife went on vacation."

"I wish you would have told me that before I gave you all my damn money!" Pharaoh snapped as he sat down.

"It won't happen again Mr. Dickson. So, how are you holding up?"

"I to get bond. When can I get bond?"

"They're not going to give you bond."

"Then why am I paying you?"

"To defend you, of course. Listen Mr. Dickson, this isn't state court. The government doesn't give two rats' asses about money. It's all about cooperation."

"Well you can forget that, cause I ain't nobody's fuckin' rat!"

"Listen, everyone has agreed to testify against you with the exception of your friend Ollie. I suggest you do some serious thinking because it's you against the world right now."

"Man how I know the government ain't make none of that shit up. They probably lying on my guys."

"These are court documents. They can't forge these statements. You sent what's his name, Tez, to pick up the shipment, am I correct? How do you think the Feds knew?

'Cause he told them. Do you know where he's at? Well he was out on bond, in protective custody. Right now he's downtown at 1300 Beaubien, on homicide charges, which is why I'm here. They have one witness against him, but the state's case would be a lot stronger if you cooperated."

"How do you know I know anything?" asked Pharaoh.

"Well, do you?"

"If I did, I wouldn't tell them bitches. By the way, how much time am I facing?"

"At least, two life sentences."

"For what?"

"One for the drug conspiracy, and one for the murder-for-hire charge."

"So when will I go to trial?"

"That depends on how many motions we file. I'd say 'bout eighteen months, two years tops. So what do you want me to tell the government?"

"Tell em' I said suck a fat baby's dick." With that, the visit was over. Mr. Cunningham gathered his papers into his briefcase, and hit the buzzer for an officer.

"Your making a big mistake here," said Cunningham.

"Tell me about it, I made the mistake of hiring yo' rat ass."

The officer let Mr. Cunningham out, then escorted Pharaoh back to his unit. All eyes were on Pharaoh, as he entered. Boo-Shay met Pharaoh at their cell, and was itching for the details.

"Who was that?" asked Boo-Shay.

"My pussy ass lawyer," answered Pharaoh, as he climbed in his bunk.

"What he talking about?"

"Not shit. He want a nigga to roll over and tell something."

"What you tell him?"

"Told his ass to beat the road up. I'm firing his pussy ass, first thing in the morning."

Boo-Shay ran downstairs to report his findings to

Burch El and the rest of 'Let's Tell Something Records.' The members of the record label all huddled in Nick's cell next to the laundry room. Nick's cell was their headquarters. The only thing being discussed was top secret squirrel missions, some rat shit.

"So what's the verdict, is he gon' sign to the label?" asked Burch El.

"I doubt it, he on some anti-rat shit. His lawyer just came and seen him. He told his lawyer to kick rocks, 'cause he was trying to get him to cooperate," answered Boo-Shay

"Well plan B. When that nigga gets his court papers sent in, you know what to do," said Buch El.

"He don't never come out the cell. If he do, it's only to use the phone, or take a shower and it's right back to the cell. Hell, I can't even jack my dick," laughed Boo-Shay.

"I'm going to fix that. Tomorrow I'll sign his ass up for sick-call. He won't have no choice but to leave the unit, once the nurse calls him over to the hospital," said Bay.

"Yo' old ass always thinking. Remind me to never cross you," said Black, giving Bay a play.

"A'ight that's a bet," said Burch El, as the record label filed out one by one.

The next morning Pharaoh was awakened by the unit officer, and told that he had to go see the nurse. Pharaoh reluctantly got up. He brushed his teeth, and washed his face. He looked around the cell before leaving, locked his wall locker, then headed downstairs. The unit officer radioed control and sent Pharaoh out into the main corridor. Boo-Shay and the rest of 'Let's tell Something Records,' were all up, sitting in the common area. They watched Pharaoh like a hawk, as he left the unit. Burch El nodded to Boo-Shay, who headed upstairs. Black, Bay, and Nick all spread out, just in case Pharaoh came back early, they could signal Boo-Shay. He used a filed down pen top to pop Pharaoh's combination lock. He shuffled through a large white envelope and located what he was looking for. Boo-Shay was looking for Pharaoh's court docket number, and found it. He wrote it down, then scanned through a few statements made by Tez, Killer B., and Chris. Satisfied with his findings, Boo-Shay placed everything back into Pharaoh's locker, and locked it.

With Pharaoh's court docket number, 'Lets Tell Something Records' was in business. Nick, would send his wife down to the court building with the docket number. She would pull everything the government had against Pharaoh, all his transcripts, debriefing, anything. It was all public record, as long as you paid for the information it was yours. Once the record label received the information from Nick's wife, they would dissect it, and form their stories accordingly. They would say Pharaoh told them about his case.

Burch El, Black, Bay, Boo-Shay, and Nick were all beyond snitches. They were flat out liars. There's a difference between snitching, and lying, what they were doing was on a whole different level. They were actually taking full advantage of the hearsay law. In the Feds, physical evidence isn't a prerequisite. All it took to get a conspiracy, was two or more people saying something similar. "Sho...Woo..." said Burch El, trying to notify Boo-Shay that Pharaoh was back. Boo-Shay blew some baby powder in the air and swung the cell door open, as if he had just finished shitting. He stepped out onto the tier as Pharoh walked up the stairs.

"I wouldn't go in there, if I was you."

"You ain't stopped shitting since I got here," Pharaoh snapped as he leaned over the railing.

"What they want with you at medical?"

"They was asking me about some heart medicine. I don't take no medication for nothing."

"Shit, let me go down here and check on my laundry," said

Boo-Shay as he walked downstairs.

One by one, 'Let's tell Something Records' filed into Nick's tiny cell. Boo-Shay handed over his findings to Nick, who left and headed straight for the phone. Pharaoh tested the air in the cell before going in. He pulled the door shut behind him, and stared out the window at the prisoners walking the yard across the street at the prison. Pharaoh wondered how much time an old gray-haired black fellow was serving, as he walked along the track alone. Pharaoh jumped up on his bunk, at the thought of that being him.

Chapter 37

Four days later, Pharaoh was taken to court by two U.S. Marshals. They made him pack all his personal property into a brown box, excluding his legal material. Pharaoh was puzzled, because his lawyer hadn't mentioned anything about him having court. He rode alone in the caged backseat of the grey tinted van. Pharaoh asked the marshals why he was going to court, and one of them responded: "they call us and say go pick Joe Blow up, and bring him downtown. That's all we know."

Pharaoh sat back and tried to relax. With the latest events, nothing got to him. Everyday it was something new. After forty minutes riding in and out of lane traffic, the marshals pulled into the garage of the federal court building. Pharaoh's stomach dropped, it reminded him of the movies. He was escorted onto an elevator, and up to the tenth floor.

The scene started looking familiar, as the marshals stopped in front of the interrogation room agents Kemp and Thomas had questioned Pharaoh in weeks prior. One of the marshals opened the door, then stepped back, letting Pharaoh enter. In attendance were Agents Kemp and Thomas, the prosecutor, and Pharaoh's attorney. He looked around the room, as his lawyer stood to his feet and walked over to Pharaoh with a huge, phony smile.

"How's it going Mr. Dickson?" Pharaoh stared him down while the marshals removed his handcuffs and ankle bracelets.

"What's all this?" asked Pharaoh, adjusting his clothes.

"They just want to ask you a few questions. It'll be in your best interest, to at least hear what they're offering."

"Do you all mind if I speak with my attorney in private?" asked Pharaoh, looking at the agents, and prosecutor. They all looked at one another, and shrugged their shoulders. They reluctantly stood up, and excused themselves into the hallway.

"I'm sorry about this," said Mr. Cunningham, as the three walked out the room.

"I thought I told you, I wasn't fucking with these bitches. You hard of hearing?" asked Pharaoh.

"I'm simply looking out for you, they're threatening to file a superseding indictment because, apparently. you've been up there in Milan running your mouth."

"What the fuck are you talking about?"

"Some inmates, well informants have debriefed with the government, saying that you told them about your case. One of them is claiming to have bought from you in the past."

"And they can use that shit in court?"

"Can they? They'll use it to convict you beyond a reasonable doubt.. I keep trying to tell you that this is the Feds, not the State.

"I'm not a rat."

"Listen to you, I'm not a rat. Let me tell you something, in twenty years all that won't even make a difference. Nobody will remember who told on who, let alone care. By the way, the government has offered to help get your son back."

"My mom gon' get my son."

"Not if the government has anything to do with it. Besides, do you want your son to grow up without his father?"

"What the fuck do they want from me?"

"For one, they want you to cooperate against Toro, and two, the murder Tez supposedly committed."

"And what do I get, besides the label of a rat?"

"I can gurantee you'll have some daylight."

"Nah, you got to come better than that. If I'mma tell on the

Mexican connection, and a homicide ya'll at least got to give me a ballpark figure."

"Hold on," said Mr. Cunningham, as he raced into the hallway.

"He's cracking, but he wants a ballpark figure," said Cunningham.

"Richard you know the law prevents us from making specific deals. How much time he receives, depends solely on the judge," said Agent Kemp.

"So, what do you want me to tell him?"

"Tell him that we can put him in the range of 144 months to 180 months, if he cooperates fully with the government. It'll be up to the judge to decide," said the district attorney. Mr. Cunningham raced back into the room. He ran his fingers through his thinning salt and pepper hair, as he closed the door behind him.

"Twelve to fifteen years."

"Nope, not going to happen," said Pharaoh.

"Hold on, I wasn't finished. They're offering twelve to fifteen years on the guidelines, but they'll also file a motion prior to sentencing, saying that you've cooperated substantially, and the judge will have the discretion to depart. If he departs, he'll have to start at the low end of the guidelines, then give you a time cut. In your case, the low end is twelves years, so he'll have to go below twelve. He can let you walk, once the government files the motion."

"All that shit sounds good, but I lost all interest, when you said discretion, that means if he wants to. I'm straight on all that rat shit. I just wanted to see how them Yankees was coming. By the way, you re fired," said Pharaoh, mocking the legendary Donald Trump.

Mr. Cunningham had turned beet red. He tried to say something, but the words wouldn't come out. He stormed out of the room to relay the news. Pharaoh took a seat and smiled. He knew that there was a possibility he

would never see the streets again, but he could live with
that, so long as he had his dignity.

Chapter 38

Six months later, Pharaoh hired a new attorney out of Ann Arbor, Michigan. He was known to be a good trial lawyer, and more importantly, friends with Judge Townsend. His name was Douglas Mulkoff. Pharaoh found him through an old head who was in the county jail with him. Pharaoh had been back in the county since 'Let's tell Something Records' jumped on his case. He couldn't go back to Milan, because they all filed separations against him. He didn't mind, he was having it his way. He managed to get back on the floor with Sheriff Dudley and Tez was right across the hall from Pharaoh, they could see one another through the bars.

Pharaoh's new attorney filed a motion for a speedy trial. The judge ruled on the motion in Pharaoh's favor and set trial for December 14th, which was two weeks away. Pharaoh was sweating like a Hebrew slave. He knew deep down that he didn't have a snowball chance in hell, but he had to try his hand. He still hadn't accepted the truth regarding Tez, Killer B., Dee, Mike, and Chris all turning state on him. Pharaoh told himself, that he'd have to see it in order to believe it.

The Feds had kept their word on blocking Mom Dukes from getting custody of Jr. She had hired two separate attorneys and filed petitions with the court, but to no avail. The State dropped the murder charges against Tez with prejudice. They needed at least one more credible witness, because Chyna's statement was motivated by Tez beating her. Pharaoh's new attorney had been visiting him for two weeks straight to prepare for trial. He delivered the same plea bargain, twelve to fifteen years and agreement to file a motion for downward departure. Pharoah rejected the offer, but had been contemplating pleading guilty without any cooperation. His lawyer told him that he'd still be looking at life if he were to plead out and the government would want him to stipulate to a waiver of his right to appeal. Pharaoh began to realize that he was in a catch-22, "Damned if you do, damn if you don't." The Feds were playing for keeps. If you cooperate, you've sold your soul, and the government owns you. If you don't cooperate, they'll give all day to think about it, so they still own you. Just when Pharaoh thought things couldn't get any worse, Sheriff Dudley laid the news on him about her pregnancy.

"What?" asked Pharaoh. She had pulled Pharaoh into their meeting love palace.

"Shhh…"

"Man, I don't need this right now. This isn't a good look."

"What do you mean, this isn't a good look?"

"I'm facing forever and a day. I start trial in a minute, ain't no telling how this shit might pan out. I already got one son."

"How much time they offering?" she asked.

"Twelve to fifteen years, but they want me to cooperate. It ain't gon' happen."

"So, what you gon' do?"

"I'm going to trial. Look, if I get convicted just get an abortion."

"I'm not having no damn abortion."

"Well, I can't make any promises. I don't have no hella money to help you raise no baby from the penitentiary."

"I'm not worried about no money. I want you to come home."

"I'm trying. Lord knows I'm trying."

"Just tell them people what they want to know. I can do the time with you." Pharaoh stared Sheriff Dudley (Stacy) in the eyes. He realized for the first time that he had feelings for her, her feelings were obvious. Pharaoh broke the stare and dropped his head.

"You don't understand, it's not that simple, love," he said as he walked out of the mop closet.

Chapter 39

Pharaoh sat nervously, tapping his foot a hundred miles per hour on the leg of his chair at the defense table. He wore a blue business suit, with a pink power tie, his wire frame Cartier glasses, and a pair of black 'Gucci' loafers. He turned slightly in his chair to face Mom Dukes, Donald, and a few other family members who came to show their support. His lawyer and the U.S. attorney just finished jury selection, there were two Blacks, one Hispanic, and the rest were White. He wasn't content with the selection, because not one of the jurors was one of his peers; every last one of them was from some hick town. They believed the police, government, and courts could do no wrong. They weren't exposed to the crooked cops, and shady dealings, so in Pharaoh's eyes, he didn't stand a chance.

At every stage of the trial, the government offered Pharaoh the same dry cooperation agreement, which he shot down. The government forwarded Pharaoh's attorney with the witness list. Pharaoh read the forty-two names on it, out of forty-two, Pharaoh only knew seven of the names. Trial got under way; the government explained its case to the jury briefly, then called the star witness, Tez. Pharaoh couldn't believe his eyes as he watched his best friend take the witness box and raise his hand, he just knew that Tez wouldn't go through with it.

Tez proved Pharaoh wrong. When the prosecutor asked Tez to point Pharaoh out and describe what he was wearing, Tez did exactly that. He looked over to the defense table, and made eye contact with Pharaoh, it was then, and only then that he accepted the truth. He swallowed hard, and became teary-eyed. He couldn't hear anything that was going on, everything became one big blur. After the prosecutor finished drilling Tez with numerous rehearsed questions, the government rested. Mr. Mulkoff, stood to cross-examine, but Pharaoh grabbed his arm and whispered in his ear. "Let's do it."

Mr. Mulkoff could see the seriousness in Pharaoh's eyes. He walked over to the prosecution's table, and held a brief conversation. Together, the prosecutor and Mr. Mulkoff approached the judge's bench. They explained that Pharaoh had wanted to waive the trial and cooperate. The judge sent the jury into recess, while the Rule (11) cooperation was overlooked and signed by Pharaoh. Tez, who was still seated at the witness stand, looked over at the defense table. Pharaoh winked at him, and smiled. Tez waved the prosecutor over to the witness box frantically, but the prosecutor ignored him. He pointed the marshals in Tez's direction, they walked over to the witness box, and cuffed him. As Tez walked past the defense table, Pharaoh put his hand over his mouth and pointed laughing silently.

Pharaoh stood at the podium beside his attorney, and entered a plea of guilty. Judge Townsend accepted the Rule (11) cooperation agreement, and gave Pharaoh the option to withdraw from the agreement, if for some reason at sentencing the court was unable to impose a sentence within the guideline range. After the plea, Pharaoh was taken up to the tenth floor to the interrogation room. Inside sat the prosecutor, Agents Kemp and Thomas, and Mr. Mulkoff. Pharaoh was treated like a king. They ordered him carry-out from 'Tubby's Submarine Shop,' talked to him as if he was one of their colleagues, and vowed to get his son for him. He agreed to cooperate against Toro and Joey in the marijuana investigation. He told them how he met Toro and what led him to Phoenix in the first place. Pharaoh admitted to the bank robbery, but hesitated to say who was all involved. Mr. Mulkoff explained to him, that it was all or nothing. Pharaoh reluctantly implicated Ollie in the robbery, a well as the marijuana conspiracy. He told himself that all wars had causalities, and Ollie was this one. Pharaoh went on to tell them about the murder of Rolo at "007", then the murder of Annie, he drew a map of the location he and Tez had burried Annie's body. Agent Kemp got on the phone, and put together a team, they were to take Pharaoh out to the site. Pharaoh told him about the murders of Tamara, and Kellie, along with the murders of Mel and his bodyguard. He told the agents that Sheriff Dudley could testify that Tez had an argument with the guy who was killed at the 'Good Life Lounge' and that Chyna was indeed working when Tez killed Rolo. Pharaoh agreed to take a lie detector test, and passed.

The Feds got with the State and relayed it's findings, all of the murders were committed in Detroit, with the exception of Mel and his bodyguard, their murders were federal, because it was a drug-related hit. Mr. Mulkoff explained to Pharaoh how the judge would sentence with all his cooperation. He said that the judge would give a separate time cut for every investigation he assisted authorities in. Mr. Mulkoff told Pharaoh about the third party Rule 35 (b) motion, that's when someone other than the defendant, assists with government on behalf of the defendant. Someone on the streets could set someone up, and the credit would go to whoever they wished. Pharaoh shook his head in disbelief at all the different ways a person could tell, at the same time, thought about Ralph and how he vowed to repay him.

Chapter 40

Pharaoh sat in the county jail for four months, waiting for the murders against Tez to pan out. In the mean time, Toro and Joey pleaded guilty, as a result Pharaoh didn't have to testify and still would receive a time cut. He had been working with Ralph on his Rule 35 (b) motion. Pharaoh wanted to be released at his sentencing hearing, so he explored all possible avenues. He had Ralph going to all the night clubs and meeting potential drug dealers, he would arrange to make a buy from the dealer, then contact Pharaoh's attorney, who would notify the DEA, or ATF depending on the investigation. Ralph would work with the agents, making buys and all the credit would go towards Pharaoh's sentence. So far, Ralph had knocked six dealers, for an eighth of a kilo of crack cocaine each. Pharaoh could almost expect to walk free at sentencing.

"Man, good looking out, my nigga," he said talking through the small window of the visitor's cell.

"It ain't nothin' I told you I got you. When you coming home?" asked Ralph.

"Man, I got to wait until this murder shit is over with Tez, then they gon' sentence me."

"What you gon' do when you get out?"

"Shit, what else? I'ma get money. I got the key to the game now. I can sell a million pounds of whatever, and if I get caught, I'll just tell," laughed Pharaoh.

"You terrible my man," laughed Ralph.

"Nigga, the sky's the limit. When I touch, I'ma get all the money. You just gon' be on stand by. You're my get out of jail free card," said Pharaoh.

"Once word gets out, you think niggas is gon' fuck with you?" asked Ralph.

"Listen, as long as my prices are right, and the work is tight, niggas gon' shop with me. The majority of them niggas is working for the Feds anyway. Don't ever be fooled," said Pharaoh.

"Well, just hurry up and get home," said Ralph.

"Tez trial starts tomorrow. It's expected to last for two weeks, because it's multiple murders involved. So I figure within the next three months, I should be at the crib."

"A'ight my nigga, I'm up, you be smooth."

"You too," said Pharaoh, as he and Ralph touched the glass with their fists.

"Why you so happy?" asked Sheriff Dudley, as she walked Pharaoh back to his ward.

"Cause I'll be home to you in no time," said Pharaoh, as he slapped her on the ass playfully.

"Quit it," laughed Sheriff Dudley, as she looked up and down the hallway to see if anyone had seen Pharaoh slap her butt.

"Where yo' partner at?"

"He went out on lunch. You want to get a quickie in?"

"What kind of question is that?" asked Pharaoh, as he grabbed her hand, leading her into the mop closet.

"We got to hurry up."

Pharaoh had her pinned up against the wall, tongue kissing her. He lifted her shirt above her head, and worked his way down to her breast. "Oh, Pharaoh..." sighed Sheriff Dudley. She was starting to show, and it was preventing Pharaoh from getting in the position he wanted, so he turned her around. He pulled his pants down around his ankles, and slid his dick through the hole of his boxers. He gripped her soft yellow ass with both hands, as he gently inserted the head of his dick. "Ah..." they both said in unison. She was wet as ever. Pharaoh, had always heard that pregnant pussy was the best, boy was it the truth. He got four good strokes in, then let off a luggie inside her. "When I said quickie, I ain't mean that damn quick," joked Sheriff Dudley. Pharaoh went back to his ward, and straight to his cell, he laid across his bed, looking off into space. He thought about what life had come to, and how no one was winning except the government. Pharaoh had grown tired of all the thoughts and fell asleep.

The next day, Pharaoh was called down to registry for court. Two sheriffs walked him through an underground tunnel to Frank Murphy Hall of Justice, it was the state court building. Pharaoh was taken to a small holding cell, with a visitor's window. At the window, sat the state's prosecuting attorney, she prepped Pharaoh on what she would be asking him, and the potential questions Tez's court appointed attorney might ask. She started with the murders of Annie and Rolo because they were the ones being tried first. She drilled Pharaoh for close to two hours, up until the trial was set to start.

Pharaoh was exhausted from the long debriefing; he stretched out on the cold cement slab, and attempted to fall asleep. Just as he closed his eyes, he heard the voice of Tez in the hallway. Tez had just gotten off the elevator, and was being escorted by two sheriffs to a holding cell across from Pharaoh. Pharaoh didn't bother getting up, he laid on the cement slab listening to Tez run his head about how he was going to beat the murders.

"They ain't got but one witness that can say I did the shit. It's my word against his," said Tez, as the sheriffs slammed the cell door behind him.

"Yeah, but I'm not the one you've got to convince. They got twelve jurors for that," said the sheriff, as he checked to make sure Tez's cell was locked, then walked away. Tez could see someone lying in the cell across from him, but couldn't see the person's face. He stared over at the other cell for a moment, but was interrupted by his attorney at the visitor's window.

"How it's looking? We gon' beat this bitch or what?"

"We're going to try," his attorney replied.

"You don't sound too convincing. What the fuck you mean try? This is my life we're talking about. We're going to do more than try!"

Pharaoh laughed, at the sound of Tez snapping on his attorney. 'Boy oh boy, it's funny how the table's turn' he thought.

"Listen, you've got two witnesses saying the same thing on one of the murders, and one of them happens to be your best friend."

"Once they find out his motivation for telling, that I was cooperating against him, then all of a sudden now the murders. I mean, come on, man. Ain't a jury in the world gon' believe that shit."

"That may be the case on four of the bodies, but your baby's mother, Annie, how else would he have known where her body was. Like I said, you've got two other witnesses, one circumstantial, and the other an eye witness. I'm just being honest with you, sir. Your friend, Mr. Dickson, is here and ready to testify. I'll see you in the court room, okay."

Tez walked back over to the front of the cell, and looked over into Pharaoh's cell. Pharaoh hadn't budged; he was enjoying his ear hustling session.

"Hey my man! My man across the hall!" yelled Tez. Pharaoh heard Tez calling, but remained still.

"Hey my man. You know what time it is?" asked Tez. Pharaoh rolled off the cement slab, and walked over to the door. Tez looked puzzled as he met eye contact with Pharaoh.

"This for us," asked Tez.

"It was for us when you were testifying against me."

"Nigga, you put a hit on me!"

"Nigga, you crossed all boundaries fucking with my baby mama."

"So, this is all about a bitch?"

"Nah, it's about respect."

"Ain't that a bitch. I'm facing life 'cause you can't stomach a nigga fucking yo' hoe. If you get on the stand, I'm finished."

"Better you, than me," said Pharaoh.

EPILOGUE

Ollie pleaded guilty to the conspiracy charge. He was sentenced to 240 months, and sent to Tarre Haute, United States penitentiary in Indiana. Ollie, was a victim of circumstances, and a casuality of a war between Pharaoh and Tez. Ollie, was the one who wishes he had cooperated. Everyday he kicks himself in the ass because he didn't.

Tez, was convicted on all six murder charges, and sentenced to six natural life sentences. He's currently serving time in Mound Road Prison in Michigan. His kids, and family cut all ties with him, because he killed their mother, Annie. Tez, is the one who didn't have anything to tell. All the telling in the world couldn't save him.

Pharaoh was sentenced to time served. The government filed every possible downward departure motion on his behalf. He was greeted by Mom Dukes, Jr., and Sheriff Dudley (Stacy), in the hallway of the federal building.

"Hey lil' man," Pharaoh said, as he reached down to pick Jr. up. "Oh, boy your getting heavy." He said, rubbing Jr.'s hair.

"You ready, baby?" asked Stacy.

"Yeah, let's get out of here."

They drove over to 'Fish Bone's' a high class restaurant in downtown Detroit. Pharaoh was so geeked to be out, he didn't have much of an appetite. Mom Dukes, volunteered to take Jr. home, while Pharaoh and Stacy got caught up on time. Pharaoh's lease wasn't up on his apartment, so he decided to go there because it wasn't far from the restaurant. The manager recognized Pharaoh, and gave him a spare key to his place.

Pharaoh and Stacy began kissing, and taking each other's clothes off soon as they entered the apartment. In between kisses, Pharaoh managed to close the front door. He led Stacy into the living room, where they dropped the rest of their clothes. Pharaoh stood at attention, with his dick in his hand. Stacy dropped down to her knees on the deep plush carpet. She took Pharaoh's dick from him, and began slapping herself across the face with it. She teased and kissed the head of Pharaoh's dick, then finally mouthed it. She took his entire manhood into her warm, moist mouth. "Shit!" sighed Pharaoh, reaching down to palm Stacy's head with both hands. He fucked her mouth as if it were her pussy. She free handed Pharaoh, using her hands to grip his ass cheeks, she pulled him in and out of her mouth, while looking up into his eyes. Pharaoh was about to have an orgasm, so he pulled away breathing hard. "Ahh," he sighed, flopping down on the couch behind him. Stacy was on him like a bitch in heat. She climbed on top of Pharaoh's still hard gleaming dick and slid down on him, riding him cowgirl style. Pharaoh laid back as Stacy fucked his brains out. "Ah..Oh.. Pharaoh!" yelled Stacy as she had her first, then second orgasm. Sweat began to trickle down the small of her back and forehead as she fucked herself into a frenzy. Pharaoh grabbed Stacy's waist, and began sliding her up and down violently on his dick.

"Fuck me" yelled Stacy.

"Take this dick," said Pharaoh, as he could feel himself about to explode.

"Oh my God!"

"Ah.. take this dick!" yelled Pharaoh, as he erupted into Stacy.

Boom!

Stacy fell back against Pharaoh's chest and slumped over. The loud gunshot frightened him. He lifted Stacy's lifeless body and stared at the figure before him. "What the fuck?" yelled Pharaoh, looking into the eyes of Sasha. She stood over Pharaoh, with a 9 mm pointed at his heart. Pharaoh looked over at Stacy's obviously dead body, and thought about his daughter who was expected to be delivered in three months. Sasha broke Pharaoh's stare by shooting Stacy in the stomach twice. *Boom! Boom!* "Bitch!" yelled Pharaoh, as he attempted to lunge at Sasha. She quickly turned the gun back to him, stopping him dead in his tracks.

Boom!

Sasha shot Pharaoh in the right side of his upper chest, sending him flying back on the couch. His life flashed before his eyes as Sasha inched toward him. She raised the gun to Pharaoh's head and fired two rounds. *Boom! Boom!*

The End

Sample Chapters

From Hoodfellas

By
Richard Jeanty

Chapter 1
The Natural Course

"Mr. Brown, we're not really here to negotiate with you. It's more like a demand, or whatever you wanna call it," said Crazy D.

"What makes you think I'm gonna do what you're telling me to do?" Mr. Brown asked. "Yo, Short Dawg, bring her out," Crazy D ordered.

Short Dawg appeared from behind Mr. Brown's storage area with a knife to Mr. Brown's wife's neck while her left hand is covered in blood. "She still has nine good fingers left, but next time we won't be cutting off fingers, oh no, we ain't interested in the same body part twice. Next time it might be one of her eyeballs hanging out the socket," Crazy D said as he signaled for Short Dawg to bring the knife to Mrs. Brown's eyes. "Tell me what you want and I'll do it, just don't hurt her," said Mr. Brown. "We've been watching you for a while now and my guesstimation is that you make about fifty to a hundred thousand dollars a month. Forty percent of that is ours and we're gonna collect it on every first of the month," he said. "How we supposed to survive? The shop doesn't even make that kind of money," Mr. Brown pleaded. "Do you need motivation to make that kind of money?" Crazy D asked as he raised his hand to Short Dawg, ordering him to start taking out one of Mrs. Brown's eyes. Before he could stick the knife in, Mr. Brown chimed in and said, "Okay, I'll do it. I'll give you forty percent of what we make." Crazy D smiled and said, "No, you'll give me forty percent of a hundred thousand dollars every month. He ordered Short Dawg to drop the knife with a swift movement of his head.

As Crazy D and Short Dawg were making their way out of the shop, Mr. Brown reached for his shotgun. However, before he could cock it back, Crazy D had his .45 Lugar in his face saying, "It's your choice, old man, you can die a hero or you can become a zero." Mr. Brown wisely placed his shotgun down, and then apologized to Crazy D. What Crazy D did to the Browns was routine since he came out of the State Pen. Crazy D walked out of jail wearing some donated clothes that were twenty years out of style and fit a little too snug around his six foot-plus frame. The difference this time was the tightness of the fit. He had gained a considerable amount of weight in muscle. The shirt was tight around his arms and his pants barely made it past his thighs. He was ridiculed as he rode the bus back to his old neighborhood. The kids were pointing at him, adults shook their heads at him and women just laughed at him. Crazy D was fed up with the treatment he received his first day out of jail. He looked like a buff homo. With no money and no skills to get a job, Crazy D had no choice but to turn back to a life of crime. After serving a twenty-year sentence for robbery and second-degree murder, the system failed him miserably, but even worse, they failed the rest of society by letting a loose canon out of jail without the proper rehabilitation.

While in jail, Crazy D's mom only visited him the first few months. She soon fell victim to the crack epidemic and ultimately had to turn her back on her son at his request. There came a time when she could hardly remember that she had a son. While constantly under the influence of crack cocaine, his mother did her own stint in prison for prostitution and other petty crimes only to get out and start using again.

Crazy D went to jail at the young age of seventeen and it was there that he learned his survival tactics. Wreaking havoc on people before they got to him was what he learned when he was in prison. The attempted rape on him the first week after he arrived at the Walpole facility in Massachusetts brought his awareness to a level he never knew existed. He was lucky that one of the toughest inmates in that prison was a friend of his father's. Word had gotten out that Crazy D was being shipped to Walpole and his father's best friend made a promise to his mother to look after him. Crazy D's dad, Deon Sr., and Mean T were best friends before his dad got killed, and Mean T was sent to prison for thirty years after a botched armed robbery against a store owner.

Chapter 2

Mean T and Sticky Fingers

Mean T and Sticky Fingers aka Deon Campbell Sr. were best friends throughout their entire lives. They were more like vagrants from the time their mother decided to allow them to walk to school by themselves. In fact, the very first day that they walked to school without any supervision, they decided to make a detour to the corner store. Mean T was the lookout while Sticky Fingers robbed the store of candy, potato chips, juices and other valuables that matter to kids. It was a little distance from Evans Street to Morton Street in Dorchester, Massachusetts, but their parents trusted that they would walk directly to school everyday. The Taylor Elementary School was where most of the kids who lived on the Dorchester side of Morton Street went to school. Stealing became a fun habit for the duo and every morning they found themselves down the block at the corner store stealing more items than their pockets could afford. Mean T was the bigger of the two, but Sticky Fingers was the conniving thief. He could steal the bible from a preacher, and Mean T would knock the daylights out of a pregnant woman.

Over the years, the duo broaden their horizons from stealing candy to stealing sneakers and clothes out of a store called 42nd Street located in Mattapan Square. By then, they were in high school being promoted because of their age and not the work that they did. The two were dumb as a doorknob, but one was an expert thief and the other an enforcer. The two friends were the best young hustlers from their block. The Korean owner of the store was forced to install cameras because Sticky Fingers and Mean T kept robbing the store and there was never any proof to prosecute them. Usually, the cops didn't respond on time and by then the two had made it home safely with their stolen goods. The shop owner was growing tired of this and decided to arm himself in order to keep from getting robbed.

Mean T and Sticky Fingers wore the freshest gear to school. Everything was brand name because they stole the best of everything from the different stores downtown Boston. Their favorite stores were Filene's, Jordan Marsh, Filene's Basement and of course, 42nd Street in Mattapan Square. On top of that, the two of them sold some of the stolen merchandise to some of the kids at the high school when they needed money. Their bad habit became an enterprise. The two thieves outfitted their bedrooms with stolen goods from stores all over the Boston area. They had enough merchandise to supply a whole high school of kids with clothes, shoes and other clothing items such as socks, t-shirts, underwear and long johns needed for at least a month. However, Mean T and Sticky Fingers would run into some difficulty when they decided to rob the 42nd Street store once more. The Korean owner had had enough and he felt he needed to protect his livelihood, so he bought a gun.

By this time, Mean T and Sticky Fingers were pretty known to the entire Korean family who worked as a unit in the store. While Sticky Fingers walked around and stuffed his bag with stolen items, so he could dash out of the store using the same tactics they had used in the past with Mean T knocking out the father who stood guard at the entrance, the father looked on. However, on this day, they would meet their fate. As Sticky Fingers rushed towards the exit, all he felt was a hot bullet piercing through his heart. Mean T didn't even have time to react as the small Korean man raised his gun and stuck it in Mean T's mouth. Pandemonium rang out in the store as everyone tried to make it to the exit. Meanwhile, Sticky Finger's lifeless body lay on the ground with his hands clutched around a duffle bag filled with stolen items. The cops arrived in no time. Someone's life had to be taken in order for the cops to respond in a timely manner.

Mr. Chang, as the community later found out the store owner's name, had to defend himself against the whole community. No one came to his defense when he was being robbed blindly, but everyone was angry because another young black life had been taken. Sticky Finger's mom came out shedding tears as if she didn't know what her son was doing in the street. A search of the victim's home revealed about fifty thousand dollars worth of stolen items from different stores, including Mr. Chang's 42nd Street. Sticky Finger's mom had to have known that her son was hawking stolen merchandise because the officers could barely take a step into his room without stepping over stolen clothes while serving the search warrant. The whole place was cluttered with clothes scattered all over the room.

To top off an already insane situation, the cops found a loaded gun on Mean T after searching him at the scene. Mean T aka Tony Gonsalves, an American born Cape Verde heritage young man was handcuffed and taken to jail where he faced aggravated robbery, illegal possession of a handgun, first degree armed robbery and a list of other charges concocted by the district attorney to ensure his proper place away from society for the next thirty years. It didn't help that Tony and Deon weren't in good standing at school. No teachers, counselor or principal would vouch for them as good people. The media smeared their names even further and there was no way that Tony was going to walk even though his friend was killed.

A few months after Deon's murder, the media revealed that he had left behind a pregnant woman with an unborn child. That child would be named Deon after his father. Mean T would receive a thirty-year sentence, the maximum allowed under

Massachusetts law. He was transferred from the correctional facility in Concord to the facility in Walpole after his sentence. As a young man, Mean T didn't really understand the extent of his sentence, so he chose to act in a machismo way and accepted his fate. On the van ride from Concord to Walpole, while shackled to other hardcore criminals, reality started to set in for Mean T and he understood clearly that his life had taken a drastic turn for the worst and he had better start thinking about his survival tactics. Mean T rose to prominence very quickly at the prison as he engaged some of the tougher inmates in fights and defeated quite a few of them while earning their respect.

Mean T was tested the very day he was headed to Walpole to start his sentence. One repeated offender wanted to impress all the impressionable first timers in the van, and he made the unthinkable mistake of picking on Meant T.

"You're gonna be my bitch when we touch down," he said to Mean T with a tempted grin. The whole van was laughing except Meant T. He was sitting in the row in front of Mean T and had to turn his neck around to talk to him. Before he could turn around to say something else, Mean T threw his handcuffed hands around his neck and choked him until he passed out. Words had gotten around about the incident and Mean T was given his props for almost killing a man who was known as Nutty Harold in prison. Nutty Harold was released on a technicality and he unfortunately had a confrontation with Mean T on his way back to prison after killing a man six months out of prison.

It was almost eighteen years later, a few months short of his eighteenth birthday, when Crazy D aka Deon Campbell Jr. would walk into the prison in Walpole to meet the guardian angel known to him as Abdul Mustafa Muhammad. Mean T had converted to Islam while serving his sentence. He had gotten into many fights after arriving at the prison, including one that involved sending a prison guard to the emergency room, which earned him an additional ten years to his sentence. Mean T was casually walking to his cell after code red was called. This one particular guard, who hated him for garnering the respect of his fellow inmates, felt Mean T was not walking fast enough. He used his stick to rush Mean T back to his cell thinking that the other two guards behind him provided a safe haven from an asswhip. Mean T was much too quick and strong for the guard as he found his neck wrapped inside Mean T's massive biceps. The two guards stood back as Mean T threatened to choke the life out of the guard who unjustly pushed and hit him with the stick. The white guard started turning pink and his eyes bulging out of their sockets as he fainted from the chokehold feeling that life itself was about to end. The other two guards could only watch in horror before stepping in to provide some relief for the guard using their night stick. He became a lifer. Abdul, formerly known as Tony Gonsalves also formerly known as Mean T on the streets, was a highly respected man in prison. As a lifer, he had earned the reputation of a tough, intelligent and manipulating leader. He protected those close to him and destroyed those who went against him.

Deceived

Rahsaan Stink Jones was given a second chance at life when he moved from his slum ridden North Carolina neighborhood to Newport News Virginia to live with his grandparents. It didn t take long for him to see that all ghettos across America were just the same. After being introduced to a crack epidemic sweeping through the country, he met Cross, A crazed New Yorker who would stop at nothing for his thirst for life s finer things. Cross embedded his sadistic way of doing things into Stink s life. However, after meeting the beautiful Bonni, Stink s focus on life began to change. Faced with the reality that his lifestyle would only lead to death or prison, Stink was ready to make a choice. With the atrocious acts of his partner looming over his head, Stink was sure that he too would be Crossed.

In Stores!!

My Partners Wife

In this twisted tale of seduction, Marcus Williams finds himself taking refuge in the arms of a woman completely forbidden to him after he discovered his cheating ☐iancée s sexual trysts. His life spirals out of control after the death of his partner while the killer is still on the loose. Marcus is conflicted about his decision to honor his partner or to completely allow his heart to decide his fate. Always the sucker for love, Marcus starts to fall head over heels for his partner s wife. However, with more deaths on the horizon, Marcus may soon find himself serving time with the same convicts he had been putting behind bars.

In Stores!!

Coming March 2011...Hoodfellas III

Deon and his crew are forced to return back to the States because of unfortunate situations in Haiti. However, lurking around in Deon s mind are those killers who took out his boys, Short Dawg and No Neck. He won't rest until the heads of the killers are delivered to him. This personal vendetta will have to be settled before Deon can have peace of mind, but will he allow a personal vendetta to become his downfall as he tries to become a legit businessman?

Miami Noire

After Chasin' Satisfaction, Julius finds that satisfaction is not all that it's cracked up to be. It left nothing but death in its aftermath. Now living the glamorous life in Miami while putting the finishing touches on his hybrid condo hotel, he realizes with newfound success he's now become the hunted. Julian's success is threatened as someone from his past vows revenge on him.

In Stores!!!

The Bedroom Bandit

It may not be Histeria Lane, but these desperate housewives are fed up with their neglecting husbands. Their sexual needs take precedence over the millions of dollars their husbands bring home every year to keep them happy in their affluent neighborhood. While their husbands claim to be hard at work, these wives are doing a little work of their own with the bedroom bandit. Is the bandit swift enough to evade these angry husbands?

In Stores!!

NEGLECTED SOULS

Motherhood and the trials of loving too hard and not enough frame this story...The realism of these characters will bring tears to your spirit as you discover the hero in the villain you never saw coming...

As Katrina become destitute, she has to fight to keep her children from harm. However, the children soon discover they have to look after their mother. Can they make it in this cruel world alone?

In Stores!!!

Neglected No More

Jimmy and Nina continue to feel a void in their lives because they haven't a clue about their genealogical make-up. Jimmy falls victims to a life threatening illness and only the right organ donor can save his life. Will the donor be the bridge to reconnect Jimmy and Nina to their biological family? Will Nina be the strength for her brother in his time of need? Will they ever find out what really happened to their mother?

In Stores!!!

Chasin Satisfaction

Betrayal, lust, lies, murder, deception, sex and tainted love frame this story... Julian Stevens lacks the ambition and freak ability that Miko looks for in a man, but she married him despite his flaws to spite an ex-boyfriend. When Miko least expects it, the old boyfriend shows up and ready to sweep her off her feet again. She wants to have her cake and eat it too. While Miko's doing her own thing, Julian is determined to become everything Miko ever wanted in a man and more, but will he go to extreme lengths to prove he's worthy of Miko's love? Julian Stevens soon finds out that he's capable of being more than he could ever imagine as he embarks on a journey that will change his life forever.

In Stores!!!

The Most Dangerous Gang In America: The NYPD

The police in New York and other major cities around the country are increasingly victimizing black men. The violence has escalated to deadly force, most of the time without justification. In this controversial book, noted author Richard Jeanty, tackles the problem of police brutality and the unfair treatment of Black men at the hands of police in New York City and the rest of the country.

In Stores!!!

Sexual Exploits of a Nympho II

Just when Darren thinks his relationship with Tina is flourishing, there is yet another hurdle on the road hindering their bliss. Tina saw a therapist for months to deal with her sexual addiction, but now Darren is wondering if she was ever treated completely. Darren has not been taking care of home and Tina's frustrated and agrees to a break-up with Darren. Will Darren lose Tina for good? Will Tina ever realize that Darren is the best man for her?

In Stores!!

Sexual Jeopardy

Ronald Murphy was a player all his life until he and his best friend, Myles, met the women of their dreams during a brief vacation in South Beach, Florida. Sexual Jeopardy is story of trust, betrayal, forgiveness, friendship and hope.

In Stores!!!

Sexual Exploits of a Nympho I

Tina develops an insatiable sexual appetite very early in life. She only loves her boyfriend, Darren, but he's too far away in college to satisfy her sexual needs.
Tina decides to get buck wild away in college
Will her sexual trysts jeopardize the lives of the men in her life?

In Stores!!!

Me and Mrs. Jones

Faith Jones, a woman in her mid-thirties, has given up on ever finding love again until she met her son's best friend, Darius. Faith Jones is walking a thin line of betrayal against her son for the love of Darius. Will Faith allow her emotions to outweigh her common sense?

In Stores!!!

Extreme Circumstances

What happens when a devoted woman is betrayed? Come take a ride with Chanel as she takes her boyfriend, Donnell, to circumstances beyond belief after he betrays her trust with his endless infidelities. How long can Chanel's friend, Janai, use her looks to get what she wants from men before it catches up to her? Find out as Janai's gold-digging ways catch up with and she has to face the consequences of her extreme actions.

In Stores!!!

Cater To Her

What happens when a woman's devotion to her ☐iancée is tested weeks before she gets married? What if her ☐iancée is just hiding behind the veil of ministry to deceive her? Find out as Sean Mitchell takes you on a journey you'll never forget into the lives of Angelica, Titus and Aurelius.

In Stores!!!

Serosa becomes the subject to information that could financially ruin and possibly destroy the lives and careers of many prominent people involved in the government if this data is exposed. As this intricate plot thickens, speculations start mounting and a whirlwind of death, deceit, and betrayal finds its way into the ranks of a once impenetrable core of the government. Will Serosa fall victim to the genetic structure that indirectly binds her to her parents causing her to realize there s NO WAY OUT!

In Stores!!!

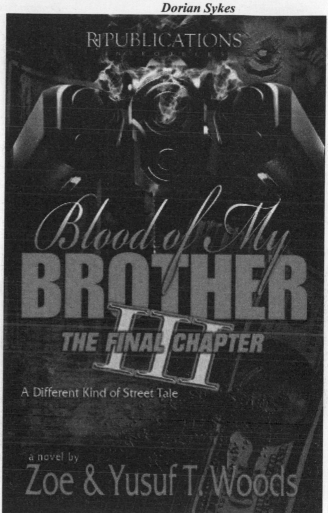

Retiring is no longer an option for Roc, who is now forced to restudy Philly's vicious streets through blood filled eyes. He realizes that his brother's killer is none other than his mentor, Mr. Holmes. With this knowledge, the strategic game of chess that began with the pushing of a pawn in the Blood of My Brother series, symbolizes one of love, loyalty, blood, mayhem, and death. In the end, the streets of Philadelphia will never be the same...

In Storess!!!

Roc was the man on the streets of Philadelphia, until his younger brother decided it was time to become his own man by wreaking havoc on Roc's crew without any regards for the blood relation they share. Drug, murder, mayhem and the pursuit of happiness can lead to deadly consequences. This story can only be told by a person who has lived it.

In Stores!!!

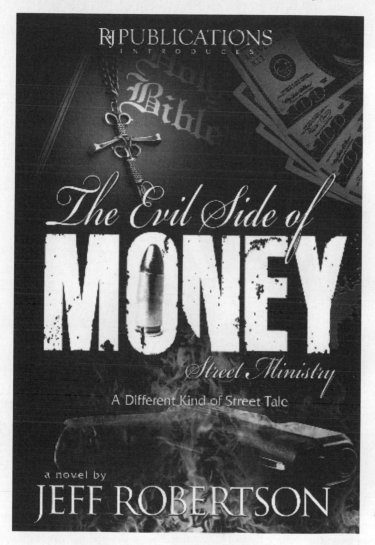

Violence, Intimidation and carnage are the order as Nathan and his brother set out to build the most powerful drug empires in Chicago. However, when God comes knocking, Nathan's conscience starts to surface. Will his haunted criminal past get the best of him?

In Stores!!

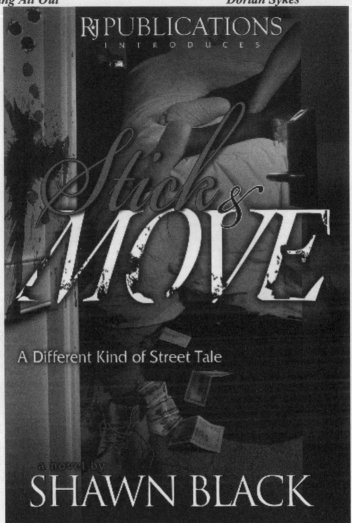

RJ PUBLICATIONS
INTRODUCES

Stick &
MOVE

A Different Kind of Street Tale

a novel by

SHAWN BLACK

Yasmina witnessed the brutal murder of her parents at a young age at the hand of a drug dealer. This event stained her mind and upbringing as a result. Will Yamina's life come full circle with her past? Find out as Yasmina's crew, The Platinum Chicks, set out to make a name for themselves on the street.

In stores!!

Ashland's mother, Bianca, fights hard to suppress the truth from her daughter because she doesn't want her to marry Jordan, the grandson of an ex-lover she loathes. Ashland soon finds out how cruel and vengeful her mother can be, but what price will Bianca pay for redemption?

In stores!!

Malcolm is a wealthy virgin who decides to conceal his wealth From the world until he meets the right woman. His wealthy best friend, Dexter, hides his wealth from no one. Malcolm struggles to find love in an environment where vanity and materialism are rampant, while Dexter is getting more than enough of his share of women. Malcolm needs develop self-esteem and confidence to meet the right woman and Dexter's confidence is borderline arrogance.
Will bad boys like Dexter continue to take women for a ride?

Or will nice guys like Malcolm continue to finish last?

In Stores!!!

A beautigul woman from Bolivia threatens the existence of the drug empire that Nate and G have built. While Nate is head over heels for her, G can see right through her. As she brings on more conflict between the crew, G sets out to show Nate exactly who she is before she brings about their demise.

In Stores!!!

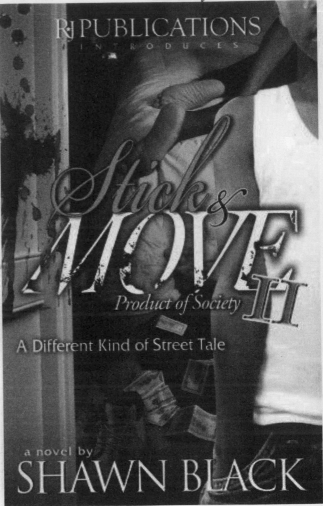

Scorcher and Yasmina's low key lifestyle was interrupted when they were taken down by the Feds, but their daughter, Serosa, was left to be raised by the foster care system. Will Serosa become a product of her environment or will she rise above it all? Her bloodline is undeniable, but will she be able to control it?

In Stores!!

An ex-drug dealer finds himself in a bind after he's caught by the Feds. He has to decide which is more important, his family or his loyalty to the game. As he fights hard to make a decision, those who helped him to the top fear the worse from him. Will he get the chance to tell the govt. whole story, or will someone get to him before he becomes a snitch?

In Stores!!!

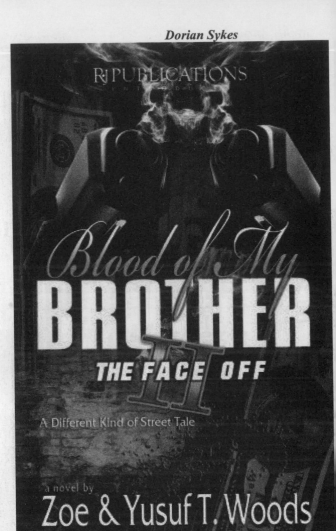

What will Roc do when he finds out the true identity of Solo? Will the blood shed come from his own brother Lil Mac? Will Roc and Solo take their beef to an explosive height on the street? Find out as Zoe and Yusuf bring the second installment to their hot street joint, Blood of My Brother.

In Stores!!!

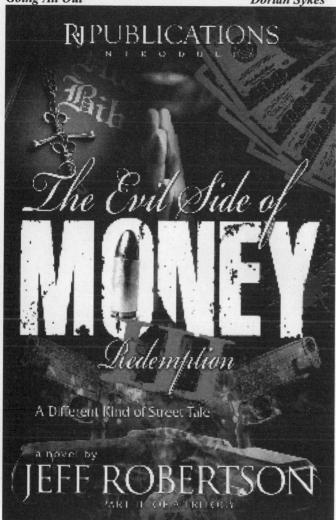

Forced to abandon the drug world for good, Nathan and G attempt to change their lives and move forward, but will their past come back to haunt them? This final installment will leave you speechless.

In Stores!!!

Nafiys Muhammad managed to beat the charges in court and was found innocent as a result. However, his criminal involvement is far from over. While Jerry Class Classon is feeling safe in the witness protection program, his family continues to endure even more pain. There will be many revelations as betrayal, sex scandal, corruption, and murder shape this story. No one will be left unscathed and everyone will pay the price for his/her involvement. Get ready for a rough ride as we revisit the Black Top Crew.

In Stores!!

Dave Richardson is enjoying success as his second book became a New York Times best-seller. He left the life of The Bedroom behind to settle with his family, but an obsessed fan has not had enough of Dave and she will go to great length to get a piece of him. How far will a woman go to get a man that doesn't belong to her?

In Stores!!!

Deon is at the mercy of a ruthless gang that kidnapped him. In a foreign land where he knows nothing about the culture, he has to use his survival instincts and his wit to outsmart his captors. Will the Hoodfellas show up in time to rescue Deon, or will Crazy D take over once again and fight an all out war by himself?

In Stores!!!

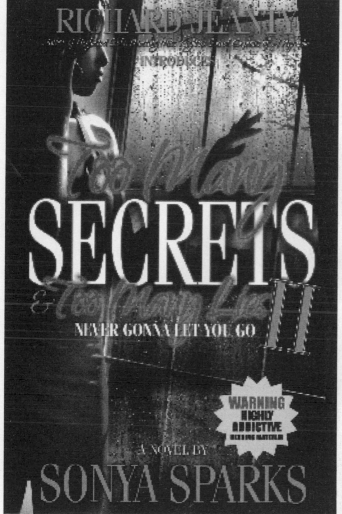

The drama continues as Deshun is hunted by Angela who still feels that ex-girlfriend Kayla is still trying to win his heart, though he brutally raped her. Angela will kill anyone who gets in her way, but is DeShun worth all the aggravation?

In Stores!!!

RICHARD JEANTY

Author of Neglected Souls and Neglected No More

Ignorant SOULS

THE FINAL EPISODE TO THE NEGLECTED SOULS SERIES

Buck Johnson was forced to make the best out of worst situation. He has witnessed the most cruel events in his life and it is those events who the man that he has become. Was the Johnson family ignorant souls through no fault of their own?

In Stores!!!

When an Ex-con finds himself destitute and in dire need of the basic necessities after he's released from prison, he turns to what he knows best, crime, but at what cost? Extortion, murder and mayhem drives him back to the top, but will he stay there?

In Stores !!!

What happens when someone falls insanely in love? Stalking is just the beginning.

In Stores!!!

Use this coupon to order by mail
1. Neglected Souls, Richard Jeanty $14.95 Available
2. Neglected No More, Richard Jeanty $14.95 Available
3. Ignorant Souls, Richard Jeanty $15.00, Available
4. Sexual Exploits of Nympho, Richard Jeanty $14.95 Available
5. Meeting Ms. Right's Whip Appeal, Richard Jeanty $14.95 Available
6. Me and Mrs. Jones, K.M Thompson $14.95 Available
7. Chasin' Satisfaction, W.S Burkett $14.95 Available
8. Extreme Circumstances, Cereka Cook $14.95 Available
9. The Most Dangerous Gang In America, R. Jeanty $15.00 Available
10. Sexual Exploits of a Nympho II, Richard Jeanty $15.00 Available
11. Sexual Jeopardy, Richard Jeanty $14.95 Available
12. Too Many Secrets, Too Many Lies, Sonya Sparks $15.00 Available
13. Stick And Move, Shawn Black $15.00 Available
14. Evil Side Of Money, Jeff Robertson $15.00 Available
15. Evil Side Of Money II, Jeff Robertson $15.00 Available
16. Evil Side Of Money III, Jeff Robertson $15.00 Available
17. Flippin' The Game, Alethea and M. Ramzee, $15.00 Available
18. Flippin' The Game II, Alethea and M. Ramzee, $15.00 Available
19. Cater To Her, W.S Burkett $15.00 Available
20. Blood of My Brother I, Zoe & Yusuf Woods $15.00 Available
21. Blood of my Brother II, Zoe & Ysuf Woods $15.00 Available
22. Hoodfellas, Richard Jeanty $15.00 available
23. Hoodfellas II, Richard Jeanty, $15.00 03/30/2010
24. The Bedroom Bandit, Richard Jeanty $15.00 Available
25. Mr. Erotica, Richard Jeanty, $15.00, Sept 2010
26. Stick N Move II, Shawn Black $15.00 Available
27. Stick N Move III, Shawn Black $15.00 Available
28. Miami Noire, W.S. Burkett $15.00 Available
29. Insanely In Love, Cereka Cook $15.00 Available
30. Blood of My Brother III, Zoe & Yusuf Woods Available
31. Mr. Erotica
32. My Partner's Wife
33. Deceived 1/15/2011
34. Going All Out 2/15/2011

Name_____
Address_____
City_____State_____Zip Code_____

Please send the novels that I have circled above.
Shipping and Handling: Free
Total Number of Books_____ Total Amount Due_____
          Buy 3 books and get 1 free. This offer is subject to change without notice.
Send institution check or money order (no cash or CODs) to:
RJ Publications
PO Box 300771
Jamaica, NY 11434
For more information please call 718-471-2926, or visit www.rjpublications.com
Please allow 2-3 weeks for delivery.

Use this coupon to order by mail

35. Neglected Souls, Richard Jeanty $14.95 Available
36. Neglected No More, Richard Jeanty $14.95 Available
37. Ignorant Souls, Richard Jeanty $15.00, Available
38. Sexual Exploits of Nympho, Richard Jeanty $14.95 Available
39. Meeting Ms. Right's Whip Appeal, Richard Jeanty $14.95 Available
40. Me and Mrs. Jones, K.M Thompson $14.95 Available
41. Chasin' Satisfaction, W.S Burkett $14.95 Available
42. Extreme Circumstances, Cereka Cook $14.95 Available
43. The Most Dangerous Gang In America, R. Jeanty $15.00 Available
44. Sexual Exploits of a Nympho II, Richard Jeanty $15.00 Available
45. Sexual Jeopardy, Richard Jeanty $14.95 Available
46. Too Many Secrets, Too Many Lies, Sonya Sparks $15.00 Available
47. Stick And Move, Shawn Black $15.00 Available
48. Evil Side Of Money, Jeff Robertson $15.00 Available
49. Evil Side Of Money II, Jeff Robertson $15.00 Available
50. Evil Side Of Money III, Jeff Robertson $15.00 Available
51. Flippin' The Game, Alethea and M. Ramzee, $15.00 Available
52. Flippin' The Game II, Alethea and M. Ramzee, $15.00 Available
53. Cater To Her, W.S Burkett $15.00 Available
54. Blood of My Brother I, Zoe & Yusuf Woods $15.00 Available
55. Blood of my Brother II, Zoe & Ysuf Woods $15.00 Available
56. Hoodfellas, Richard Jeanty $15.00 available
57. Hoodfellas II, Richard Jeanty, $15.00 03/30/2010
58. The Bedroom Bandit, Richard Jeanty $15.00 Available
59. Mr. Erotica, Richard Jeanty, $15.00, Sept 2010
60. Stick N Move II, Shawn Black $15.00 Available
61. Stick N Move III, Shawn Black $15.00 Available
62. Miami Noire, W.S. Burkett $15.00 Available
63. Insanely In Love, Cereka Cook $15.00 Available
64. Blood of My Brother III, Zoe & Yusuf Woods Available
65. Mr. Erotica
66. My Partner's Wife
67. Deceived 1/15/2011
68. Going All Out 2/15/2011

Name_____
Address_____
City_____State_____Zip Code_____

Please send the novels that I have circled above.
Shipping and Handling: Free
Total Number of Books_____Total Amount Due_____
Buy 3 books and get 1 free. This offer is subject to change without notice.
Send institution check or money order (no cash or CODs) to:
RJ Publications
PO Box 300771
Jamaica, NY 11434
For more information please call 718-471-2926, or visit www.rjpublications.com
Please allow 2-3 weeks for delivery.